The Karma
of
King Harald

A Canine Cozy

by Richard Audry

Published by Conger Road Press

Minneapolis, Minnesota

ISBN: 978-0-9850196-2-4

Cover design by Jesse Pelkey

Cover photo by D. R. Martin

Visit drmartinbooks.com

Contact the author at drmartin120@gmail.com

Chapter One

King Harald proceeded up Willow Street with regal bearing.

Proud.

Erect.

Monarch of all he surveyed.

Up above, the maples and lindens had budded out, promising a summer's worth of delicious shade. Harald stopped at almost every trunk, sniffed robustly, and—discreetly here and there—lifted a leg to add his own signature to the others.

The huge, ginger-colored canine was of unknown provenance. Part Chesapeake, from his looks. But the other part remained a mystery. Some folks in New Bergen joked that a moose must have had a romantic tryst with one of Harald's forebears.

Not that long ago, Harald had been a down-on-his-luck adult dog, left at an animal shelter by a family that couldn't afford him anymore. But then one day the boss walked in through the shelter's doors. Harald knew instantly that this was the human for him and he made sure he got noticed. There was much tail-wagging, but no slobbery jumping up on. His sales pitch had been perfect and Harald departed with the boss that very same day.

Now, at Walleye Avenue, Harald hung a right. He trotted along with perfect self-assurance and an utter disregard for the niceties of navigation. The big goofy mutt was an existentialist of the purest sort—ever seeking for the true essence of the moment at hand. In that spirit, he paused to scarf up the remnant of an abandoned sandwich, chew a bit of gravel, pee on a gingko tree, and woof resonantly, but amiably, at a passing brown delivery truck.

By and by Harald made his way across the playground of the Georgia Dardenson Elementary School, through the parking lot, and into the maples and basswoods beyond. There he spent a constructive half hour terrorizing squirrels, noshing on twigs, and urgently inhaling the aromas of tree trunks. When he emerged on the other side of the woods, onto a plowed field of shattered cornstalks, he set his compass for a farmhouse about a hilly half-mile farther north. He spotted a person moving around up there in the yard and maybe that person wanted to play.

Harald bounded across the muddy field, dooming himself to a good scrubbing when he arrived home. That was in the future, though, and of no concern at the moment.

The dog halted just short of the farmhouse, cut to the quick. His putative playmate had climbed into an old, dark-colored pickup and was even now bouncing away down the long driveway to the east.

King Harald entertained the notion of giving chase. But the truck vanished out of sight down a long hill. The thought of human company—if it even was a thought—vanished from the dog's mind like a bubble bursting in the sun. For suddenly, he was in the backyard, a place of inconceivable enchantment.

Early tulips were nearly ready to bloom, and Asiatic lilies and peonies had poked up amidst the dirt beds scattered throughout the long grass. Lilacs and apple trees were starting to show nubbins of flower buds. The pin maples were bright and crisp and lovely to sniff. And glittering, dancing baubles of color dangled from their branches.

Harald was no ponderer, but the spectacle delighted him and held his attention for better than fifteen seconds. Until the most interesting, most enchanting aroma hit the 220 million smell receptor cells tucked way back up his substantial snout. Hit them like a Mack truck without brakes. The smell came from just over *there*.

He bounded across two tulip beds—leaving disorder in his wake—and, as if sliding into home base, came to a quick stop under a flowering crab apple tree. He peered up at the most marvelous thing he had seen in, well, forty seconds.

There, dangling from a low branch, was the item that had called to him with an allure that was not to be denied. An object whose complex bouquet of scents would have challenged the vocabulary of an Elizabethan poet to describe—had the poet possessed 220 million smell receptor cells.

King Harald stared thunderstruck at the object that moved gently in the morning breeze, inhaling deeply through his nostrils.

He reared up on his hind legs, bracing himself against the crab apple trunk. With a certain reverence, he twisted himself around and began to gently prize the pretty, pretty thing from the string that suspended it among the glittering baubles.

Chapter Two

Andy Skyberg and his fellow New Bergenites liked to say they had two seasons—winter and antiquing.

Winter had slouched away about four weeks earlier, at the beginning of April, and the gently rolling countryside was greening up nicely. The fields were mostly planted, the furrows neatly aligned this way and that. The woods and farmsteads showed the lovely green lace of mid-spring leafing out—delicate and ethereal. Even from his perch in his sister's Plymouth Voyager, cruising northwest up the Interstate, Andy could see yellow swatches of daffodils around farmhouses and out in garden plots.

Andy had struggled awake at four that morning, fed King Harald, and put him out in the backyard with bowls of water and dog chow. Elsie Bjorklund would have stopped by at mid-morning to check on the big mutt. Now, on toward lunchtime, Andy was coming back from Lindbergh International Airport with cases of Copper River salmon and crab packed in dried ice, for a big catering gig that evening at the Flèche Droite Nation Casino.

From some distance he could see the giant figure of Lovely Lena—all blond curls, dimples, and pink-checked gingham—slowly, creepily waving at traffic from atop the noodle factory. Lovely Lena Macaroni Corporation, on the south end of Elbow Lake, was New Bergen's biggest employer. Along with agribusiness, St. Magnus College and Prep, and the casino, Lovely Lena kept the Beaver Tail County economy humming along.

For New Bergen, though, the summer gravy came from antiquing tourists and seekers after rural charm. The fourth- and fifth-generation Norwegians and Swedes of New Bergen held a certain small-town disdain for big-city types. But they happily put petty prejudice aside when folding money and plastic emerged from wallets and purses.

Andy pulled off the Interstate and turned right. It was a resplendent May morning, with rich blue sky and billowing cumulus clouds. Off to his right the white spire of the Elbow Lake Lutheran Church soared out of the tops of the trees, looking positively New Englandy.

Just before arriving downtown, Andy cruised by the sprawling New Bergen High School, built a few years before in the cold, sterile brick-and-glass style he thought had gone out in the '60s. Did good-looking cost that much more to build, he wondered, than ugly?

Andy barely noticed the cop's car in front of the main entrance, until he realized that Cass Conlin, his girlfriend and a deputy sheriff, was standing beside it, chatting with someone. Easing up on the pedal, Andy rolled down his window, honked, and waved. Cass squinted across the boulevard and then waved back.

Andy realized that her companion was the assistant principal, Dick Schaeffer—a thickset fifty-something with a trim, gray buzz cut. Schaeffer glared at him, as if Andy deserved to be put in detention. The man was a notorious hard-ass, even for an assistant principal, and Andy felt sorry for anyone who incurred the disciplinarian's wrath.

That's when Andy saw the strange decoration in the back seat window of Cass's black-and-white. For a few seconds it made no sense. He couldn't quite conceptualize the object. Then he got it.

The rear end of some adolescent male, naked, plastered against the glass, and anatomically correct.

A full moon at mid-morning, one might say.

Andy laughed, grateful to no longer have a teenaged boy's brain inside his head. Cruising half a block farther, he turned onto Skjegstad Street, New Bergen's main drag. At last count the street and the surrounding neighborhood had seventeen antique shops and a big antique mall.

Andy rolled by the Norwegian Fellows Lodge International Headquarters and Museum. Next door was the Swedish B&B, in the old Ostrander Hotel. Farther down were the Finn Sisu ski shop, Tonia's Troll Haven toy store, and Trudi Bock's Karma Kubbyhole in the old video rental store.

Flipping the turn signal, he swung the Voyager left on Perch Avenue, then took a quick right into the alley. He crept about midway down the block and parked. Propping open the back door of Ansel's Café, Andy began to haul the chilly boxes of Alaskan seafood down to the walk-in fridge in the basement.

* * *

Andy peered out into the dining room from the kitchen, over the line counter where the wait people picked up dishes. He gazed around the eatery named in honor of his sister Kirsten's favorite artist, Ansel Adams. A dozen of the master's own handmade prints graced the walls. Those glorious landscapes went wonderfully with the Prairie School decor that Kirsten favored for her restaurant.

She had put up a couple of Andy's own landscape canvases, as well. His piney, rocky lake scenes from the northeastern part of the state. Some of the best oils he'd ever painted.

Only then did Andy notice the lunchtime crowd, such as it was. Weekday business was always a bit thin before Memorial Day.

A couple of obvious out-of-towners—he lean, silver-haired, clad in a red Gore-Tex windbreaker, and she trim, sunbaked, in a royal blue tracksuit—sat along a side wall, nibbling on crusty bread and sipping red wine. Opposite them, Bob Ludeman perched on the edge of his chair. Bald, diminutive, and dressed to the nines in a pin-striped suit, he was leaning toward the couple, speaking in an animated but confidential tone. A specialist in Art Deco and Art Nouveau jewelry, Bob sold to collectors all over the world. Big spenders who visited his shop were often treated to a meal at Ansel's.

Carter LaPorte, the managing editor of the *Beaver Tail County Chronicle* up in Hobartville, slouched at a tall table by the opposite wall, slurping a latté. He had today's issue of the *New York Times* spread out in front of him. Sitting with him, chatting away, was local sawbones Doc Hilgenberg, whose Croque Monsieur luncheon special had so far not been touched.

As Andy's eyes wandered over to the three women occupying one of the window tables, he suddenly took a deep, sharp breath.

Trudi Bock, owner of the Karma Kubbyhole, looked as if she was making an earnest sales pitch to Andy's aunt, Bev Engebretson. Observing was Charlene Adams, Trudi's second-in-command, better known as Charlie. She leapt in now and then to underscore some point or other.

Aunt Bev appeared to be interested, asking the occasional question.

Andy very nearly succeeded in tiptoeing silently back out of sight when he heard Aunt Bev holler.

"Anders, I see you there. Come on over here."

A forced half-smile fought its way onto his face. He waggled a wan wave at the trio, then accepted his fate and walked over to join them.

"Anders," his aunt chirped, craning her neck to maintain eye contact. "Just the boy I wanted to see."

Aunt Bev had on her green St. Magnus College sweatshirt and blue jeans with flowers embroidered on the legs. It looked as if she'd recently had her hair done, with the gray roots nicely covered up in that garish henna tone that had been her trademark ever since Andy could remember.

"How are you doing, Anders?" cooed Trudi, shaking back her long auburn locks coquettishly. "You look positively scrumptious."

Andy blushed and laughed nervously. He thought he looked about the same as ever. Tallish at six-four. A head of close-cropped, dark blond hair. Blue eyes—the one on the right a little lazy. A long face with a strong chin. A teeny bit over his ideal weight.

"Well, Trud, okay, you know," he finally mumbled.

"You'll be interested to hear this, Anders, since you're a painter just like your Aunt Bev."

Andy earnestly hoped this was not true. His paintings were nothing like his aunt's artwork.

"Your fifth chakra controls your artistic spirit," Trudi informed him.

This knowledge, Andy confessed, had not come to his attention before.

"Now Bev's fifth chakra is right here." Trudi reached over her baby-greens-and-endive salad to lightly touch the older lady's neck with an aquamarine index finger-nail. "As is yours. Now if you and she were to give Aerobello's Artistry scent a try—that's for the fifth chak-ra—I could almost guarantee that your painting—"

"Rosemaling," Aunt Bev said, a little snappishly. "*I rosemal.*"

Andy didn't know if such a verb existed, but Aunt Bev used it liberally, nonetheless. He wondered how he could get out of here graciously, leaving no female egos bruised.

Trudi smiled apologetically and shook her head. "Of course, I knew that. You're famous for it." Her voice became calming for a change, deep and gentle, like a cat's purr. "Isn't she, Charlie?"

Trudi's stout second-in-command nodded. "Oh, for sure, Trud." Charlie beamed at Aunt Bev, a broad grin spreading across her pale moon face as she pushed up her wire-rim spectacles.

"If you tried Artistry, Bev, Anders," Trudi continued, "I wouldn't be the least bit surprised if your rosemaling *and* painting made a quantum leap. You two would probably be *in the zone.*"

The ardent rosemaler looked confused. "What zone?"

"It's a figure of speech, Aunt Bev," Andy said. "Trud means it'd take our art to a higher level."

"Well, that would be a good thing, wouldn't it?" said Aunt Bev, blinking up at her nephew.

I'll put on that perfume, Andy thought, when hell freezes over. But he continued to hold up the corners of his mouth as he nodded.

"However, I didn't come here today because of chockers or whatever you call them," Aunt Bev continued. "I came because I wanted to talk to you or your sister, Anders."

Bingo! Another clever sneak attack on Kirsten. From

the flank. Through the wobbly younger brother.

"I know that Kirsten doesn't want me to rosemal these precious white walls of hers," Aunt Bev said, reading Andy's mind, "because it would mess up those *black-and-white* pictures. But I figure that we could put up my rosemaling pieces as paintings. They don't have to be permanent, you know."

"Kirsten's pretty adamant about not changing the look that she has going in here," Andy replied. "But I'll talk to her about it one more time."

Just as he was trying to extricate himself gracefully from Aunt Bev's sales pitch, Andy saw J. J. Lindquist, Kirsten's head waitress, churning straight at him, balancing a pair of *salades niçoises* on a tray on her upturned left hand.

J. J. stopped briefly. "Hey, Andy, Doris Schattenheimer called a while ago. Said she saw King Harald out wandering around. Tried you on the phone."

The young, athletic waitress proceeded on to another window table, where a middle-aged couple awaited their order.

Andy groaned inside. Harald had become quite the escape artist lately. Luckily, most everyone in New Bergen knew him and liked him. And it was a providential break that the city of eight thousand souls couldn't afford an animal control officer.

"You're gonna hafta get that stupid dog a chain, Andy," chided Charlie. "Or a new fence."

What was with Charlie and old Harald? Andy

wondered. She used to like him. And the big mutt adored her, heaven only knew why. But Charlie had been coming down hard on Harald ever since she started working for Trudi.

"Harald?" said Aunt Bev. "Chain up Harald? Noooo."

"A taller fence, I guess," Andy sighed. Make that item number one-million-and-one on his agenda of stuff to do that he couldn't afford.

"He's a real sweet dog, though," Trudi put in, looking at Andy with an uncomfortable note of chumminess.

Andy grinned without enthusiasm, desperate to change the subject away from himself and his dog. "You like wine, Trud. I was gonna tell Kirsten about a new wholesaler I heard about down in the Cities. They got some real nice Malbecs and Zins and—"

Aunt Bev let out an involuntary yelp as she gazed over Trudi's shoulder. "Judas Priest and take me to heaven!"

Andy and Trudi twisted around and looked through the window out onto the sidewalk.

There, almost leaping with excitement, whimpering happily, was King Harald, with something green and floppy in his mouth. He looked as if he'd been mud wrestling.

Andy, Aunt Bev, Charlie, and Trudi rushed out the door. That's when they all saw just what it was that the dog had gripped firmly in his jaws.

"Oh, my God!" gasped Trudi, going white as a plate of lutefisk. "It's Adonis!"

She blinked furiously at Andy. Tears welled up in her eyes. "Your bloody, damned mutt killed my iguana!"

Chapter Three

Trudi lunged forward, as if to wrest the late Adonis from the jaws of the seemingly rapacious King Harald. But the subterranean growl that emanated from the homely canine brought her up a few feet short, and she backed off.

"Holy cow, Trud, I'm so awful sorry," Andy sputtered, stunned at this macabre turn of events. "Harald's never done anything like this before, unless it's killing a squirrel. And he hardly ever catches one."

"And he didn't do this hit job, either," announced a gravelly voice out on the sidewalk.

Everyone looked up to see New Bergen's self-styled socialist philosopher standing there in his trademark Navy pea jacket and red stocking cap. Thorstein Veblen Hofdahl's square, weathered face looked like a roadmap of Beaver Tail County. His pale blue eyes, magnified somewhat by the horn-rimmed bifocals that he always wore, came to rest on Andy.

"I took a good look at the decedent, once I got Harald up in the back of my pickup," the wiry septuagenarian continued. "He wouldn't let me take it off him, though."

"Look at that *beast*," Trudi sobbed, wiping her tears with the sleeve of her pink knit pullover. "He's guilty as sin."

"Guilty as sin," Charlie echoed, jutting out her receding chin as best she could. She glared pointedly at Andy.

Bob Ludeman, the antique dealer, had joined the gathering to see what the fuss was about. He wrinkled his nose. "That is disss-gusting!" he hissed. "Poor, poor Adonis." He pulled out his red silk pocket square and covered his mouth, then edged over next to Trudi in a show of solidarity with his fellow merchant.

Harald sat on his haunches, slobbering all over the defunct iguana, looking very pleased with himself and delighted to have such a large audience. That's when he noticed Charlie and trotted over, gently laying the reptile at her feet.

Charlie made a loud "Eeeeuwww" sound and skittered back from the limp, green offering.

Thor pressed on. "It's a bum rap, Trudi. Harald didn't snuff your lizard. Unless he carries a knife."

"What?" said Andy and Trudi, more or less simultaneously.

"Just look at the critter's neck, will you?" Thor said.

Andy squatted down in front of King Harald, patted him on the head, and told him what a fine old boy he was.

Then he delicately picked up Adonis the iguana—all eighteen limp, slightly nauseating inches of him.

Andy stood and examined the dead reptile. "Thor," he said with amazement, "you're right. Look here, Trud. Adonis had his throat cut."

Holding Adonis's corpse right up to a still sniffling Trudi, Andy showed off the clean, deep incision. "I think that Harald must've licked the blood off," Andy said. "But that lizard for sure got his throat slashed."

Doc Hilgenberg had sidled out the door. Nearly eighty, he swore that he'd abandon his one-man practice only when they pried that last tongue depressor out of his stiff, cold fingers.

Behind him came Carter LaPorte, his skinny reporter's notebook and cheap ballpoint at the ready.

"Andy," the doc said, "I'd watch your dog, just in case that thing had salmonella."

Trudi squeaked with outrage and glared at the doc. "My Adonis was perfectly clean, you old quack!"

Andy stepped in front of the New Age retailer, as she surged toward the white-haired physician, fists clenched. Trudi halted, snuffled a bit, and looked helplessly up into Andy's eyes. Then she leaned over to take a closer, squinting look at her late pet, still gripped in Andy's hand. Her bleary eyes widened a bit further, until, without warning, she began blubbering like a baby. Aunt Bev—who'd consoled more than a few fresh widows in her day—took over, enveloping Trudi in a hug. Charlie, loathe to miss an opportunity to embrace her employer, elbowed her way into the scrum and made similar sympathetic noises.

"He gave a lot back, for an iguana," Trudi sniffled. "He loved shiatsu."

"Everyone likes Chinese food, honey," Aunt Bev agreed. "Even lizards."

"Aunt Bev, Charlie," Andy said gently, "why don't you take Trud inside and get her something to drink." He pointed through the door with the dead iguana, then thought better of it.

"A good, stiff shot of bourbon should do the trick," Thor volunteered.

Andy glowered at his curmudgeonly pal.

Trudi, Aunt Bev, and Charlie started to head inside.

"Hey, what's going on?" a sharp female voice asked.

Andy's head snapped to the left and saw the newest arrival. Brenda Erickson. With a sense of dread, he explained the situation to her. But instead of making sympathetic tut-tuttings, as any decent New Bergenite would have, Brenda sneered.

"If I believed in all that New Age garbage, I'd say Trudi had a little karma thrown back in her face."

Andy and everyone else knew how Brenda's siblings, after their mom died, had sold the family farm to Trudi instead of Brenda. Trudi had promised to keep the land in cultivation. Brenda and her husband wanted it to build a bunch of McMansions and a nine-hole golf course. There'd been lawsuits, newspaper articles, and accounts of confrontations between the two women. Nonetheless, jaws dropped at Brenda's insensitive remark, and Trudi started bleating again.

Charlie strode over to the arrogant brunette. Though shorter than Brenda by almost a head, Charlie managed to puff herself up so the two antagonists were nearly eye-to-eye.

"You leave Trudi the hell alone, you bitch!" Charlie snarled. "She's told you she's not selling the farm. And if she did, you and that money-grubbing husband of yours are the last people she'd sell it to."

Then Charlie actually belly-bumped the well-dressed former captain of cheerleaders, who gasped and hopped backward, almost tottering over onto her posterior.

Andy could hardly believe it. He silently hoped that Brenda might defend herself and give Charlie a reason to clean her clock.

But Brenda was not tempted to resort to fisticuffs and backed away from the truculent young woman. She glared at Charlie. "I won't forget about this vicious attack, Charlie Adams." Then she wagged a finger at Trudi. "And I won't forget about my land. I'll do whatever it takes to get it back. *Whatever it takes.*"

She turned abruptly and headed down the sidewalk.

Everyone stood in shocked silence. Finally, Aunt Bev spoke up. "Well, *that* was different."

Bob Ludeman headed back inside to tend to his customers. Doc Hilgenberg followed, presumably aiming to polish off his Croque Monsieur. Aunt Bev, Charlie, and Trudi returned to their table, trailed by Carter, who said something about getting a few quotes.

Remaining outside, Andy and Thor blinked at each other, as if to say, *Do you believe what just happened?* Harald sat contentedly on the sidewalk, admiring his hand-iwork and eyeing the iguana in his master's hand.

Just then, up roared a Beaver Tail County Sheriff's squad car, angling into the parking slot directly in front of the door. Its tires squealed a little as the big Ford lurched to a stop. And out hopped Deputy Sheriff Cass Conlin.

"So just what in the dickens is goin' on here?" Cass gruffly asked, her skinny legs spread and her hands on her hips. "And what is that you're holding onto, Andy?"

He waved the former Adonis vaguely around. "Trud's pet lizard got himself assassinated."

"You are pullin' my leg," the sheriff's deputy said.

"I sure wish I was," Andy replied, recounting what had happened.

Then Thor chimed in with his version of events.

"Harald was trotting along east up Trollhaugen Road. About a mile beyond Trudi's place and mine. I recognized his ugly mug, of course. I coaxed him into the back of my truck with a Salted Nut Roll, but he wouldn't let me near the iguana. I gave him the candy bar anyway. Hell, I didn't want to touch the damned lizard."

Cass cogitated a moment. "I think we oughta look into this a little more, go out to her place. It's a cruelty to animals charge, at the very least."

"Poor old Adonis," Andy muttered. "Who'd want to do such a thing?"

"Well," Cass said, "those church ladies have been

picketing the Karma Kubbyhole ever since last fall. And earlier this morning Dick Shaeffer bent my ear about how Trudi is corrupting his daughter. For whatever reasons, she seems to get people riled up. I just want to make sure one of them hasn't gone off the deep end."

"This town certainly doesn't lack for fruitcakes," Thor observed. "Now if you'll excuse me, I have to get back to my errands." He nodded to Andy and Cass, and ambled off.

"If we go out to Trud's place, she should come, too, Cass," Andy said. "She'd know if anything was tampered with."

"Fine by me," answered the ponytailed cop. "I'll take that lizard, though. I'll get an evidence bag out of the car."

As Cass put Adonis in the bag, Andy asked, "Who was that in your squad over at the high school? Cheeky little punk." He grinned, very proud of his double entendre.

His humorous *bon mot* flew right over Cass's head. "Coupla kids mixin' it up in the study hall. Had to break 'em up."

Back inside Ansel's, Andy found the bereaved New Age retailer picking desultorily at her food with her right hand while Charlie held her left hand across the table. Aunt Bev had a comforting arm around her shoulder. Carter LaPorte hovered next to Trudi with his open reporter's notebook. There was a story to be written here.

"And when did the picketing begin, Trudi?" he asked in a mild voice. He was vaguely handsome and professorial—especially when he had his half-glasses on. But like a lot of writers, he favored tweedy, ill-fitting sports jackets.

"Well," Trudi said in a dispirited tone, "I guess when I opened last November. I love this area, but some people here are so small-minded. I'm all for the Judeo-Christian-Islamic God, if that's what floats your boat. But there are other options. Personally, I like the notion of Buddhism a lot. Karma, you know. But not the way Brenda Erickson thinks of it. And the Eleanorian people are really onto something, too."

Andy groaned inside. Trudi and her Eleanorians. A bunch of oddballs who communed with the departed spirits of Eleanor of Aquitaine and Eleanor Roosevelt.

Just then, Trudi caught sight of Andy and jumped up. "Oh, Anders," she said, brushing by Carter.

Before he knew it, Andy was in a Trudi bear hug.

"I'm awfully sorry I called your Harald those horrible things out there," she gushed. "Please say you'll forgive me."

"By the way," Aunt Bev asked, "who's got Harald?"

They all looked out on the sidewalk, where Harald had been placidly sitting at kerfuffle's end.

The oversize mutt had vamoosed. Again.

Chapter Four

After Andy made sure that J. J. and the other waitresses didn't need him, he climbed into the black-and-white police cruiser with Trudi, Carter, and Cass. By happenstance they spotted Harald on the way out of town, peeing on an ash tree on Pike Avenue. Rather than waste time incarcerating the hound back at Andy's place, they took him along on the ride out to Trudi's farmhouse.

The last time Andy had sat in the back of a black-and-white was 24 years earlier, when he and two buddies abducted one of Old Man Palruud's giant pumpkins. They'd conspired to drop it off the top of the Olaf B. Overholt Memorial Observation Tower out at the county park, from which point you could see four counties. But a young deputy sheriff named Ed Vandegraff smelled a rat, arriving just as the trio had wrestled that miserable squash up the first flight of stairs.

His pals skittered. Andy didn't. He couldn't abandon his green Chevy pickup, well known to everyone in New Bergen. It was a long ride back into town to face the awful majesty of the law and—worse yet—his dad's icy disappointment.

This time, though, he didn't mind it, doubly so because the New Age maven was in the front seat, pushing her new line of chakra scents on a visibly apathetic Cass. Andy had never really chatted with Carter LaPorte before. The two of them compared bios, while trying to avoid large, sloppy kisses from Harald, who was wedged between them.

Carter said that he had grown up in the Cities, then spent a number of years in the army. After he left the service, he earned a journalism degree and went into newspapering.

Harald, getting no satisfaction from Carter, twisted around and gave Andy's face a quick, lubricious lick. His rear end almost gyrated from the effort of wagging a tail in such cramped quarters.

"Ah, geez, Harald!" Andy sputtered, hauling out a wad of tissues and giving his cheek a swab.

Carter chuckled. "And what about you? How'd you end up back in New Bergen?"

Andy recounted how he'd earned a pretty much useless history degree at the big university down in the Cities.

"You know, Carter," Trudi said, twisting around, "Anders and I were an item in college. We went together for six or seven months. Isn't that right, Anders?"

"Yeah, that's right. An item. We had some fun, Trud and me."

"Yes we did," confirmed Trudi, facing forward again.

Andy thought he could hear Cass groan.

He continued with his story. There were a couple years of vagabonding after college. Then he came back to the Cities and took a job driving for a limo service. He never thought it would be a regular career, but the pay was decent and there was rarely a dull moment.

He married a woman who worked for a rock concert promoter and Andy thought everything was tickety-boo. Until Mrs. Skyberg decamped for LA with a Pilates coach for a heavy metal band. After that, Andy had spent a couple of months not answering the phone. Drinking way too much beer and eating way too much junk food. Watching way too much ESPN. Going out only at night, like one of those pale newts that lurks in deep, dank caves.

A couple of years ago his sister Kirsten had started up Ansel's Café and asked Andy to be her right-hand man. She gave him a studio above the restaurant rent-free, for his painting projects. Ever since he'd visited Europe's great art museums as a college student, and been bowled over, he cultivated the dream of becoming a landscape painter. He started taking classes and proved to have a knack for brush, oil, and canvas. He worshipped people like Monet and Turner and Friedrich. Painting fulltime was his ambition, as yet unrealized.

Cass pulled into Trudi's driveway, spraying gravel out onto Highway 77. They bounced along the narrow track through the muddy fields. A couple of ravens flapped slowly up and away, cawing like angry witches. The two-story white house looked just as Andy remembered from that fateful night two-plus decades earlier, when he'd picked up Brenda Erickson, née Fundingsland, for his one and only date with her. It had been a disaster, which is why, to this very day, he shuddered when she hove into view.

The four humans and one canine piled out of the squad car. Andy was amazed to see how thoroughly Trudi had transformed the old place.

Neat flower beds surrounded the house, awaiting their plantings. In places where oaks, maples, and ashes provided shade, Trudi had hostas, columbines, and bleeding hearts. Colored glass, crystals, bells, and metal baubles dangled off branches, catching and brilliantly refracting or reflecting the light. Numerous sets of wind chimes filled the air with a sweetly dissonant soundtrack. A regular fairyland, Andy thought.

"My goodness," Carter said, gazing around, taking a few notes. "Very nice, Trudi. Very charming. I'd like to tell our lifestyle editor about it, if that's okay. I'm thinking the Sunday home section?"

It was plenty okay with Trudi, who observed that any publicity was good publicity.

Cass—whose taste ran to wildlife art and country western music—issued a noncommittal grunt.

Andy took Harald by the collar, and the oversized mutt started to tug him right into one of the tulip beds. "Sorry, Trud," Andy said over his shoulder, trying to slow down the muscular canine. But there was no denying Harald. He made a beeline for a flowering crab just on the other side of the orchard, Andy slogging behind him in a hunched-over position.

The other three made their way to the flowering crab, too, sidestepping the mud where they could. The deputy sheriff bent way over to get under the tree. Andy and Carter eased down on their haunches to watch, Andy maintaining a good grip on Harald.

Cass peered around, banging into a few crystals and other baubles. Then she let out an excited "Yeah!"

"What do you see, Cass?" Andy asked.

"I'll be a—" she began. She jockeyed around so she could display what she'd found. "It's a little noose with blood on it. Made from a long shoestring. I think Harald found your lizard hanging here, Ms. Bock, and pulled him out of it somehow."

"How awful!" Trudi exclaimed. "Poor Adonis."

"I'm gonna leave it here for now," Cass continued, pulling a small digital camera out of her equipment belt. She took a few shots of the little noose from different angles. "Now I think we oughta check your house."

They went back through the garden beds, Trudi having claimed Carter LaPorte's arm for physical and emotional support. Cass asked Trudi when she had last seen Adonis alive. Trudi said early that morning, before she left for work.

"Front door looks fine," observed Cass. "Look okay to you, Ms. Bock?"

"Yes, fine," said Trudi. "And will you please call me Trudi."

"Of course, ma'am," said Cass. "And when's the last time anyone was here driving a truck?"

"Not lately," Trudi said. "Why?"

"'Cause you got fresh truck tire tracks in the mud in your yard. Fairly worn tires. Not much tread left."

The others looked down. Cass was right. Someone had been there in a pickup or van a short while ago. The deputy sheriff snapped off a few pictures of the tread marks.

Then they all went around the north and west sides of the house, checking every window. When they came to the south side, it was instantly clear how the lizard killer had gotten to Adonis: someone had kicked in the mudroom door and left a note stuck to the doorframe with masking tape.

Cass went up the two short steps and read the missive silently. Her eyebrows furrowed and her jaw clenched. She muttered something under her breath about a male child's canine lineage.

"What's it say, Cass?" Andy asked.

The deputy sheriff drew a deep breath and read the block letters written in pencil on the sheet of lined tablet paper: "I killed your pet and put him in the tree. No devil's work allowed here. Take your evil filth and get out of town now. Or next thing to hang is you."

A dramatic moan escaped from Trudi and she cast her gaze downward, shaking her head. Then she looked up, her chin quivering, and she shrugged.

"I just have no idea what to say," she whispered. "Now they're going to kill me if I don't give up the store?

Hang me up in a tree like my poor, dear Adonis?"

Trudi—as Andy knew all too well from personal experience—was a vibrant, vivid sort of personality, in addition to being, well, pretty darned attractive. She always wore bright shades, like the pink top and purple broomstick skirt that she had on this morning. She favored large jewelry and her hair always looked gorgeous. But right at the moment, all the color and verve had gone out of her. As if she'd taken a body blow, as if she'd deflated.

"Are you all right, ma'am?" Cass queried. "Would you like to sit down?"

Trudi took a deep breath and blinked at her three companions, one at a time.

"I'm okay. I'm fine. Just let me catch my breath."

"You sure, Trud?" Andy asked anxiously.

Trudi nodded. "You just go inside and check out the house, okay?"

"Carter," Cass said, "stay here with Trudi. And hold onto Harald."

"Sure thing, Deputy Conlin," the newspaperman said.

"Andy, you come with me."

The skinny deputy hoisted herself up to her full five foot six inches, including spit-shined black police oxfords. She sniffed loudly, shrugged her shoulders, and pulled down her dark brown cap with the silver badge as tightly as her blond ponytail allowed. Then she snapped open the canvas safety strap on the top of her holster. She pulled the Glock 9mm out, clicked off the safety, and racked the slide.

Not for nothing did people refer to her, behind her back, as "Barney Fife in a brassiere."

"Geez Louise, Cass," Andy sighed, "do you have to do that? You don't need your gun."

"Andy, we have no idea whether or not we have a perp lurking in there."

"Then why don't you call for backup?"

She sniffed again. "I don't need any backup."

"Dammit, Cass, you're gonna get yourself killed one of these days."

She turned and eyeballed her current squeeze. "You don't want to come in, I'll understand. You're just a civilian."

"And you're one macho little shit."

Cass allowed herself a tiny grin and a happy, demented glint twinkled in her eyes. "That I am. You comin' or not?"

Chapter Five

"Yeah, I'm comin'," Andy said. "So long as you protect me."

"Don't you worry your pretty little head," Cass said. Then she nodded at Carter and Trudi. "You two stay put. Got it?"

Cass and Andy went up the mudroom steps through the smashed door, through the mudroom—filled with gardening clothes and implements—and into Trudi's kitchen. The cabinets looked old, but freshly painted in pastel green. The signs of the zodiac were stenciled up on the wall, in each of the four corners. There was a huge metal rack hanging over the food-prep table in the middle of the room, full of fancy gourmet pots and pans. The window glittered with little dangling crystals and stained-glass doodads.

Andy noticed it first.

"Cass," he said, pointing his nose at the floor. She looked down, too.

Near the center of the kitchen, the yellow tile floor was

stained, splattered with some reddish-brown liquid, about a square foot's worth. They could see where Adonis's feet had skittered in his blood as he tried to save himself—a strange calligraphy of death. Off to the side, a bloody utility knife lay next to the fridge, where the lizard killer had evidently tossed it.

"I'll get photos later," Cass told him. "Now come on."

She preceded Andy, Glock still hoisted skyward, gripped two-handed. Into the living room they crept. He'd never seen anything in a farmhouse like this. A setting right out of the pages of a chic interior design magazine.

The walls were a gentle shade of gray, the trim painted a classy semi-gloss white. Across the plaster ceiling Trudi had installed weathered oak beams. Dominating the room, against the far wall, was a giant, blue velvet sofa, with a crazy quilt thrown offhandedly but stylishly over the back. The walls were bedecked with antique prints, mostly 18th century and British. Portraits of noble ladies and gentlemen, champion horses, pastoral scenes. Underneath everything, atop the refinished oak floor, was a dense, ornate oriental rug of rich blue and red.

Trudi's most recent husband, the day trader, must've made a whole pile of money, Andy thought.

"See anything in here?" asked Cass.

"Nobody's hiding, anyway," Andy answered. "No damage. There's Adonis's cage in the corner. He, or she, must've just reached in and grabbed him."

They tiptoed into a hallway and checked out the two downstairs rooms—one an office, the other a dining room.

Then they climbed slowly, gingerly upstairs, Cass still holding her weapon at the ready. They stuck their noses into the bathroom. It looked like a Chinatown bordello, with red-flocked wallpaper in an oriental pattern. There were framed copies of Japanese woodcuts showing couples in energetic poses doing impossibly naughty things.

Cass and Andy were halfway up the hallway when the sound of something falling emerged from the bedroom on the left.

"Down, Andy!" Cass whispered and took a shooting stance. She drew a few deep breaths.

Andy dropped to the floor.

"Deputy sheriff!" Cass bellowed. "Come out now! Hands on top of your head!"

Not another sound emanated from the bedroom. The next half-minute seemed like an eternity to Andy.

Cass began to inch toward the door, back plastered to the wall. Andy followed, on his hands and knees, his heart pounding like a trip hammer.

"Last chance," she bellowed. "Come on out!"

Again, no response came from within.

The deputy sheriff sucked in another big gulp of air and pivoted around into the doorway, bringing her Glock to bear.

Before she could move another inch, a terrified calico cat burst out into the hallway between her two widespread legs. It spurted right over Andy's shoulder and launched itself down the stairs like a major-league curveball.

A loud THWUMP and a shouted "Oww!" issued from

the stairway, followed by a startled, basso-profundo "*Wooo-ooof.*"

Cass wheeled around, back into the hallway, and aimed right over Andy just as Trudi fell flat on her face at the top of the stairs. Into the line of fire. Surprised and tripped up by the plummeting pussycat.

Harald clambered over her and paused in the hallway, panting earnestly.

"Dogdammit!" Cass spat. "You there." She jabbed an angry finger at Trudi and Harald. "*Stay!* Got it?"

Trudi, still sprawled inelegantly on the hallway floor, nodded, her hazel eyes wide as moonstones. "He shouldn't have been in here," she whispered, apparently to Harald. "He's an outside cat."

Harald replied by licking Trudi's cheek.

"One more time," Cass muttered under her breath, pivoting into the next room. She swung her Glock smoothly from side to side, taking in every detail she could. Andy scrabbled after her on his hands and knees, and peered in between the deputy's legs.

It was an opulent bedroom. A full-tester mahogany bed, draped with some kind of saffron-colored oriental silk, occupied the middle of the room. A gorgeous dresser of birdseye maple sat in one corner, drawers pulled out, clothes scattered all around.

Cass looked under the bed, into the closet, behind the door. Whoever had been here was long gone. But he or she must have had a bit more in mind than eradicating a pet iguana. The deputy sheriff made a quick study of some of the intimate clothing distributed among the piled drawers and on the floor.

"Andy, look at this," she said, holding up a matched set of skimpy panties and bra, in a kind of peach-colored, seashell pattern.

Andy's eyes brightened as he stood up. "You like 'em?" he whispered. "I'll get you some."

"That's not what I mean!" Cass whispered back. "And none of that when I'm on duty. Look at 'em, will you?"

Andy took the bra, examined it, front and back, and floodgates of memory opened up. Visions of a topless Trud came surging over him, from long-ago college days. She really had been quite something in that department, and still was. Looks were never the issue with Trud.

It took him a little bit to notice what had caught Cass's eye: the bra had been stabbed repeatedly, right through the cups. He put his right index finger into a couple of the slits, then blushed. Cass refused to crack a smile. Trudi's panties were in the same punctured condition, as were a dozen more items of intimate apparel.

"What's it mean, Cass?"

The deputy chewed on her lower lip. "Well, Andy, I think it means Ms. Bock's in a lot more trouble than we thought she was."

Chapter Six

Cass pulled her Ford squad car up next to its exact twin in front the defunct Pure Oil station at the north end of Skjegstad Street, now the New Bergen outpost of the Beaver Tail County Sheriff's Office. The squads were white with black trim, the county crest emblazoned on the front doors. It depicted a beaver rampant upon a beaver dam, about to be shot by an early Norwegian settler.

Cass, Andy, Trudi, and Carter piled out. Andy hauled Harald from the back seat.

Carter said his good-byes and strolled away. When Cass asked Trudi to come into the sheriff's office, the downcast retailer turned to Andy. "I'd feel better if you were there," she said, with a quick, shaky smile.

Andy looked at her, then at Cass. "Okay with you, Cass?"

The deputy sheriff nodded curtly. Andy pulled out his smartphone and called Ansel's to make sure he wasn't needed.

The trio trooped in and Andy deposited Harald in the

restroom. He was getting tired of hanging onto the big hound's collar.

The old brick gas station had been reamed out, carpeted, plastered, and painted in a plain white, utilitarian manner. Except for the rosemaling up on the walls, a gift from Aunt Bev to the taxpayers of Beaver Tail County. The furniture was all office-surplus gray.

At one of the desks sat Assistant Sheriff Ed Vandegraff, Andy's nemesis from that youthful pumpkin-nabbing caper. He was munching on a burger and slurping a soda.

"Kind of a tough day, huh, Ms. Bock," Ed said, wiping a drop of ketchup off the corner of his mouth. "Please sit down. You too, Andy."

Trudi nodded tiredly and plopped down in the chair facing him. "One of the worst," she said.

"Now let's talk a little bit about the harassment you've been dealing with."

"I really can't imagine why anyone would hate me so much that they'd do something like this," Trudi said. "First Adonis. Now this— This—"

"Breaking and entering, along with damage to property," drawled Cass dryly. "Specifically, criminal defacement of intimate apparel."

Ed tut-tutted and Trudi nodded.

"Heaven knows I've tried to be a good neighbor," said Trudi. "I donated aromatherapy products to the auction to help fund the new scoreboard at the high school."

Andy nodded but was too polite to mention that no one

had bid on them, until Thor's wife Sonny swept up the whole lot for two dollars and change.

"I even sponsored that girls' softball team last summer. The Crystals."

"They were pretty darned good, too, if I recall," said Andy. "Came in fourth out of six. Right, Cass?"

"Right, Andy," said Cass, who had played second base on the team that eliminated them in the semis.

"So why am I being persecuted?" Trudi asked. "Why do these Philistines want to drive me out?" She blinked from Ed to Cass and back, then reached over and squeezed Andy's paw. Gently, he extricated his hand.

"Okay, Ms. Bock, fill me in again on those church ladies giving you the hard time," said Ed. "Cass, take notes, will you?"

"Well, they started up when I opened my store last fall," Trudi began. "Picketed, tried to get the city council to bounce me out of town, take away my license. They asked customers to boycott me, passed around petitions."

"They're from Beacons of the Faith Church, right?" Ed asked. "Didn't like you, your products, or what?"

"Yes to both. They've told me to my face that I'm promoting devil-worship and witchcraft, and I'm trying to corrupt the children of Beaver Tail County. Dreadful stuff!

"I had a window smashed in the middle of the night last December. Maybe you remember that. Not that I think any of those old ladies did it. But it was a big nuisance. And this spring I've received three or four nasty anonymous letters."

"Saying what?" the beefy assistant sheriff queried.

"That I'd burn in hell, that I was a whore of Satan, that God would smite me down unto the lowest in creation." She waved an aquamarine-nailed hand vaguely around in mid-air. "And if God didn't do anything about me, they would handle it."

"You still have the letters?" Ed asked.

"I should have kept them, I suppose," Trudi answered. "But they were so vile, I burned them up."

"Do you remember anything about them?"

"Just that they were very spiteful and insulting and... Well, one thing was that they seemed to have been written on an old typewriter. They weren't printed with a computer."

Cass rubbed her cheek—which was freckled and wholesome, despite her efforts to look hard-boiled, pale, and intense. "Andy, what's the deal with this Beacons of the Faith bunch? You know these people, right? What kind of burrs have they got up their butts?"

"Well," Andy said, "they're extremely conservative and anything mystical like what Trud is peddling is bound to get them in a lather. When I was a kid, Mrs. R practically ran an astrologer out of town on a rail. I mean, they think the mainstream Lutheran church is run by flaming commie-pinko-liberal heathens. That's why they came up with their own synod."

"How many churches in the synod?" asked Cass.

"Just the one," Andy said.

"Can just one church make a synod?"

"I guess so," Andy said with a shrug.

"Okay, so these folks are nutcases who have a low regard for pretty much everyone except themselves," said Cass. "You think they're sociopaths? You think they'd do stuff like this?"

"I doubt it," Andy answered. "Not the ladies, anyway."

"Why?"

"'Cause they wouldn't touch an iguana, for a start. They take that snake in Genesis pretty darned seriously. And any of his relatives, too. Satan's spawn, you know."

"Horrible people!" Trudi exclaimed. "Adonis was a sweetie."

"So," Andy continued, "for the last fifteen or twenty years Mrs. R, Mrs. Runestrand, has been the real power behind the pulpit in that outfit. The pastor does whatever Mrs. R says."

"But why does he feel compelled to obey that woman?" Trudi wondered.

"Well, Mrs. R's husband Oscar is the biggest heating and air conditioning contractor in the whole county. Owns Beaver Tail HVAC up in Hobartville. Most of the church's donations come from the old man's checkbook. So Mrs. R owns the synod."

"If you ask me, they are some awfully self-conflicted people," Trudi said. "They keep saying they love the sinner but hate the sin. They brought me plates of cookies when I opened up, but said they'd do their best to put me out of business. Mrs. Runestrand herself told me that if I wasn't stopped, the virginal young women of New Bergen—"

Cass hooted spontaneously, then rubbed her right eye. "Sorry," she muttered, "but there aren't many of those."

"Anyway," Trudi continued, "she said the pure young women will be turned to black and vile corruption."

"I mean, Ed," Cass said, "that bunch has to be at the top of our list of possible perps."

Ed shook his head. "It's too soon to say, Cass."

"Unfortunately I've managed to get on the wrong side of some other people in town, as well," Trudi said, shaking her head. "Everyone knows that Brenda Erickson thinks I stole her family farm out from underneath her. The old Fundingsland place."

"There was a kind of family dispute about the farm, wasn't there?" Ed asked.

"Yeah, there often is," Andy observed. Spats among siblings over inherited Beaver Tail County farmland were as common as mosquitoes.

"As I recall, the mother's will left the land and house to Brenda's sister and brother." Ed looked to Cass, then Andy. "And she hauled those two into court."

Andy nodded. "They got the case dismissed pretty quick, though. Brenda did get her third of the estate, more or less. Just not any farmland. Stocks, some cash, a condo in Florida. The old girl knew what her daughter would do with the land."

"Why didn't the other two siblings keep it?"

"Nancy wanted to," Andy explained, "but Rod needed

the money. They couldn't put it up for auction, because then Brenda might get it."

"My real estate agent contacted me about the property," Trudi explained. "And I promised, if they sold to me, that I'd keep the land in cultivation as long as I owned it. I swore that I wouldn't sell to Brenda. But that woman won't take no for an answer!"

"Do you know of any other people who might wish you ill?" asked Ed.

"Well, what happened with Dick Schaeffer from the high school," Trudi sniffed, "was totally beyond my control."

"Tell me about it," Ed replied, then peered at Cass. "You gettin' all this, Cass?"

"Sure am," the deputy said.

Trudi launched into her account. "Schaeffer's daughter Amber liked to stop by my shop and try the scents and the natural makeup. What sixteen-year-old girl wouldn't? We talked a bit and I shared my philosophy with her. Well, she bought some books in the store, one of them about the Wiccans."

"Wiccans?"

"Witches, Ed," Andy put in. "A perfectly legitimate pagan religion."

Trudi beamed at Andy, then looked at Ed again. "After reading the book, Amber decided that she wanted to be a Wiccan, not a Methodist."

"That certainly explains why Schaeffer's PO'd at you," Ed said.

"I suppose it does. But what's happened is between father and daughter. I can't help it if the girl has an open mind."

Trudi's reply was a teeny bit disingenuous, Andy thought. She always did have a gift for wandering into other people's quarrels—then taking sides. She didn't like to back down.

"Aren't you forgetting someone else who might be a little unhappy with you, Trud?" Andy asked.

Trudi and Ed blinked at him. Then a light bulb went on over her head.

"Oh, of course. How could I forget?" She peered back at Ed. "I'm on the board of the Beaver Tail Animal Humane Society. We operate the no-kill shelter in Hobartville. We also keep an eye on animal issues around the county. And we heard rumors early this past winter that animals were being abused up at Jerry Dittbrenner's hog operation. We asked around and a young man who worked there told us that he'd seen sows confined in terribly small pens and piglets smashed against the wall."

"And you managed to get a story in the *Chronicle*," noted Andy. "Which got quite a rise out of Dittbrenner. Didn't you compare him to Ivan the Terrible?"

"No, Anders, it was Vlad the Impaler."

"And didn't you ask for the state agriculture department to check into it?"

"For as much good as it did," Trudi sniffed. "They claimed they found no violations. But they're all in bed together, those big hog farmers and the government bureaucrats."

"I heard that Dittbrenner was hugely steamed by that article," Andy said. "From what I understand, the guy has a pretty hot temper. He has a reputation for being a mean drunk. Beat the snot out of more than a few guys in bar fights."

"Think Mr. Dittbrenner could be sending these threatening notes?" asked Ed. "Maybe he killed your pet lizard?"

"I wouldn't put it past a man like that," said Trudi. "He asked me for a public apology. But I absolutely refused."

* * *

After the interlude with Ed Vandegraff, Cass dropped off Andy, Trudi, and Harald at Andy's house, where they fed and watered the dog. Then, minus canine, they drove back to Ansel's in Andy's Silverado.

Trudi was unusually subdued, for Trudi. Which wasn't any surprise, given the huge mess she found herself in. Andy felt for her and wished that he could do more to help. But he was bound and determined to keep her at arm's length. He'd made the mistake, soon after she'd appeared in New Bergen, of asking her to meet him for drinks. "For old times' sake," as he put it.

He was interested in what she had been doing with her life and how she happened to end up in New Bergen running a metaphysical retail shop. And, admittedly, he was curious to know how loaded she was. He knew she'd been through three divorces, each with a well-to-do guy.

But she took Andy's interest to mean something more and had been subtly trying to reignite what they had going back in college. Most women would have given up after a few discouraging signs from Andy. But Trudi, when she set her sights on something, wasn't one to throw in the towel. She was nothing if not dogged.

Andy had grown up in Beaver Tail County, Trudi in neighboring Herkimer County. They'd never met until his junior year at the university, her senior year. It had been pretty hot and steamy there for a few months. But Kirsten, who'd disliked Trudi at first sight, had been correct in her observation. Trudi was a bit of a weirdo, totally the wrong person for Andy.

As they walked into Ansel's, Andy saw Aunt Bev through the open kitchen door, merrily drying wine glasses and yammering at Kirsten, who was washing.

"Why don't you sit down at the wine bar, Trud, and I'll rustle up some lattés," Andy said. "My treat. You've had an awful rough day."

"A latté would be nice," Trudi said, hoisting herself up onto one of the chairs. Before Andy could get to the espresso machine behind the wine bar, Kirsten and Aunt Bev had emerged from the kitchen.

Aunt Bev trotted over, still wiping a glass. "Hi, Anders. Trudi, you are just the lady I wanted to see. I'm wondering if you've given any more thought to the idea I had this morning."

"You mean rosemaling the wall of the store by the parking lot?" Trudi asked.

Aunt Bev nodded eagerly. "Yup, uh-huh."

As Trudi and Aunt Bev yakked away, Kirsten sidled up to her brother. "Had quite an interesting day, haven't you? Hope you're available for the rest of your shift."

"Take my word for it, Kirsten" Andy whispered. "I'd rather have been washing dishes than prowling through Trudi's bedroom, studying her underwear."

Kirsten's eyes widened as she glanced over at Trudi, then back at her brother. "You'll have to explain that to me later."

Andy picked up Aunt Bev and Trudi's negotiations in mid-sentence.

"...And including designs and your approval, plus expenses for supplies, I'm thinking maybe eight-fifty an hour, Trudi. No more than fifty, sixty hours." Aunt Bev crossed her arms over her St. Magnus College sweatshirt, the very picture of a modern hardball dealmaker.

Trudi cogitated for half a minute, then grinned. "You've got a deal, Bev. A celebration of aromatherapy flowers, dedicated to the memory of my sweet Adonis." She sighed. "Adonis would always be sitting there in the corner of his cage, staring at me, when I came into the living room. I know he enjoyed being petted and held, and he loved his collard greens and apples. I hate to think about walking into an empty house."

Bev patted Trudi on the shoulder. "Why don't I follow you home, kiddo? I can sit with you a while."

Trudi's face brightened. "Would you, Bev?"

"Oh, yah, you betcha. And if you like, I can have

Frank—"

"That's your husband?"

Bev nodded. "He can come over and patch up that door of yours."

"Oh, Bev, that'd be fantastic."

Andy watched the two women walk out of Ansel's, feeling overwhelming relief that his role in the case of the lacerated lizard had come to an end.

Chapter Seven

Andy stopped by the Karma Kubbyhole a bit before ten the next morning, during his break, to see how Trudi was bearing up. It startled him to come upon a slow-moving procession of somber-faced women, bearing various items of cuisine. This sort of thing was common at the passing of a husband or wife or child. Comfort them with casseroles, so to speak.

Normally, the death of a pet wouldn't occasion such an outpouring of sympathy. But New Bergen was buzzing about this lizard atrocity, and some of the town's women wanted to show their solidarity with Trudi. After all, many of them had cats.

Doris Schattenheimer was first in line, with a piping hot Tater Tot Hamburger Delight. Andy knew it well. Mary Iverson followed, holding her famous tuna-and-potato-chip hot dish. Sharon Voxland was celebrated for rustling up vast quantities of creamed chipped beef in times of bereavement, and she didn't fail on this occasion.

Moved almost to tears, Trudi invited everyone inside.

Andy stood back and watched her work the crowd, graciously accepting the brimming Tupperware and ovenware she was presented with.

As Andy stepped inside the Karma Kubbyhole, he was amazed once again at how Trudi had managed to transform the former video rental store. Dark wood paneling created a calm, peaceful mood, while rays of color bounced through the stained-glass window hangings. A strong scent of patchouli filled the air.

All around were displays of New Age accessories. Crystals and dream catchers and wind chimes. Statuettes of wizards and witches. A big shelf unit with hundreds of vials of aromatherapy scents and, next to it, a display chockablock with homeopathic cures. Shelves and racks overflowing with books and CDs and DVDs. Beautiful turquoise Native American jewelry and exquisite Celtic pendants.

Trudi's handyman, Gus Johnson, walked over to Andy. "That girl oughta run for office, huh, Andy?" he said, shaking his head in admiration. "Look at how she's charming them. Why would anybody go and kill that lizard of hers? Most folks around here like Trudi, even if she's operating in another cosmic dimension a lot of the time."

Somewhere in his mid-fifties, Gus had turned up in New Bergen last fall in his orange VW bus, fresh from a 30-year surfing sojourn in southern California, Hawaii, and the Mexican Baja. An old acquaintance of Trudi's, he lived in the Karma Kubbyhole's basement in exchange for keeping the place fixed up and running errands. Apparently they'd briefly been an item out in California, after Trudi's first marriage imploded.

Gradually, the crowd of well-wishers cleared out, leaving Trudi exhausted but smiling. Gus joined her behind the counter.

"You know," she said, "the food doesn't matter so much. I don't even *like* creamed chipped beef. It's the outpouring of love and support. A lot of those ladies are good churchwomen and they don't mind that I'm bringing the New Age to New Bergen."

"It's hard not to like Trudi Bock," Gus teased.

Trudi giggled and pushed him away, sneaking a quick peek at Andy. He did not reward her with anything resembling a show of jealousy.

Andy knew that Gus—who vaguely resembled a much-older Brad Pitt gone to seed—also batted his eyelashes at every woman above the age of consent who walked into the store. Through the long, slow winter season, more than a few local women had come by and bought a little of this or that, hoping to get chatted up by Gus. Trudi didn't seem to mind.

"So what do the Eleanors have to say about all this?" Gus inquired, swinging an ornate little brass pendulum and chain he'd plucked off a countertop display.

"I had a visit from Queen Eleanor last night," Trudi said. "No help at all. Couldn't understand a fraction of what she had to say."

Gus shook his head. "Man, that medieval French is a

bear, isn't it?"

"I think she was on again about the Crusade. And Henry. She never stops talking about Henry. Unfortunately, she had nothing to say about Adonis."

Gus scratched his head. "Henry the, uh—"

"The Second, you silly man. Peter O'Toole."

A nervous smile plastered on his face, Andy said so long and started to head outside, just as Lauren Kastner was coming in.

The opening door made the sound of an owl hoot. Gus had concocted an array of digital door "chimes" for the store.

"Oh, hi, Andy," Lauren said. "Man, it's just so sad what happened to Adonis. He was a really mellow life-form."

Andy had only seen Adonis a couple of times, in Trudi's store, when she brought the animal to work. But he had to agree. Adonis had seemed pretty laid-back, to the point of hardly moving.

Lauren, a half-time store employee, had been part of Trudi's little menagerie for about three months—one of those stray critters the colorful retailer tended to adopt. Andy had heard that Lauren had done time in the Oak River House, for addiction issues. Like a lot of folks who'd dried out at the prominent treatment center—smack dab in the lovely woodlands near Malden—she had stuck around Beaver Tail County.

She was a skinny, plain-looking girl in her early twenties. For a close-to-middle-aged guy such as Andy, her multiple piercings were a little off-putting. As were the Celtic designs tattooed on her forearms and neck. And the short, spiky, bleached blond hair wasn't exactly to his taste. But on the whole, he thought Lauren was a pretty nice young woman. She said exactly what she thought, and for the most part Andy agreed with her.

Trudi had told Andy she'd never met a harder worker. And there were encouraging signs that Lauren might even be interested in becoming an Eleanorian. She had been spotted reading a biography of the old First Lady.

"Do they have any idea yet who might have done it?" Lauren asked. "I mean, what kind of monster would slash an iguana's throat?"

"No, not yet, Lauren," Andy said. "We'll just have to wait and see."

* * *

When Cass had called him at the restaurant that morning, Andy had resisted with all his might.

He huffed, he puffed, he whined, he begged.

He had plaster-patching to do at Ansel's. He had to print up the inserts for the new evening menu. He was going to help Troy Dahlgren, the head cook, bake up a batch of key lime pies.

Andy flat-out did not want to go with Cass to Mrs. Oscar Runestrand's house. He had neither the time nor the intestinal fortitude for an encounter with the holiest roller in all of New Bergen. Besides, he happened to know Mrs. Runestrand pretty well. Enough to know that an encounter with her was likely to be only slightly more enjoyable than a root canal.

In fact, without her, Anders Skyberg almost certainly would have spent the last 37 years and the rest of eternity inside a cramped, little maple box six feet under the turf at Elbow Lake Cemetery.

As a three-year-old he'd nearly drowned. Mrs. Runestrand had been the heroic bystander who hauled him out of Gaasedelen Creek by the scruff of his neck and forced the water out of his lungs. He often wondered why it couldn't have been someone a little more fun. Someone who guzzled beer, played the banjo, and told off-color jokes. Someone you'd want to hang out with.

Comfortable or not, there was always a sort of wary connection between Andy and Mrs. Runestrand. Nowadays he knew she regretted that she hadn't, as yet, been able to "save his soul, in addition to his life." Not that she hadn't tried.

But Cass refused to let Andy off the hook. And she knew he usually could sneak away from Ansel's in mid-afternoon. Kirsten was fine with a little flexibility in his schedule, so long as he pulled his weight otherwise.

Cass said that she figured having Andy along would help in her questioning of Mrs. Runestrand. No one called the woman by her Christian name, Adeline, not even her husband.

The Runestrands lived out in the country east of New Bergen, near the failed chopstick factory. Their house was a tidy, suburban split-level, without the suburb, set in a grove of gnarly oaks, surrounded by newly seeded corn and bean fields. The Runestrands had raised eight children here. Two kids had successfully escaped. In fact, one of them, a son, operated a B&B in the Castro district of San Francisco and had won several drag-queen competitions. The six remaining offspring had been unable to break out of their mother's gravitational field.

Mrs. Runestrand met Cass and Andy at the door in a shapeless, blue-and-white striped cotton housedress. Her long gray hair was held in a single braid that hung down her back. She was square and solid, much like the oaks outside. Without so much as a smile or dab of small talk, she looked at Cass, then Andy.

"Been expecting you," she said, leading them into a living room cleaned and tidied and ordered within an inch of its life. "Set yourself down. I'll get some coffee."

Andy tried to say no thanks, but she ignored him as she tottered out into the kitchen.

Gaudily colorful Biblical scenes—the kind common in Sunday school decor—adorned the walls. On a side table near the picture window sat a clutch of family photos.

Cass peered intently at one of the portraits. "Is Zeke Haugen related to her?" she whispered in Andy's ear.

"Yup," Andy whispered back. "He's Mrs. R's second daughter's oldest. A real pain in the keister, from what I hear. Done some vandalism, graffiti tagging, petty theft, fights."

"Tell me about it," Cass answered. "He's your 'cheeky little punk.'"

Andy grinned. So Cass had caught his play on words,

after all. And Mrs. Runestrand's grandson was the boy behind the full moon that Andy had seen in the squad car window.

Mrs. Runestrand reappeared with a tray that held three steaming white coffee mugs, two of which she gave to Andy and Cass. She sat down with her own and took a dainty sip.

"I have been praying for your immortal soul, Anders Skyberg," the old lady said. "I have never stopped. Since the day the Lord put me in the way of saving your earthly life."

Andy laughed nervously. "Thanks, Mrs. R. Every little bit helps."

Cass owed him *big time* for this.

"As I said on the phone," the deputy began, "I wanted to ask you a few questions about—"

"That filthy whore of Satan and her den of evil?"

Andy and Cass blinked at each other. "Whore of Satan" had been one of the phrases Trudi had quoted from those threatening letters. A coincidence or what?

Cass, in general, took no guff from anyone. And she had that look Andy knew so well, especially when she had the uniform on: *Don't mess around with me.*

Cass locked eyes with Mrs. Runestrand. "Now I'm no lawyer, ma'am, but calling someone a whore in front of an officer of the law sounds to me an awful lot like the civil offense of slander. I'm not a particular fan of Ms. Bock, but I doubt very much that she accepts money for the performance of sexual acts. That would be prostitution. And should Ms. Bock care to haul you into court, I would be more than happy to testify to what I just heard. As, I'm sure, Andy would, too."

To Andy, Mrs. Runestrand looked a little chastened, as if she knew she'd overstepped a bit.

"As I was saying," Cass began again, "I wanted to ask a few questions about your campaign against Ms. Bock's store. I understand you're doing this because her religious beliefs conflict with yours."

"Moral and religious relativism paves the road to hell, Miss Conlin," Mrs. Runestrand said without a dollop of doubt.

"Mrs. Runestrand," Cass growled, "I am not a 'miss.' I am a deputy sheriff. Please address me by that title."

The old lady's eyes narrowed. "Very well, Deputy Sheriff. I was about to say that we have enough to deal with in New Bergen. Methodists, Presbyterians, Baptists, Catholics, not to mention so-called 'mainstream' Lutherans. We don't need witches and warlocks, as well, shilling their foul—"

"Were you aware, Mrs. Runestrand," Cass interrupted, "that Ms. Bock has received menacing letters. And yesterday morning her home was vandalized, her life threatened in a crude note, and her pet lizard killed?"

"Spawn of the devil," Mrs. Runestrand said under her breath.

Andy poked Cass in the ribs with his elbow and whispered out of the side of his mouth. "Told you so."

"Cruelty to animals is against the law, Mrs. Runestrand," Cass stated. "So are destruction of property and terroristic threats."

Mrs. Runestrand shrugged. "Earthly laws are very often not sufficient to the task of fighting Satan."

Cass pursed her lips. "Do you think any of the people involved in your protest against Ms. Bock's store would take earthly laws into their own hands?"

"Seven of us have adopted the task of ridding our community of this threat," said Mrs. Runestrand. "We're all grandmothers with a little time on our hands. Our men are mostly still working, our younger women raising children. It's only right that we should undertake to sound the trumpets and tumble down this woman's den of sin. But to answer your question in a way that you *might* understand, Miss Conlin—"

"It's *Deputy* Conlin," Cass snapped.

Mrs. Runestrand glared back. "We make our crusade within the letter of the law, *Deputy Conlin*. We protest, we picket, we petition public officials, we plead with the people of the town—even the sinners. I have never even been out to the Fundingsland place. Moreover, what we may possess in moral rigor, we lack in physical vigor."

She recounted the medical woes of her little troop of righteous soldiers. A recent knee replacement. Obesity problems. Hypertension. Failing eyesight. Persistent urinary tract infections. She herself had high cholesterol, "the bad kind."

What Mrs. Runestrand was saying, Andy realized, was that it was a wonder any of them could hoist a picket sign and peck out a letter to the editor, let alone murder an iguana and punch holes in Trudi Bock's underpants.

Before they left, Cass went up to Mrs. Runestrand and asked her, with obvious pleasure, "How's your grandson doing? I had to take him into custody yesterday."

Mrs. Runestrand cringed, the first time anything had really ruffled her dour old feathers. "You mean Ezekiel, I suppose. He is a vexation to those who love him. I haven't seen him in some months now. I pray for him every day."

"Do you think he could have anything to do with Ms. Bock's problems?"

"I do *not*," she said emphatically. "Ezekiel was raised with family values." Then she flicked her right hand at them, like the queen dismissing a pair of commoners. The interview had concluded.

After they climbed into the squad car, Andy told Cass again that Mrs. Runestrand and her sour band of Lutheran ladies just weren't capable of the brand of unpleasantness Trudi had been enduring.

"Mean-spirited, for sure," he said, "but in their own narrow, dogmatic, theocratic way. Their style is to pummel you black and blue with the word of God, not with their old arthritic hands. Now, Zeke Haugen, that's an interesting deal."

Cass made a snorting noise and sped down the long Runestrand driveway, as if she were especially eager to escape from the place.

"It wasn't that bad, was it?" Andy asked.

"People like that, women like that, get under my skin,"

Cass answered with a grimace. "Religious nuts. They're the kind who think females ought to be staying at home and breeding babies. If it were up to Mrs. Runestrand, I wouldn't be wearing this uniform and doing whatever the hell I want to do. With whoever the hell I want to do it with.

"Andy, I'd be lying if I didn't tell you that woman just creeps me out."

Chapter Eight

"So what'd Zeke do to arouse the awful fury of the law?" Andy asked as Cass fishtailed out onto the highway, spraying gravel into the ditch. "Nowadays it takes something pretty *outré* to get hauled outta school in a squad."

"*Outré* about says it," Cass replied. "*Outré* is Zeke's middle name."

Andy rode along in silence for a moment, studying the bumper sticker emblazoned on the dashboard between the air-conditioning vents. "Hug A Cop Today" it said. Andy had done considerably more with the cop next to him just the weekend before. But he figured that particular verb would never find its way onto any bumper sticker affixed to a vehicle owned by John and Jane Q. Taxpayer.

If someone had told Andy a year earlier that he'd be dating Cass Conlin—the cute but notably severe officer of the law—he would have said, "Pull the other one." But a mutual acquaintance introduced the two shortly after Cass had dumped a younger, philandering boyfriend. The instant Andy saw Cass, he remembered where they'd met before. She had once given him a ticket for speeding.

Against all odds, the two hit it off pretty well. So long as they didn't talk much about politics and TV crime shows. Cass had strong opinions on both topics. They shared some fun, had a few laughs, and enjoyed each other in the sack. Andy's theory was that Cass, for a change, wanted someone who was older and mellower. For his part, he simply enjoyed her energy, her no-holds-barred outlook, and her plain, old-fashioned babe-i-tude.

"So what'd Zeke do?" Andy repeated. "You're keeping me in suspenders here, Cassie."

"He got into a heckuva fracas with the Norquist kid, Jason. You know, the one who's getting a free ride from Stanford 'cause he's some kinda genius in software engineering."

"I read about that. Judge Norquist's boy."

"The very same. Anyway, Jason got in Zeke's way with regard to a certain young lady's attentions. And Zeke called him out on it. And young Mr. Norquist, though a tad nerdy, has a bit of a spine and stood up for his rights in the open dating market. So Zeke jumped him in the hallway and started pounding the Stanford-bound sap out of him."

A large brown delivery truck came barreling at them over the crest of a hill. Cass offered the standard mid-highway greeting in this part of the world. A raised index finger at the top of the steering wheel. The woman driving the truck returned the salutation.

"After two teachers had peeled Zeke offa Jason," Cass

continued, "he was incarcerated in Dick Schaeffer's office, awaiting my arrival. Before I got there, a young lady stopped me in the hallway outside of the biology lab. Did you know those places still stink like hell? Man, that brought back memories."

Andy almost laughed. Cass's memories meant only ten years ago. When he said "brought back memories," it meant over twenty years. "So, what about the girl who stopped you?"

"Said she had caught Zeke messing around in a storage room out behind the gym. She'd been working on some posters in the girls' Phy Ed office. I asked her what he was up to. Well, he'd been doing something with the old typewriters that had gotten retired back in the late '80s. She'd heard him pecking something out on one of the old manual machines. But she didn't see what he was writing."

"You know, Cassie," Andy said, "that's quite a coincidence. Trud getting threatening notes made on an old typewriter. And Zeke Haugen getting caught using an old Underwood or whatever."

Cass nodded. "The thought had occurred to me. We'll have to check it out. But with Trudi having burned the letters, it's hard to prove anything."

"So anyway, what happened with the girl?"

"Well, when he caught her standing in the door, scoping him, he chased her out into the gym and grabbed her. Said she'd be sorry if she told anyone. But the young female told me she wasn't the least bit scared of him. She observed, and I quote, 'Zeke Haugen's the most pathetic little shit on the face of the earth.' Nice turn of phrase, I thought."

Andy agreed with a nod. "A regular poet. So you hauled him off to the sheriff's office, full moon flying, and—"

"Then took him home to cool his heels. He's expelled from school for a week. One more occurrence and he's out the rest of the year."

They cruised into the outskirts of New Bergen, past the new MegAmerica gas station with a giant inflatable monster truck in front. "Well," Andy noted, "he only has to make it a few more weeks, till summer vacation. Even Zeke should be able to manage that."

"I wouldn't count on it," Cass opined. "Any kid who plasters his pimply bare butt on a squad car window has a serious attitude problem, as far as I'm concerned."

As they headed up Skjegstad Street, Andy asked Cass if she was free a week from Saturday. Walleye fishing opener. Lake Bonga. Shore lunch. A cold six-pack of Biberschwanz Pilsner. A nice romantic evening afterwards.

Cass's face lit up like a Fourth of July sparkler. "I thought you'd never ask."

* * *

Andy arrived back at Ansel's at about three. He peeked into his twin sister's office, where she was tapping furiously on her laptop, probably working on one of her spreadsheets. This was the sort of thing Kirsten Skyberg had done when she started out as a number-cruncher in

Silicon Valley. From there she zoomed into senior management at a famous software company. Kirsten retired at thirty-five with a bundle of bucks. No one knew exactly how much, but it was rumored to be somewhere in the lowish eight figures. Then she moved home to New Bergen with her husband and two kids. The easy life of the wealthy retiree finally drove her up the wall, and she decided to get busy again. Ansel's was the result, primarily because she wanted desperately to have a good New Bergen restaurant to eat in.

"Checkin' in," Andy said, inserting his lanky self into the doorframe. "Done with law enforcement for the day. Anything on the docket?"

She smiled distractedly, looking up at him. "And when isn't there something on the docket?"

"True enough," he said, plopping down in a folding chair next to an old oak bookshelf full of cookbooks and cooking magazines—all of them festooned with scores of yellow sticky notes, marking recipes for future consideration.

"Three things, Anders," Kirsten said. "Bill Tompkins has the cutlery ready."

Andy nodded. That meant a trip out to Bill's farm the next morning to exchange the worn knives for the newly sharpened set. He made the trip every two weeks.

"Next, I'll need you in front tonight. Five o'clock. I have a teacher's meeting for Aurora.

"Okeydokey." Andy thought of his niece Rory as a kind of kindred spirit, a lot more easygoing than her mom.

The Skyberg "don't-sweat-it" gene, which he possessed, had been passed on to her, as well.

"This last thing's a little speculative," Kirsten said, "but I have no one else to chase it down."

Andy leaned over and placed his elbows onto his knees, and his chin into his hands. "Sounds mysterious. What's up?"

"You remember that Elbow Lake Days comes first weekend in August. And we're going to have a Dane Dunk, as usual."

"Didn't we just about run outta Danes last year? Least those willing to take a dunking?"

Kirsten, chairwoman of the chamber of commerce's Elbow Lake Days committee, nodded. They indeed did suffer from a shortage of Danes in New Bergen.

"I didn't tell you," she said, "that the Danish National Home Association gave the chapter up in Hobartville the authority to appoint as many honorary Danes as we need. J. J.'s volunteered. So has Troy. Uncle Frank's good for a few dunks. Ed Vandegraff figures there're at least a hundred people he's written speeding tickets for who would love to dunk him. He's big, too. Make a nice splash. I'm gonna put in a shift. You game?"

Plunging feet first into a barrel of icy cold water wasn't Andy's idea of a good time. But the cause was plenty good. The Beaver Tail County Mentorship program received some money. So did the New Bergen girls' softball league. And the county food shelf.

"Yeah," Andy sighed. "I'll go for eight or ten dunks."

"Great," Kirsten said. "But that's not all I need you to do. Ansel's is going to have an ebelskiver booth out at the park."

Andy searched his memory banks for a few seconds. "Those Danish ball-shaped, pancakey things that you need those funky pans for?"

"Right," Andy's twin sister confirmed. "I have plenty of ebelskiver pans. I've made ebelskivers at home. But I'm looking for a certain ebelskiver recipe."

Andy peered quizzically at Kirsten, who normally had recipes coming out her ears.

His twin had dark blond hair turning to gray, which she wore in a bob. Her piercing blue eyes were narrowly almond-shaped, turned up at the ends, almost oriental. Her nose was small, and her cheekbones high and handsome. She resembled her twin brother only a little. Altitude was the primary thing she had in common with him, measuring six foot one in bare feet. She shocked everyone at New Bergen High when she refused to go out for girls' basketball.

Andy often wondered why it was Kirsten who'd gotten the smarts and the drive and the incredible luck. After all, his twin was just twenty minutes older. Not that he begrudged her. It was just something he'd never figured out.

"You mean you don't have some recipes already?" Andy asked.

"Sure I do," Kirsten answered, waving a big, hardworking hand at her archive. "But a few of the old dears at church told me about this legendary ebelskiver that some pastor's wife had made at church breakfasts back in the '50s and '60s."

She flashed a wicked grin. "You'd think they were recollecting what they used to do with their boyfriends in the back seats of '52 Plymouths. Only problem is they can't remember who it was that made this heavenly ebelskiver. I want you to find the recipe, Andy. If it's the real deal, that's the one I'll use. And I just don't have time to go banging around the countryside playing at food detective."

"And I do?" Andy asked.

Kirsten nodded and swiveled back to view her computer screen. "I don't see any other hired help in this room, little bro."

Chapter Nine

Andy lived in a small, stuccoed bungalow on Willow Street, between two elderly widowed sisters who relied on him to mow their lawns, snow-blow their sidewalks, and listen to them tell the same ancient stories again and again and again. The sisters said that they liked to live together, but separately.

The extent of their affection for the six-foot-four ex-chauffeur manifested itself in their steadfast refusal to spread gossip about Cass Conlin's frequent six a.m. departures from Andy's back door, usually preceded by Harald's energetic woofing. Andy knew that they did not approve of such doings. They were terrifically prim and proper, even for old ladies of their vintage. But the two sisters weren't about to bite the hand that mowed their lawns and shoveled their walks.

It was Saturday, a few days after the notorious iguana incident. Andy was taking a couple of vacation days and planned to run out to Thor's place. His pal had spied a big patch of trilliums out in the woods on the edge of his property. Andy wanted to get some photos, so he could use the lovely white flowers in a new landscape painting.

Andy gobbled a quick breakfast, and twenty minutes later, he and Harald were bouncing up Thor's long driveway. Andy admired how quickly and neatly his old friend's son-in-law had gotten the fields ready and planted with soybeans. Some of the rows had little colorful signs on the ends, from a leading seed company, proclaiming provocative things like "Gardill 2848" and "Gardill 9031" and, most suggestive of all, "Gardill 3338XXX."

Opposite the farmyard from the Hofdahl manse stood two spiffy, white-and-green pole buildings, housing the goat cheese operation—one for the goats, the other for cheese-making. Thor's wife Sonny had been making boutique goat cheese for five years now. Her Montrachet, Colby, and Muenster could be found in co-op grocery stores and deluxe supermarkets down in the Cities.

A bunch of the kids and their mamas were out in the pasture behind the pole buildings, and they bleated almost in unison as Andy arrived.

The instant he and Harald emerged from the blue Chev Silverado, Thor popped out of his mudroom door and gestured urgently at them. *Come inside, now*. Andy almost shouted back: *What's the problem?* But he waited until he was pretty much in Thor's face.

"What's shakin', there, Supergeezer?" he laughed. "Besides that belly?" He and Thor traded insults like an old vaudeville team. Adequately barbed, but not too sharp.

"Get in here," Thor whispered, then turned and bolted back into his mudroom.

Andy stood there gape-jawed for a few seconds. He

had expected a zinger in return. But none came.

Andy wondered what was up. He held the screen door open for Harald, who had been recently soaped and rinsed enough to be allowed inside someone's house. Then man and dog padded after Thor.

The mudroom and kitchen looked pretty much like any on a Beaver Tail County farm. The kitchen had worn linoleum floors and ancient cabinets with glass doors as opaque as a nonagenarian's cataracts.

"So what's makin' you so darned terse and unsociable?" Andy asked as they proceeded through the living room, all dressed up in its white and pink Victoriana. Sonny's turf.

"If you'd just shut up and wait a minute, I'm gonna tell you," Thor said, heading into his sanctuary in the former parlor.

Andy followed him in and felt, as he always did in there, as if he'd wandered into the stacks of an old college library.

Every wall was covered floor to ceiling with shelves of books, mostly political stuff—and mostly socialist and communist. The complete works of Marx, Lenin, and Mao glowered out into this new gilded age of capitalism run amok. There were comprehensive sections on the Great Depression, the McCarthy-era witch-hunts, and the protests of the Vietnam War. Every book written by and about Thor's namesake, Thorstein Veblen, the great sociologist and economist. Thor had started a new section on the Great Recession of 2008 and beyond.

A gray, forty-inch-tall fireproof safe in the corner contained all Thor's research material on *Skjorfjeld's Retreat from Vinland*, a Viking saga that he was in the process of translating into English. Thor had told Andy all about this labor of love, and Andy struggled to seem the least little bit intrigued. The old boy was obsessive about it.

For some incomprehensible canine reason, Harald took a strong interest in a stack of ancient law books on the floor, slobbering and sniffing it simultaneously.

"Sit down, Andy," Thor barked.

Andy cleaned a few copies of *The Progressive* magazine off a gray secretary's chair by Thor's desk. "Whatcha gotcher knickers in a knot for, anyway?" he barked back.

"They're after me."

"Who's after you?"

"The feds."

"The feds? Like in the—" Andy ruminated for a few beats. "Feds?"

"*The* feds."

"You mean the FBI, CIA, Naval Intelligence, the National Security whatchamacallit?"

Thor nodded, pushing his bifocals back up his nose.

"What makes you think so?"

"There's two guys out in a white panel truck up behind the south forty, near where those trilliums are that I told you about. Been sittin' out there for two, three days. They only climb outta the thing to take a leak. They have a clear view of the house with whatever super-duper cameras they shoot with. What they don't know is I'm lookin' back at them with my Russian spotting scope. I can see a tick on a deer's ass from a mile away with that thing."

If Thor said he'd seen a panel truck out on that country dirt road, there undoubtedly was one. Andy didn't think Thor would have hallucinated it. But there had to be some other explanation than the feds coming all the way to New Bergen to spy on a highly opinionated crackpot.

"I can actually answer that famous riddle," Thor said, with his first hint of a smile.

"What riddle?"

"Does a federal agent *you-know-what* in the woods?"

"Huh?"

"The answer is, 'Yup.'"

Andy scratched his head. "You sure they aren't out there surveying for that fiber optic cable that's coming through?"

"No surveying equipment that I can see."

"You try to talk to them?"

Thor nodded. "I walked up there yesterday and hammered on the rear doors. I could hear 'em yakkin' when I approached the van. But they shut up and pretended not to be home. Couldn't see a thing through the front windows."

"Okay," Andy said. "Suppose somebody is doing surveillance on you. Why?"

Thor snorted, as if the answer was self-evident.

"Why?" Andy repeated, a little snappishly.

Thor crinkled his weather-beaten brow. "I've become too dangerous."

"In what way?"

"Through my articles. My op-ed pieces. My political blog. My letters to the editors. My essays. My YouTube videos."

"Oh."

Andy wanted to say that all of twelve people bothered to read any of the journals or papers Thor managed to get published in. But that would be mean.

"The political-corporate complex has gotta be aware of them and understands how dangerous my ideas are."

"Oh."

"You see, Andy, I've figured a way to tame capitalism that'll *work*. Domesticate it, housebreak it, make it serve the people instead of oppressing 'em. And they're scared shitless of it. The feds, the banksters, Wall Street, the East Coast intellectual power elite. The Federal Reserve. The Trilateral Commission. Homeland Security. The lot of 'em. That's why those boys are sittin' up there in that panel truck."

Andy slowly shook his head. "I think Castro tried that nationalization thing," he said finally, "and it didn't turn out too good."

"What I have in mind is kinder and gentler, Andy, and you know it. The government only takes what it needs to support the programs that the working classes have to have. Universal health care. Free college education. A national passenger train system that works. No one starves. A roof over every head. All foreign wars shut down. Banksters and CEOs and other rich sonsabitches get smaller troughs to stick their snouts in. All federal elections paid for by the government. Zero personal or corporate or union dollars in all federal races."

"But what about the terrorists they're protecting us from, Thor?"

"Listen, you pup, we get out of their turbans, they'll get out of ours."

Andy didn't want to get into all that with Thor again. Hell, the old guy's plan might even work. But Thor Hofdahl of rural New Bergen seemed a mite too insignificant to single-handedly shift the rudder of Wall Street capitalism.

"Does it occur to you, Thor," Andy said, "that if all those powers-that-be found you the least eeny-teeny bit threatening, they'd just arrange to have some Jason Bourne wannabe come out here and shoot you in the head?"

Thor nodded thoughtfully. "It baffles me, too."

Chapter Ten

Whenever Andy was out in the woods, anything that had been bothering him simply vanished into thin air. For a little while he was no longer a middle-aged, slightly out-of-shape guy who'd never really accomplished much. All that angst flew up and away and vanished into the sky like a dove—at least for the moment. Instead, he figuratively linked arms with Thoreau and Wordsworth and Muir, kindred spirits who all found sustenance in the woods and the fields.

Under the maple and oak and ash—that was where Andy Skyberg found peace and enlightenment.

Harald became so giddy and bumptious out amongst the twigs and rocks that Andy could almost read the big mutt's mind: *"Let's you and me just run away and live out here and chase squirrels and eat grass!"*

Andy thought it might not be such a bad idea.

Today, though, there were trilliums to be photographed—according to Thor, the biggest damned aggregation of trilliums he'd ever seen. Out in some shaded bottomland on his property, bordering his south forty and a parcel of state forestland. Andy knew just how he wanted to paint them—with a big nod to Claude Monet.

What Andy saw when they arrived at the spot Thor had described took his breath away. A carpet of white stretched a full city block, seventy or eighty feet in breadth. Embracing a trickle of a creek and swaying gently in a subtle breeze.

Andy whistled softly. "Isn't that just gorgeous as the dickens, Harald?" he asked his dog. "Can't you see it on a big canvas, hanging in a gallery? With my name on it and a price that includes more than three numbers?"

Andy sensed that Harald wanted to charge through those very same trilliums, after a chittering squirrel that was tormenting him from a tree across the way. So Andy took the precaution of tying his mutt to a small cottonwood. Then he pulled out his digital camera and shot the field of trilliums from straight on, from one side, then the other. It meant carefully treading all around the margin of the flowers, to get that and this angle. Again and again. But Andy couldn't get enough of it. He took dozens and dozens of pictures, visualizing his new artwork as he snapped.

Harald didn't seem to mind being tied up to the cottonwood. There would always be another squirrel. He gnawed placidly on the rawhide strip Andy had given him and snoozed. For a dog, it was a fine way to spend a morning.

Andy was sitting on a log, flipping through his pictures on the camera's viewing screen, when he heard Harald grumbling softly behind him—his serious, subterranean growl.

"What's the problem, ol' scout?" Andy said. He went over and squatted by the dog.

Harald stood and growled again, baring his not inconsiderable fangs.

Andy looked in the direction Harald was gazing. He couldn't see a thing.

Then he heard it—the faint snap and crackle of someone tramping into the bottomland. Someone who didn't care if he was being heard.

Andy detached Harald from the cottonwood and found a muddy hummock, a spot that offered a clear view of the trillium field. They hunkered down behind it.

Harald growled again. Andy grabbed his snout, clamping it tight. *"No,"* he whispered.

The big mutt vibrated a bit, as if he were going to argue the point, but settled down and shut up.

A slightly overweight man in jeans and camo jacket hove into view, loudly huffing and puffing. He wore a dun-colored backpack. His balding pate glinted in the dappled light under the trees. A few strands of brown hair trailed over the top.

Andy might have taken him for merely another sojourner amongst the splendors of Mother Nature, but not with the tripod-mounted gear he had on his shoulder. It looked like some kind of video camera. But fancier than a TV photographer's setup, that was for sure. Possibly military equipment. Infrared, maybe.

And Andy very much doubted that this fellow was out here to film the trilliums.

The man in the camo jacket came slip-sliding down the rise. He nearly lost his balance, but caught himself. He cursed sharply, the f-word, then kept on coming. He plowed right into the trilliums, kicking and crushing his way through masses of the graceful white blooms. Then he tramped out of sight, into the woods on the other side, heading straight for the perimeter of Thor's son-in-law's biggest bean field. Which, Andy well knew, offered a clear, straight-shot view of the socialist gadfly's house, his farmyard, and his wife's goat operation.

"Holy Moses, Harald," Andy told his dog, "Thor wasn't kidding. It *is* the feds! It has to be. And look what that sonofabitch did to the trilliums!"

* * *

After driving back to town, Andy stopped at the sheriff's station and told Ed Vandegraff what he'd witnessed out in the woods. Ed seemed awfully disinterested. Andy understood that it was a Saturday afternoon and Cinco de Mayo to boot. The police were gearing up to handle partiers who got a little too lively that evening. Ed said he'd check into the trillium-masher caper or send "Deputy Conlin" out to have a look-see "early next week."

After that oddly unsatisfying encounter, Andy and Harald headed back home. But as he swung his Chev pickup down Skjegstad Street, Andy spotted a gaggle of onlookers down by Trudi's store, out in the parking lot.

What the heck was going on?

Parking his crew-cab Silverado across the street, Andy attached Harald's leash and hauled the canine toward Trudi's store. What he saw made him whistle with admiration.

There, up on a sturdy, tall, aluminum stepladder, was Aunt Bev, daubing colorful paint onto the skeletal sketch of a giant rosemaling design. The mural stretched a good twenty-five feet wide and ten feet tall along the outside, white-stuccoed wall of the Karma Kubbyhole.

From what Andy could see, there were lots and lots of cascading flowers in the design. Colorful blooms were the big thing in rosemaling. They all looked pretty much the same to him, and like nothing that he knew of in nature. Also he spotted a sketched-out object that, if his eyes didn't deceive, looked suspiciously like a giant iguana.

Aunt Bev had secured a homemade wooden tray to the top of the ladder, to hold her paint pots and brushes. Arrayed around her was an audience of a good two dozen spectators.

Rosemaling as performance art, Andy thought to himself. Who else but Aunt Bev could pull that off? He politely threaded his way through the crowd.

"Hey, Aunt Bev," he said, a little loudly, blinking up into the sun. Her hearing wasn't the greatest. "Whatcha up to there?"

Aunt Bev twisted around and grinned down at her nephew. "Just the biggest commission of my career, is what, Anders," she answered, then clambered down with admirable nimbleness for a sixty-something.

"That sketch you made," said Andy. "Charcoal?"

"Yup," said Aunt Bev.

"You do that freehand or some other way?"

"Well, last night I had Ronnie—"

Myron Engebretson was Aunt Bev's older son and Andy's cousin, as well as a senior manager at Lovely Lena Macaroni Corporation.

"—come here and set up his laptop computer and a digital projector from work to put my design up onto this wall. It took me two hours to trace it out. Trudi hired me to memorialize her lizard, Anders. We're calling it 'Helse Gjennom Aroma.'"

Andy chuckled and shrugged. His Norwegian was pretty rusty at the best of times. "Ummm, okay, that would mean?"

"'Health Through Aroma.' Underneath will be the dedication, 'Inne Hukommelse av Adonis.' In memory of Adonis. I got the translation off of Google."

"Well," Andy said, "I shouldn't keep you when you're working. But as long as I'm here, I wanted to ask you about a little detective job Kirsten gave me. You know she's heading up the committee for Elbow Lake Days."

"So I heard," said Aunt Bev. "A considerable respon-sibility."

"And there's gonna be a big ebelskiver feed at the park that Sunday morning."

"Just *loooove* ebelskiver. Who doesn't? I will be there, you can count on me. But why does Kirsten need detective work?"

"She has her heart set on tracking down a legendary ebelskiver recipe that's hidden somewhere in the mists of history. Back in the '50s or '60s or thereabouts. Some pastor's wife came up with it and to hear Kirsten talk about it—well, it was supposed to be just heavenly. And I wondered if you had any thoughts about where to start looking."

"Anders, do you have any idea how many pastors came through Beaver Tail County back in those days?" asked Aunt Bev, peering up at him. "And how many pastors' wives? This here was the minor *minor* league for Lutheran ministers. There would have been dozens and dozens of them. I'd start with this lady I know up in Hobartville. Give me a day or two, and I'll track down her number." She moved back toward her ladder.

"Now if you'll excuse me, Anders, I still have to start painting Adonis before I call it a day."

Andy ambled inside the Kubbyhole, intending to pick up a piece of jewelry for Cass's upcoming birthday. Trudi had some gorgeous handmade turquoise-and-silver items. Cass loved that kind of stuff.

Lauren Kastner was showing him several necklaces, when he heard the peal of baby laughter—another of Gus's digitized doorbell "chimes." He looked up as the shop door swung open and gasped a bit when he saw the new arrival. Not someone who had much in common with a giggling infant.

It was none other than Jerry Dittbrenner.

The hog breeder—a pugnacious fireplug of a man somewhere in his mid-forties—strode up to the iPad cash register, where Charlie Adams was presiding. He had on a blue sport jacket and tan chino trousers. Hardly Andy's image of a typical Beaver Tail County farmer. His face was square and ruddy and he didn't look like he'd come for a social call. This was the guy whom Trudi had called "Vlad the Impaler," because of alleged mistreatment of his hogs.

"Is your boss here?" Dittbrenner asked Charlie, his voice a steely monotone.

Charlie—pretty good in the pugnacious department herself—scowled at Dittbrenner. "Yeah, what do you want?"

"I need to talk to her."

Apparently the Karma Kubbyhole didn't have an intercom, because Charlie cupped her hands to her mouth and bellowed, "Trudi, someone to see you."

Fifteen or twenty seconds later Trudi emerged from the back room, wearing the smile of a person expecting to see a friend or customer. Instead, a look of pure hatred flashed across her normally genial face.

She marched up to Dittbrenner, still scowling, and snapped, "Yes, what do you want?"

Charlie came around the counter and stood next to Trudi, arms crossed.

Dittbrenner looked Trudi up and down and glared at her. "I have something for you, Ms. Bock."

Trudi appeared a little puzzled.

"Here you go," the hog farmer said. He reached inside his coat, withdrew a white envelope, and thrust it at Trudi.

A little surprised, she took it. "What *is* this?"

"A subpoena. You've been served. I'm suing you. For defamation. I'm also suing your so-called humane society. You know nothing about the way a hog-breeding operation works. And lady, you're gonna regret tangling with Jerry Dittbrenner."

Trudi was speechless—a rare occurrence.

Charlie looked as if she were about to pop a blood vessel.

Dittbrenner turned on his heel to leave. As he wheeled around, he caught sight of Andy and Lauren by the jewelry display. He looked away and trod out the door.

Then something weird happened.

Lauren muttered, "Excuse me, Andy, I'll be right back," and walked right out of the shop—hot on Dittbrenner's heels.

Chapter Eleven

Compared to the trillium-tromping atrocity and the bizarre encounter with Jerry Dittbrenner, the next day was positively pleasant. Simply a delightful Sunday.

Thor came over to Andy's after lunch and they watched a big league, twi-night doubleheader on the forty-two-inch flatscreen. Coincidentally, they each imbibed some Biberschwanz Pilsners and on toward suppertime grilled a few bratwursts. Harald enjoyed a brat or two, as well—in fact, practically inhaled them.

After all that beer and chow, Andy should have slept like the proverbial baby. But he didn't.

So Monday morning when he plucked his copy of the *Chronicle* off the front stoop, his eyelids were saggy and puffy, his brain barely ticking over. He shuffled bare-footed back through the living room and into the kitchen, tossing the paper on the green laminate counter next to the coffee maker. King Harald was sitting on his haunches by the back door, watching Andy intently—as he did every morning.

Andy trudged over to unlock and fling open the door and screen. Harald trotted out and headed straight for the *faux* fire hydrant out by the back fence—a cast cement piece painted red, slightly smaller than the real thing.

Andy fixed up six cups of java. Three for an eye-opener and three for the thermos he planned to bring to his studio above the restaurant. Ansel's was closed on Mondays during the off-season. He had a morning of painting ahead of him. He figured the caffeine would enhance his creative juices.

After savoring his first few sips of the lovely brew, he plopped down at the kitchen table. The coffee began to course through his arteries, gently nudging lethargic parts of his brain with delightful little tendrils of caffeine molecules and bringing him back to a semblance of consciousness. He grabbed the newspaper off the counter, put his reading glasses down on the tip of his nose, and sat again.

Top headlines: Extensive coverage about the unceasing efforts by Jumbo Mart to obtain the necessary county permits for a superstore out by the Interstate near Hobartville. New Bergen's leading chiropractor and former city councilman to run for County Board of Commissioners. Tinsdale-Schwartzwald-Smithtown High baseball team makes it to Single-A regional quarter-finals, winning a 3-2 squeaker. Semitrailer full of potato chips tips over on the Interstate, as driver falls asleep. No injuries.

Andy flipped through the A-section's inner pages and arrived at the editorial page. Pro and con columns on the Jumbo Mart proposal, along with letters from lovers and haters of the mega-retailer. A letter about Trudi Bock's upcoming Eleanorian Festival in the town park on the same day as the Syttende Mai shindig, signed by Anders Skyberg…

Andy's eyes nearly popped out of their sockets!

The letter signed in his name said that *he, Anders Skyberg, believed that Trudi Bock's Eleanorian cele-bration was, in fact, the equivalent of an itinerant religious meeting and therefore in contravention of an obscure New Bergen city ordinance of 1923 that forbids "traveling preachers and other religious personages from holding services or lectures on any public property."*

Just then the kitchen wall phone started jangling. Still dumbfounded from the letter to the editor, Andy stood and picked up the receiver. "Yeah," he muttered, "Andy here."

He recognized Trudi's voice but not the wailing and sobbing that erupted between words like "*jerk*" and "*trai-tor*" and "*liar*" and "*snake in the grass.*" Any efforts to get a word in edgewise were in vain over the course of about 90 seconds of vituperation and lamentation. Right up to the point where Trudi hung up on him.

Andy sat again and stared into his coffee mug for several long minutes, trying to get his brain around the mess that had just dropped from the clouds into his lap. The phone started to ring again, and Andy began to hoist himself upright.

"Nope," he told Harald, easing back down, "this is exactly the situation that voicemail was made for."

After four rings the phone went silent.

Andy stared at it warily.

Finally, if reluctantly, he went over to the phone and took it off the hook. He punched in several numbers.

"You have. One. Message," pronounced the creepily bland and disembodied female voice.

"Good morning, Anders," said an old woman. "This is Mrs. Oscar Runestrand."

Andy shuddered.

"I just saw this morning's *Chronicle* and read your fine letter to the editor. I want to thank you so much for bringing that old ordinance regarding itinerant preachers to our attention. I believe there's still time to use it to persuade the city council to withdraw Miss Bock's permit for her pagan rite in the city park a week from this coming Saturday. I knew that down deep you are on the side of holy righteousness. *I knew it*. God bless you, Anders Skyberg."

* * *

In Carter LaPorte's position, Andy would have felt pretty embarrassed by such a mess-up. But while contrite, the newspaperman didn't seem too broken up. He was sorry because it was his job to be sorry, in this kind of situation. He said he'd print an apology and call Trudi to explain what happened.

Andy was sitting on a dilapidated folding chair in front of the managing editor's desk in the newsroom of the *Beaver Tail County Chronicle*. It was actually the windowless basement of the old American Legion hall in Hobartville—where they used to store the beer kegs and pickled eggs. There were about a dozen-and-a-half desks jammed into the room, each with a dusty, out-of-date computer, and heaps of newspapers and notebooks.

It was the reporters, photographers, and editors who found themselves relegated to these lower depths. In fact, a photographer had once explained to Andy that the *Chronicle*'s editorial staff had a lot in common with mushrooms. Stuck in a dim, depressing cave, up to their ankles in shit.

"So what happened, Carter?" Andy asked, uncomfortable with being so accusatory. "Trudi Bock is furious with me. And now 20,000 of your readers will see that bogus letter you printed and think I'm in cahoots with religious wingnuts like Mrs. Runestrand."

The managing editor was the kind of person who smiled a lot, like any proper member of the chamber of commerce. "I've already e-mailed Madge about this."

Andy knew Madge Juntenen, who co-owned the paper with her husband Pete. She was the editor-in-chief.

"She and Pete are on a cruise and won't be back until next week. I'm sure she'll want to tell you how sorry she is, too."

As if that'll get me out of hot water with Trudi, Andy thought glumly.

"All I can say is that no one who read and approved this letter had any reason to doubt that it was from you," Carter continued. "The tone was civil. Nothing inflammatory in it. The writer cited an existing city ordinance, which we checked out. It's on the books. From the 1920s. We couldn't have known that you didn't write the thing.

As I said, we'll print a correction and an apology in tomorrow's paper."

"That's well and good, Carter," Andy said, now exasperated. "But I still look like a horse's arse. And Trudi's the one who'll pay the price for this."

Carter nodded earnestly. But Andy wasn't buying the look of concern on his face.

"She's put a *heckuva* lot into her Eleanorian clambake," Andy noted pointedly. "She has people coming from around the country, even a few from overseas."

"I know, I know," Carter said. "But there's nothing more I can do."

Andy sighed and shook his head. "Do you still have the letter? Can I see it?"

The managing editor pulled open a desk drawer and extracted a folder, then the letter. "At least we didn't toss it," he said, handing it across the desk.

"Just cheap copy paper," Andy said, examining the single sheet. "The correspondent's definitely not into inkjets or laser printers. This is made on an old manual typewriter. Look at the wonky letters there."

Andy didn't repeat what Cass had told him about Zeke Haugen messing around with the retired typewriters at the high school. Nor did he mention Trudi's recollection of what those threatening letters looked like. But this sure did put Zeke Haugen in the frame, as they said in hard-boiled detective novels. Only thing is, would Zeke have had the smarts to look up some obscure New Bergen city ordinance? Was the kid hiding his light under a bushel? Andy made a mental note to tell Cass about this typewriter clue.

"You still have the envelope, Carter? Might help to see the postmark."

"Sorry. Circular file."

"You know," Andy grumbled, "you really ought to check with people to make sure they're the authors of their letters. Man, I wish you'd called me."

Carter slumped back in his chair. "Andy, no newspaper checks out letters they run to make sure they were written by the people who signed them. If the letter's reasonable and not libelous and makes a good point, we might run the thing. Sorry, that's just the way it is."

Andy was getting up to leave when he noticed a stack of yellowed clippings on Carter's desk. They were articles about Horace Frenchman, a famous architect back in the early years of the 20th century who hailed from Beaver Tail County.

"Are you working on something about Frenchman?" Andy asked, genuinely curious. He was an admirer of the old architect, now dead sixty or seventy years.

"Yeah," Carter answered. "I'm doing a big feature on him. No one's written anything about him in years."

"If you're interested," Andy said, thinking to proffer an olive branch, "I have a couple of out-of-print books about him. You can borrow them, if you want."

Carter's face brightened. "Why, that'd be real nice, Andy. I'd like that. It's hard to find material on Frenchman around here. Tell you what, why don't you come to my house for dinner some evening. You can bring the books along, and Harald, too."

* * *

Andy munched on a Nut Goodie and sucked on a Mountain Dew in the parking lot of the trucker oasis on the Interstate outside Hobartville.

He scanned the front page and inside news sections of the complimentary *Chronicle* he'd picked up in the newspaper office. He shuddered a bit when his eyes bounced over the offending letter yet again.

At least, there'd been a few good things to come out of this commotion. Carter had extended his *Chronicle* subscription for the next six months gratis and given him one of the coupon books that premium subscribers received. Among the deals inside was a half-price bucket of minnows at Herman the German's Fishing Supplies. Perfect for the fishing opener with Cass.

And Andy was glad that the encounter had ended on an upbeat note. He didn't enjoy conflict one little bit and he didn't want any hard feelings lingering between him and Carter.

Now it was time to deal with Trudi's hard feelings.

He pulled out his cell phone and punched in her number.

As soon as she picked up, he blurted, "Trud, don't hang up. I just talked to Carter LaPorte and let me tell you what happened…"

Chapter Twelve

It was a simple matter for King Harald to take himself for a walk, should he happen to be in the mood.

He would back off a few feet, blast out of the starting blocks, and hop right over the backyard chain-link fence. A cockapoo or even a beagle would have had a heck of a time gaining that kind of altitude. But for high-jumping Harald, it was a snap.

Since Harald was a famously gregarious hound, hardly anyone he encountered seemed to mind having him on the loose. In fact, he collected many a pat on the noggin during his perambulations. While at liberty, he tended to behave himself. He hadn't much interest in digging, refused to chase cats, and had bumped off only a couple of squirrels in his entire career. Since the big dog had undergone a certain type of embarrassing surgery long before the boss had brought him on staff, he had no interest whatsoever in hot dates with canines of the opposite sex.

Once in a while, some killjoy or other would grab him by the collar and return him to Andy Skyberg's backyard. But Harald possessed a forgiving nature and took those repatriations with good humor.

Today's was much like any other of Harald's mid-afternoon tours of the town. Under a partly cloudy sky, he went up one street and down another. He woofed companionably at several fellow canines whom he saw in windows and behind fences.

At one point in his itinerary, Harald swung by the broad parking lot of the high school. Students were coming out of the building, heading for their buses, bicycles, and automobiles. At the far edge of the lot, Harald came upon several teenaged boys who were jabbering animatedly. The dog paid them no particular attention until one of the boys—who Harald could not possibly have known was called Zeke Haugen—flourished an object in the air.

Harald stopped in his tracks, transfixed.

It was wiggly.

It was wonderful.

It looked very much like that other wiggly, wonderful thing Harald had prized out of a tree in the country just a week ago. Perhaps a bit smaller. And he wanted so much to have this one, too.

The ginger mutt trotted over to the boys, who took a moment before they noticed him.

He wagged his tail and whimpered in an obsequious manner.

"What the eff do you want?" Zeke Haugen growled at Harald.

That didn't sound too friendly, at least to Harald.

Harald wagged some more tail and whimpered a bit—his best possible begging.

Zeke approached Harald and jammed the object in his direction. "Do you want this, huh?" the delinquent sneered. "You want this?"

Harald was disappointed that this thing didn't smell nearly as good as the first thing. More like the tires on the boss's truck than that nice wiggly, wonderful object he had found out in the country.

Zeke came closer, holding the rubber lizard by the tail, as if he were going to let Harald have a good sniff. But instead, the teenager snapped the thing down and rapped Harald right on the snout.

The dog yelped and hopped backward, shocked at this nasty turn of events. Getting whacked on the nose had not been called for. Not at all. He'd done nothing to deserve that. A feistier dog might have taken offense and growled threateningly.

But not Harald. He did not want to be a dog in this fight. Determined to give Zeke Haugen no satisfaction at all, he turned tail and loped off in the direction of downtown New Bergen.

Five minutes later King Harald was cruising along on one of the side avenues that crossed Skjegstad Street, past several antique stores. As he came to the mouth of an alleyway, he heard a familiar voice emanating from it. His old friend Charlie!

But the tone of Charlie's voice was agitated, angry, almost quivering.

"You just leave her the hell alone!" Charlie exclaimed. "You don't, and I promise I'll spread your story from one end of Beaver Tail County to the other! I'm giving you a break here. Don't screw it up."

To Harald it sounded as if Charlie might be in some kind of trouble. He was just about to charge to the rescue when his friend tramped out of the alley and right into him. She nearly tumbled onto the cement.

"Jesus H. Christ!" Charlie barked. "Watch where you're going, Harald."

Harald woofed a "hello," relieved that Charlie seemed to be okay. But she stood there glaring at him, making no move at first to pat his head or scratch his back.

"Oh crap," Charlie finally said, bending over and petting him. "It's not you I'm mad at. It's Andy. Trudi throws herself at him, and he doesn't care. She's too nice a gal to get treated that way, Harald."

The dog's only response was to cock his head slightly, as if he were giving thoughtful consideration to Charlie's comments.

"Yeah, I know it's not your fault," Charlie said, giving Harald one last rub. "Now go on home. You shouldn't be out loose like this."

As Charlie turned and walked away, Harald could have sworn that he sensed another familiar aroma. Not Charlie, but someone else. But when he snuck a peek down the alley, no other human was there.

At any rate, Harald had had enough of a constitutional and, as Charlie suggested, headed home. The boss found him waiting patiently in the backyard, as if nothing had ever happened.

Chapter Thirteen

Andy wasn't enough of an obsessive angler to haul his and Cass's butts up the Interstate late on Friday evening in order to dip their lines at the stroke of midnight—the official beginning of the state's fishing opener. Oddly enough, rolling out of the sack at 4 a.m., saddling up, and heading north somehow seemed more reasonable.

Their plan was to hook up the old Alumacraft—on indefinite loan from Andy's dad—and cruise north to Herman the German's bait shop outside Hobartville. Andy would purchase a big bucket of minnows with that great coupon Carter LaPorte had given him. Meanwhile, Cass would pop into the hoagie shop next door for ginormous sandwiches and various treats, in case the walleyes didn't provide a shore lunch. Andy's cooler contained a six-pack of Biberschwanz Pilsner. Happily, state statutes allowed a fellow to drink on his boat. Just don't get caught piloting the thing after consuming too much brew.

For a while, everything went like clockwork. Cass, a hard sleeper, managed to get out of Andy's bed only a few minutes after 4. They slugged down instant coffee and instant oatmeal. Andy roused Harald, who cooperated by doing the necessary things in the backyard. Then Andy backed the Silverado in close to the garage's double door. He kept his Lincoln Town Car in there, along with his dad's Alumacraft. Then it was simply a matter of jockeying the truck up close to the boat trailer, which he wrestled up onto the hitch on the back of the Silverado. Andy, Cass, and Harald were rolling out of the alley by 5:30.

Herman the German's was a total zoo—even at six in the a.m. Andy felt on edge as he stood in line with his bucket. What if they ran out of minnows before he bought his? It'd be a shame to not be able to use that coupon. Meanwhile, Cass was next door in the sub shop, stoking up on hoagies and bags of taco chips.

Before long, Andy, Cass, Harald, and quite a few minnows crossed the line into Herkimer County, heading for Lake Bonga. Andy's grandpa had fished there with Andy's dad. And Andy's own pop took him, Kirsten, and their younger brother Karl there many a time back in the day. Not a lot of fisherfolk were aware of the lake, which suited Andy fine. About the only anglers he expected to see there were the locals who knew a thing or two about Lake Bonga's walleye riches.

A few miles short of Lake Bonga, bouncing over a badly maintained county road, Andy posed a question to his favorite deputy sheriff.

"Did you ever find out if any of those typewriters at the high school matched the typewriter used for that bogus newspaper letter?"

Cass shook her head, as she nibbled on a taco chip. "Nah, no match at all. So you can't go blaming Zeke Haugen for cooking up that letter. And I mean, what're the odds a dopey kid like him could pull a stunt that clever?"

"Clever or not," Andy sniffed, "it wasn't any fun being on the receiving end. Trud was really PO'd, I can tell you. The way it messed up her big shindig? I'm just thankful she doesn't blame me."

"And what if she did, Andy? Why should you care? I thought you and her were history."

Andy realized that Cass, along with most of New Bergen, was aware that Trudi wouldn't mind a repeat performance with him. But Cass sounded prickly about it. And that seemed a bit hypocritical of her. After all, Cass was the one who insisted she and Andy keep their relationship open.

But he wasn't looking to start an argument. Instead, he attempted to explain.

"Do you have any friends you've known for twenty years who you still like, Cassie?"

"Not many," she replied.

"Well, neither do I. So I'd like to keep the ones I have."

The Silverado arrived at the boat ramp at about seven-thirty, beneath a bright, beautiful sky with only a few puffy clouds. It was still a little bit coolish, but nothing that a sweatshirt and windbreaker couldn't handle. Half an hour later, Andy cast the first minnow into Lake

Bonga and set a slow, curved course along the far side of the apostrophe-shaped lake, his electric trolling motor humming away.

Andy had taken lady friends fishing before, and typically they didn't like to bait their hooks. Piercing the minnow's little beady eyes or tail with the barbed steel made them all squeamish.

Cass had no such compunctions. With a sniff and a snort, she blinded the tiny fish and cast it a good forty feet off the stern. How could a guy not like a girl who could cast like that?

The two anglers trolled up and down the east shore of the lake, cruising at about the pace of a brisk walk. Andy kept sneaking peeks at Cass, whose flaxen ponytail stuck out the back of her black Glock baseball cap. He still couldn't quite figure out how he'd managed to hook up with the foxiest cop in the four-county area. And how many guys meet their future girlfriend when she's giving them a speeding ticket?

It turned out they both liked tramping the woods— Cass preferably with a Winchester 30.30 cradled in her arms. They were both fond of classic rock and country western. Either of them could cook up a storm. Neither needed to fill up the air with idle chitchat. And the former chauffeur couldn't remember having hotter sex with anyone in his whole life. That girl was a firecracker.

But as for there being some deep, emotional connection... Well, deep emotion wasn't Andy's forté. Nor Cass's. Theirs was a relationship of convenience, mild affection, and good times. And wasn't that enough?

"So, where are those legendary Lake Bonga walleyes, Andy?" asked Cass, on toward noon, a tone of sarcasm clearly on display.

In their three-plus hours on the water, she and Andy had hauled in a grand total of two diminutive perch and a small northern pike with an attitude. The northern, at least, had been fun to catch.

"Dunno," said Andy, reeling in his bait and spinner. "Came here a year ago with Thor and we just about caught our limits. Nice big ones, too."

Andy was about to launch into a disquisition on the capricious nature of *Sander vitreus*—popularly known as the walleyed pike and an obsession all over the state.

But Harald, who had been utterly quiet all morning, gave a firm, resonant woof.

Andy twisted around to check out his big dog, who was standing like a hood ornament on the raised deck at the boat's bow. When the canine and human made eye contact, Harald kind of gyrated his bottom. Andy knew what that meant.

"Time for a bathroom break," Andy announced. "Might as well have lunch, too."

"So no shore-lunch walleye, huh?" sighed Cass.

"Good thing we got those hoagies."

Cass reeled in her line. Then Andy turned off the trolling motor and fired up the Evinrude outboard. He beached the Alumacraft on a little spit of sand near the bridge at the north end of the lake. Harald bounded off the bow of the boat and headed for the woods.

Carrying lunch, their cold six-pack of Biberschwanz Pilsner, and folding camp stools, Andy and Cass looked for a picnic-friendly spot. They plopped down in a grove of birches and poplars, the leaves beginning to show above their heads, dancing in a quickening, coolish breeze. It looked to Andy like it was starting to cloud over. He went back to the boat for Harald's dog food and water, then set it out for him next to the stools.

Andy had barely sat down and taken his first bite of hoagie when he realized how gorgeous this spot was. It would make for a fantastic landscape canvas.

"Hey, Cassie," he said, standing and putting his sandwich down on the folding stool, "I'm going to take some pictures while I still have this beautiful light. I think there's a painting out there. I'll just be gone a few minutes."

Cass was in the middle of a big mouthful of hoagie. "Wha' eh' 'er," she mumbled through the mass of meat, bread, and veggies.

As Andy went into the woods, Harald met him heading out. "Want to come, Harald?" Andy asked. But the dog kept on course, acknowledging his owner with nothing more than a glance and a tail wag.

Tramping back twenty-five minutes later, bubbling with the possibilities of his new idea for a painting, Andy arrived at the lunch site to find Cass and Harald looking a bit downcast.

"Hey, who died?" Andy asked flippantly.

Cass answered with a scowl. "Your sandwich."

Andy glanced at the camp stool where he had left his lunch. It wasn't there. "I don't understand."

"I was off in the bushes," said Cass. "You know, a lot of coffee this morning. And somebody snarfed the thing up while I was gone. I caught him with shreds of lettuce hanging out of his mouth." She made a head nod in the direction of Harald, who slouched guiltily on his haunches.

Andy blinked at his larcenous mutt and woefully shook his head. "It's all gone?"

"Oh, yeah," Cass confirmed, showing no sign of empathy. "That's what you get for not coming back when you said you would."

Oooookay, thought Andy. Best to let this discussion just drop. As his stomach growled, he reached for a bag of taco chips.

* * *

By the time they were back on the water, the clouds had thickened and darkened. A cutting, cold wind came in from the northwest. And a light rain gradually transformed itself into a hard drizzle. Andy broke out the rain gear as they trolled another part of the lake.

"Walleyes are supposed to feed harder when the weather's like this," he observed.

"Well, these guys sure didn't get the memo, did they?" Cass commented snarkily. She seemed personally insulted that it would dare to rain on her fishing trip.

They trolled wordlessly up and down the shore for

another hour. The only sounds were the splatter of the drizzle and an occasional, mournful woof from King Harald, the dripping wet sandwich thief.

"Hey, Cassie," Andy said, breaking the silence.

"What, Andy?" she said.

"I'd like to ask you about something."

"Ask away. I've got nothing better to do."

"You know my friend Thor."

"He's a socialist, I understand."

There was a strong tone of disapproval in Cass's voice.

Andy knew that she believed the only thing the government should pay for was law enforcement and prisons. She was a terrific libertarian, except when it came to her government paycheck, benefits, and pension.

"And he's proud of it," Andy confirmed.

"So? What about him?"

"I think somebody's spying on Thor." And Andy told Cass the story of the man in the woods with the high-end video gear, as well as the mysterious panel truck parked within eyeshot of Thor's farmstead. "Do you know anything about it, Cass? I brought it up with Ed and never heard a word back."

She pointedly declined to make eye contact with her boyfriend. "I can't say."

"What do you mean, you can't say?"

"Just that, Andy. *Can't say*."

"Maybe you mean you *won't* say."

Cass reeled in her line and seemed to be pondering

her response.

"Well?" said Andy.

"I am not allowed," Cass pronounced, as if reciting a script, "to discuss the matter you've brought up."

Andy blinked in amazement. He certainly knew that Cass was officious and severe as the dickens when it came to her job. But this seemed over the top. "So some government agency is spying on an eccentric, harmless geezer who happens to think that the filthy rich are rich enough?"

"I cannot say anything, Andy."

"But why? What did Thor do?"

Cass looked at Andy, reddening in the face beneath the hood of her dripping rain poncho. She shook her head.

Andy set his jaw. "What did he do, Cassie?"

"Ask me one more time and I'll have to report you." She set her jaw and scowled.

Andy stared at his girlfriend. "You have to be kidding."

Cass stared right back. "Just try me."

They looked at each other for what seemed a long, long time. Finally, Andy reeled in his spinner and stood up to turn off the trolling motor. He started the Evinrude and aimed his dad's old Alumacraft at the boat ramp a mile or so away.

It was going to be a heckuva long ride back to New Bergen.

Chapter Fourteen

What a difference two days could make, Andy thought morosely. He was sprawled on the sofa in his studio, just upstairs from Ansel's restaurant.

When Cass had started to speak as they drove away from Lake Bonga, Andy had felt a surge of hope. Maybe she was going to say, "Sorry, shouldn't have come across so blunt."

Actually, things got blunter.

"Andy," she had said, in a flat, hard tone as the rain bucketed down, "you need to get yourself as far away from Thor Hofdahl as you can. Drop him. Now. I'm saying this as a friend, and that's all I'm going to say."

For a while, Andy hadn't uttered another word, as he steered his Silverado through the downpour. He had been given the choice between a gorgeous, nubile girlfriend and a wrinkly, cranky old man who smelled of cheap cigars. An ultimatum. And as odd as it seemed—especially in retrospect—the choice looked pretty, gosh-darned clear.

"No," he said.

"What's that, Andy?" asked Cass.

"I said no."

"Your funeral then," came the cold reply.

And those had been the last words they had spoken to each other.

Now he was sitting in his studio with Harald, staring at the four-by-five-foot canvas that he'd started sketching on. It was going to be a scene from that grove of birches and poplars up at Lake Bonga, mashed up with the trilliums from near Thor's place. It was going to be in oil. That is, if he could ever stop moping about Cass long enough to fill up a palette with paint and dip a brush in it.

In its former life, his roomy studio had housed a solo CPA. But when Kirsten bought the building, she gave Andy the space as a perk of his restaurant employment. The place was just about perfect, with a pair of sizable windows on the north-facing side wall. Just the kind of light a painter loved. He had a big Craftech Artisan Grand Studio easel, storage shelving, a worktable, and the computer gear that let him project his digital photos onto canvas—much as Aunt Bev had done in Trudi's parking lot.

After an hour of negligible progress, Andy decided to take a break and clear out his brain. He thought he'd go over to Trudi's store to commiserate with her on the hatchet job the New Bergen City Council had done to her Eleanorian festival. Thanks to that ancient city ordinance that his doppelganger had written up in the letter to the editor, the event was officially banned from the city park.

Before he left, Andy went over to Harald, who was

snoozing on the beat-up rug near the worktable. Andy patted the mutt's bristly head. Tail wagging, Harald gazed expectantly at his master.

"I'm going over to Trud's for a little while, old boy. Don't knock anything over while I'm gone."

Andy was almost out the door when he turned around and gazed at his big, homely hound. "At least I have one loyal friend in the world. Even if he does steal my sandwiches."

* * *

When Andy walked in the front door of the Karma Kubbyhole, the sound of a conch horn greeted him.

He spotted Trudi behind her iPad cash register, checking out a talkative lady in a gaudy, neon green sweatshirt. Standing next to Trudi was handyman Gus Johnson.

Andy waved at them and they waved back. Then he waited while the woman in the flashy sweatshirt sauntered by him with a friendly nod. As she exited, the door cawed like a crow.

"Hi Trud, hi Gus," said Andy, sauntering up to the counter.

"Hey there, Andy," said Gus. "*Que pasa?*"

Gus was an intriguing character, Andy thought. He had given up the glamorous life of the peripatetic surfer to come to a winter climate and live in the basement of a retail shop. It sure seemed like some kind of demotion. Andy wondered if there was something more to it than Gus's old relationship with Trudi. Maybe the guy was down on his luck and Trudi threw him a lifeline. Andy knew for a fact that she had paid for Gus's long-overdue dental work with Doc Swanstrom. That had to cost several thousand bucks.

Beyond the mystery of Gus's reasons for being in New Bergen, Andy was fascinated by a certain rumor that hovered around him. It was whispered that in the late '70s, during a sojourn in Malibu, Gus briefly had an affair with Margot Kidder, the best Lois Lane ever. That was pretty heady stuff, here in the backwater of Beaver Tail County. Andy didn't have the nerve to ask Gus if it was true.

"What's up, Anders?" asked Trudi, with a grin that seemed out of proportion to the occasion.

Andy smiled back. He hadn't seen or talked with her since the newspaper letter incident, and he was relieved that she seemingly wasn't holding a grudge. He wondered, though, if the town grapevine had gotten word to her about his blow-up with Cass. The only thing that moved faster than light in New Bergen was gossip.

"I just stopped by, Trud, to tell you how sorry I was about what the city council did to your Eleanorian festival," Andy said.

"It *was* pretty rotten," Trudi agreed. She reached across the counter and took Andy's hand. "But I know perfectly well it wasn't your fault they figured out how to use that crummy old law. Carter took full responsibility for that letter. Mrs. Runestrand's the one who really pushed the ban through. She is one karmically messed-up old lady." Trudi made an exaggerated scowl.

"But I hear you'll still be able to unveil Aunt Bev's mural," Andy said.

Trudi nodded. "I arrived at the council meeting right at the last moment. Made me so mad. But I got them to agree to allow the New Age market in my parking lot, as well as the unveiling of Bev's mural. Your aunt has a lot of friends around town, and I think the politicians didn't want to offend them. And it'll bring oodles of visitors downtown. Folks who've come for the Syttende Mai celebration out in the park. I'm going to call it the Karma Kubbyhole Block Party."

"So you're making lemonade with the lemons they gave you," Andy said with genuine admiration. "Good for you."

"Yeah, Trudi never lets the bastards grind her down," Gus added. "She never gives up. Now, if you two'll excuse me, I'm gonna see how the kids in back are doing." Then he ambled off.

"Anyway," said Trudi, "we'll have the tables with vendors and there'll be a massage therapist *and* shiatsu practitioner. Palm-reading and Tarot cards. Music, dancing, face painting for the kids, the unveiling of the mural. Your sister's going to have her concession trailer set up."

"I know," Andy said. "I'll be getting it ready and working the window, too. Should be fun. But what's going to happen with the people coming from out of town for your Eleanorian thing?"

"They're still coming. But we'll just have our

ceremonies out at the farm early in the morning. I've rented tents and a portable potty."

Just then, Lauren Kastner emerged from the back room. Following her were a teenaged boy with a mouthful of orthodontic gear and a tall, buxom older woman. She was the spitting image of Trudi, but with freakishly black hair that was out-of-sync with the wrinkles on her face.

"Anders," said Trudi, "I'd like you to meet my mom, Toots Strassberger. Mom, this is Anders Skyberg."

"So this is the one that got away," Toots laughed. Then she marched right up and gave Andy an energetic hug. "It's great to finally meet you. I always told my girl that she should have shot for an ordinary guy without too much ambition or talent. But she goes and marries these doctors and lawyers and stock investors. So she ends up with a nice pile of money, but no one to keep her warm at night."

Andy cringed, but managed to present a wobbly, shit-eating grin.

"Mom," groaned Trudi. "Will you just hush up! That's water under the bridge, and Anders and I are great friends again. Aren't we, Anders?"

"Oh, absolutely," Andy replied, grateful to his old flame for having graciously extricated him from her mom's damnation by faint praise.

"And this fine young man is one of my part-time employees," Trudi continued. "Michael Muelhoff."

"Hi, Michael," Andy said, grabbing the teenager's

slightly damp hand.

"Nice to meet you, Mr. Skyberg," the kid said in a squeaky, adenoidal voice.

"So, Mrs. Strassberger," Andy said, "do you have an interest in metaphysical subjects, too?"

"Please, call me Toots," she said. "And it's Ms. Strassberger. I took back my maiden name. To answer your question, my little Trudi comes by her gift naturally. I'm an amateur astrologer myself and was one of the early people on the aromatherapy bandwagon. My aunt was a spiritual medium. A real one. Not one of those con artists. And my brother was a beloved pastor. He even spent a few years serving in these parts. But you wouldn't have known him, Andy. He was quite a bit older than me."

"Poor man died in an automobile accident before I was born," put in Trudi. "I never even met him, but I feel like I did. I'm still just in awe of him. He was practically a saint."

Andy had a trickle of recollection, then a flood. Uncle Herb, whom Trudi had gushed over back when they were dating in college. An improbable amalgam of Albert Schweitzer, Mother Teresa, and Superman.

The front door howled like a wolf and in stepped a delivery woman in brown shirt and shorts. She carried three boxes stacked on top of each other. Trudi signed for them.

"I was expecting these two," she said. "But not this one." She squinted at the label and brightened. "The memo says, 'Birthday gift.' But it's not my birthday for two months."

"Maybe it's for Eleanor of Aquitaine's birthday," speculated Toots.

"No, Mom," Trudi replied. "It's her anniversary in mid-May, when she married Henry. *Not* her birthday."

"Well, silly, whoever it's for, open it up."

Trudi located a box cutter and zipped open the package. She dug through the packing confetti and her jaw dropped.

"Uh...uh...uh..." she stuttered. Her face went pale.

Andy peered in the box, as Michael and Lauren darted over for a look.

Nestled in the confetti, a big rubber iguana stared up at them, its neck cut almost all the way through and liberally slathered with what looked like catsup.

Trudi had scurried out from behind the counter, and had been enfolded in her mother's embrace.

Still gripping her daughter, Toots looked at Andy. "What is it?"

"A rubber lizard with its neck sliced," he answered.

"I'm really getting tired of this sicko shit," Lauren grumbled.

"No kidding," Michael agreed in his adenoidal tenor. "Some slasher movie must be missing its psycho."

Hard to believe, Andy thought, that once upon a time nothing exciting ever happened in New Bergen. Now, though, it was getting ridiculous. Yet again, some person unknown was sending a frightening message.

And it seemed pretty darned clear what was being said: *Get the hell out of town, Trudi Bock! Or else!*

Chapter Fifteen

A couple of days later, on a Wednesday afternoon, Andy ambled into Phil's Ale and Spirits in Hobartville. The big liquor retailer featured the best selection of wine in the four-county area. It had been awfully nice of Carter LaPorte to invite Andy to a home-cooked dinner at his place. A bottle of wine or two would be a nice way for Andy to show his appreciation.

The morning and early afternoon had been spent getting Ansel's food trailer, a handsomely converted old Airstream, ready for Trudi's block party. It had felt like an oven in there. Andy was exhausted and looking forward to a leisurely evening with Carter.

He knew just what he wanted to get in the way of wine, for an unseasonably steamy evening like this. Some chilled Vinho Verde, a gently effervescent Portuguese white. Phil's was the only place in the county that carried the wine and they always had a few bottles in the refrigerator case. Just to be safe, Andy grabbed two of them.

He was on his way to the checkout counter with his bottles when a sharp female voice pinned him to the spot.

"Andy Skyberg!"

He turned around and muttered an "Oh crap" under his breath.

Marching toward him, bottle of vodka in hand, came the former Brenda Fundingsland. Still a good-looking brunette, she had a vibe that was anything but good. And Andy had known it for a couple of decades, since the days after he had taken her out on that single date, then learned how she had ridiculed him to every female friend she had. One of the original mean girls. And now Brenda was on the offensive against Trudi Bock.

"Hey, Brenda," Andy sighed. "What's up?"

There was no hello, no small talk. Brenda launched immediately into what was on her mind.

"I'm glad I ran into you, Andy. I've really tried to keep channels of communication open with Trudi Bock," she said, as if this were some noble sacrifice on her part.

"Good for you," Andy replied, with daring snarkiness. Brenda, though, didn't seem to notice.

"I'm not giving up on getting my property back. And since Trudi won't talk with me, I'm trying to figure out where she's at and how to get through to her."

"And your point would be?"

Brenda glared at Andy. "My brother and my sister sold the farm and acreage to Trudi Bock instead of me."

"I know all that, Brenda. It was in the paper. But I thought you got stocks and money from the estate."

"That's irrelevant," she snapped. "I wanted that land for our development. I promised to match any offer my siblings got. Hell, I offered to exceed any offer. But they sold to Trudi Bock."

"Refresh my memory, Brenda," Andy said, hoping to make her squirm a little. "Why did they do that to their sister?" He could almost hear Brenda grinding her teeth.

"They wanted to keep the land in cultivation. My mom's stupid do-gooder, save-the-environment thing that she had." Brenda pronounced the words describing her mother's values with the snotty tone of a belligerent teen-ager. "And Trudi Bock promised to do that."

Andy continued putting on the squeeze. "So you don't care about respecting what your mom wanted?"

Andy wondered if sparks would come out of Brenda's ears.

"Andy, you're not a businessman," she said with a dismissive shake of her head. "At least from what I hear. But my husband and I know real estate. And we think it's wasteful to leave all those acres in farmland. Lee and I can put up fifteen deluxe, chateau-style residences on that land. And a nine-hole golf course."

And make yourselves a lot richer than farmland rent could ever do, Andy thought.

"I'm just asking Trudi to sell the land to me. At a fair market value. She can keep the house. And from the way things are trending for her, I don't see how she would want to stick around much longer. And after all, that land has been in the Fundingsland family for over a century. I have *way* more right to it than she does."

"And she won't talk to you?"

"She just tells me to call that lawyer of hers down in

the Cities. And he stonewalls me. Tells me it's not going to happen any time soon."

Brenda looked like she wanted to bludgeon someone with her bottle of vodka.

"I've lost my temper with her a few times, I'll admit. But what does she expect, huh?"

"Ever heard of the honey and vinegar and fly thing?" Andy asked.

Brenda blinked at him as if he were a loon. "I don't understand."

Andy really wanted to escape. "What do you want me to do, Brenda?"

"Talk some sense into her. You're her old boyfriend, and I hear she still has the hots for you. Mrs. Runestrand and her bunch are after her. Dick Shaeffer is on her case, too. New Bergen doesn't want her anymore. She should cut her losses and leave. I'll give her a fair price for that land. I mean, give me a break here, Andy. See what you can do. For old times' sake, huh?"

"Brenda, our old time together was the worst date of my life. Like going out with Cruella deVil."

Brenda didn't look the least bit insulted. Maybe she'd never heard of Cruella. Or maybe she was flattered by the comparison.

"Dammit, Andy, that land is mine."

* * *

As Andy and Harald drove out of Phil's parking lot, Andy whistled in amazement. He often wondered if he had a big sign taped to his back that said: *Attention, all women! Please baffle and confuse and frustrate and pester this man at every possible opportunity!*

Andy loved women.

He really did.

And he was pretty sure a few of them loved him back.

But man, oh man!

They sure did make things difficult sometimes.

There were all manner of complications to look out for with the ladies. Messages that didn't mean what they seemed to. Sensitivities that were way beyond Andy's ability to detect. Expectations that couldn't possibly be met by mortal man. Bubbling, stewing emotions that existed in a far realm that a guy had no access to.

From Venus and Mars, indeed.

Well, Andy figured he needed to spend a little more time on Mars, or he would go absolutely bonkers. Dinner at Carter's house seemed like a good way to expand his narrow circle of male pals in Beaver Tail County—in other words, Thor. Most of his buddies were back in the Cities and he felt as if he had little in common anymore with the guys whom he had hung around with in high school. Carter, on the other hand, seemed to have some potential.

The journalist's house was in the middle of the block on a sleepy, leafy street in a quiet corner of Hobartville. Andy knew a bit about architecture and recognized it as a Craftsman bungalow. It had clapboard siding of slate green, with trim in a dark, dignified purple. The roofline of newish cedar shingles was low and lean, the eaves broad and shady. Just a little gem, Andy thought. No wonder Carter wanted those books on Horace French-man, the world-famous architect from Beaver Tail County. Clearly, Carter must be an architecture geek.

"Well, c'mon, Harald," Andy said, climbing out of the Silverado with his wine and books. The mutt clambered down after him, wagging his tail exuberantly.

The barefoot host, clad in khaki shorts and a colorful Hawaiian shirt, greeted them at the door. "Hey, welcome to Chez LaPorte," he said. "Great to see you, Andy. You too, Harald." He bent over and tousled the top of the big canine's head.

"Thanks for having us," Andy replied. "Harald doesn't get invited out too often, so he's pretty excited."

They walked into Carter's living room. Harald started turning around in a circle, taking everything in, carefully avoiding lamps and books and other objects his tail might sweep away. He woofed softly just once, as if to say, "Nice digs you have here."

Andy was impressed, too. The interior was every bit as handsome as the exterior. Gorgeous, built-in oak book-cases and china cabinets. More lovely oak trim and a freshly refinished maple floor adorned with Art Deco rugs. A few tasteful and probably pricey pieces of Stickley furniture. He had never thought the stuff was very comfortable to sit on. But, boy, did it look good. The walls were crisp and white, and festooned with Chinese watercolors.

"Man, Carter," Andy said, gazing around, "you've

got one beautiful house. Did you do this work, or did you buy it this way?"

Carter smiled proudly. "I had some contractors help out, but it's my baby. I bought the place at the bottom of the housing market. Forty grand. Do you believe that? It had good bones, but it needed a lot of freshening up. I hired people to do the exterior, but I did most of the inside work. Stripped the wallpaper, re-did the walls. Refinished all the cabinetry and the floors and doors. Cleaned up all the hardware. Reglazed the windows. Between work and the house, I haven't had much of a social life in two years."

"No wonder you're interested in Frenchman," Andy said. "He's from about the same era as this house."

"Yeah, and he was born in Hobartville. The paper hasn't done a piece on him in thirty years, so I figured I ought to write up something for the big home section that's coming up. There are only a couple of buildings here designed by him. Pioneer Bank and the administration building at St. Magnus College."

"Don't forget the Presbyterian Church in New Bergen."

"Yeah, that too. Anyway, those are the books, I suppose."

Andy handed them to Carter. "Both out of print. Just let me know when you're done with them."

"Sounds good. Now how about we have some of that wine before dinner."

The men and the dog proceeded back to the kitchen,

which, unlike the living room and dining room, was a slick, modern affair with all the conveniences.

As they waited on high chairs at the kitchen island for the seafood gumbo to finish cooking, Carter offered more apologies for the incident of the forged Andy Skyberg letter.

"No hard feelings," Andy shrugged.

Carter took his first sip of Vinho Verde. His eyebrows raised. "Hey, nice. Light. Can hardly taste the fizz, but it's there. Shouldn't fog you up too fast."

"Perfect drink for a warm night like tonight," said Andy. "Now I've seen your byline plenty of times, but I don't know a lot about you. You didn't say much on that ride out to Trud's farm after Adonis got iced. I think Harald kept trying to French-kiss you. So how'd you end up in Beaver Tail County?"

The journalist reported the facts.

Grew up in the Cities. No siblings. Lost his mom fairly young. Into the army ASAP. Two wives, two divorces. To college in his mid-thirties. Journalism school. Reporter and editor here and there. Peoria and Scranton, Mobile and Portland. Never made it to the big league. Laid off in Oregon and glad to get the job in Hobartville, so close to retirement age. Anyway, he'd always loved Beaver Tail County and jumped when the *Chronicle* job was posted. He enjoyed the outdoors, so what better place? He'd even rented a cabin for the summer.

Then Carter turned the tables on Andy. "And as I recall, you lost your wife to a guitar technician in a heavy metal rock band."

"Pilates coach," Andy corrected.

Carter shook his head in sympathy. "And your limo business had a flat. You beat a retreat to New Bergen. And lived to fight another day."

Andy nodded. "More or less."

"If it's not too personal," Carter said, pouring his second glass, "are you still dating that deputy sheriff?"

Andy winced. "That remains to be seen, Carter. We had a little squabble on the day of the fishing opener and she hasn't returned any of my calls since then. For my part, I'm hoping we're still an item."

"As someone who's been divorced twice, I can empathize. I hope you and Cass can work it out. But I imagine she might be a handful."

"You could say that."

"And those rumors about you and Trudi Bock?"

Andy groaned. "We had a thing back in college, but that was a long time ago. Trud's a great gal. A little weird on the metaphysical stuff. Obsessive even. That's what I couldn't handle. I like to think we can still be good friends, though."

Just then, a lightbulb went on over Andy's head. Maybe Carter was trying to suss out if Trudi was available.

"So, yeah, I have no claims on Trud. If you're, ummm…"

Carter laughed, as if he were surprised at the notion. "She certainly is an attractive woman. And from what I hear, her divorce settlements left her pretty well off. But, as you said, she is a little eccentric."

"Yup, that she is."

"Now that dog of yours looks like he could use a pick-me-up."

Harald was lying on the floor next to Andy's chair, seemingly bored with the gabfest.

Carter hopped down, went over to a cabinet, and returned with a Slim Jim, a spicy beef stick. Classic junk food. "Okay if I give him one, Andy?"

"Sure, why not," Andy said. Harald had eaten a lot worse than cheap beef sausage.

The sound of the cellophane coming off pricked up the dog's ears. He heaved himself to his feet. Then—or so it seemed to Andy—a few Slim Jim molecules wafted up into Harald's snout. He trotted over to Carter, tail pumping.

Carter offered the Slim Jim.

Harald snatched it delicately from the man's fingers, chewed two or three times, and gulped it down. He whimpered: *More, please?*

"Can he have another one, Andy?"

Andy chuckled. "Okay, but just one. I don't want to drive all the way back to New Bergen with a flatulent canine."

Three hours later—pleasantly buzzed, but not intox-icated—Andy was tooling southeast down the Interstate, reflecting on the very agreeable evening it had been. There's nothing like good food, good wine, and good conversation to restore a fellow's sense of optimism. Even Harald seemed to enjoy himself, staying awake for the entire proceedings—probably in hopes of receiving more Slim Jims.

Andy realized what he loved about living in a small, rural community is that people worked together to iron out their problems. Just as he and Carter had. And Trudi would probably come to similar accommodations with the people she had irritated. Andy had a gut feeling that in three days, when Trudi's big block party took place, everyone would have a fantastic, neighborly good time. What could possibly go wrong?

Chapter Sixteen

Since Norway's national day, Syttende Mai or May Seventeenth, had been on Thursday this year—when day-trippers and antiquers are less apt to hit the road—New Bergen's celebration took place at City Park on Saturday. There was Norwegian music and dancing, games, and a big maypole—though most of the town's residents remained in the dark about what the maypole actually symbolized. Hundreds of people attended. Many of those who drove through downtown noticed the to-do going on in the parking lot of the Karma Kubbyhole and stopped for a look-see.

Dubbed "The Karma Kubbyhole Block Party," Trudi's shindig featured entertainment of its own.

Andy watched the festivities unfold from his perch inside Kirsten's spiffy food trailer—the converted Airstream Safari.

There were Hardanger fiddle players, with their plaintive, droning tones. Morris dancers prancing around the parking lot, and up and down Skjegstad Street. Irish tumblers and jugglers. Face painters and balloon animal twisters for the kiddies. A bagpipe ensemble that made very clear why bagpipes should never be played indoors. And, of course, there were all of Trudi's healers and practitioners of the mystical and holistic arts. The local Wiccans even had a table with stacks of pamphlets.

Before things really got rolling, Trudi introduced Andy to her lawyer, old friend, and fellow Eleanorian, Carmine Bongiovanni. The six-foot-six legal eagle had come as his alter ego, former First Lady Eleanor Roosevelt. And damned if he didn't resemble her, Andy thought, overbite and all.

"I have a claim in with the Guinness organization," Carmine confided to Andy in a fair impression of Mrs. Roosevelt's reedy voice. "For world's tallest Eleanor Roosevelt impersonator. I feel very hopeful."

There was one other Mrs. Roosevelt clone circulating, as well as a few Eleanors of Aquitaine. As Trudi had explained to Andy, they were all staying at her place out in the country. They'd already had their ceremonies that morning, as the sun came up.

Andy and J. J. Lindquist worked the window of the food trailer, while Ansel's head chef, Troy Dahlgren, labored off to the side at the prep counter, putting orders together. They offered a few varieties of smørbrød—Norwegian sandwiches. Reindeer meat with apple wedges. Smoked salmon and dill, with sliced hard-boiled eggs. Jarlsberg cheese with tomato and horseradish. Herring with cucumber slices. They were supposed to be served open-faced. But in a concession to ambling eaters, Troy made them in the manner of regular sandwiches. The desserts were scrumptious, too. Krumkake filled with whipped cream and lingonberries. Rosettes dusted with powdered sugar. Jam thumbprint cookies. The espresso machine hissed and hummed nonstop all day.

Trudi was circulating everywhere, unmistakable in her gaudy Eleanorian costume dress. It was full length, scoop-necked, and form-fitting, made of crushed blue velour. On her head she had a silver tiara. Toots Strassberger, wearing a floral-print silk shirt over wide-legged black slacks, trailed behind her like the Queen Mother.

Meanwhile, Michael Muelhoff and Lauren Kastner worked the crowd, offering coupons and brochures, and free samples of various organic skin creams and vitamin supplements. And Andy spotted Carter LaPorte on the far side of the block party, interviewing one of the vendors. He had the *Chronicle*'s new photographer with him, a young woman just out of college.

Andy was relieved by another Ansel's employee at one o'clock. That meant he could give the unveiling of Aunt Bev's mural his undivided attention. The side of Trudi's store that faced the parking lot was covered with a blue plastic tarp, which hid Aunt Bev's artwork.

The day so far had gone without incident. Trudi was beaming with delight. Everybody seemed to be having a good time.

Then Andy saw Dick Schaeffer. The assistant principal was plowing through the crowd, shoving people aside. His face was red and contorted with anger. It looked as if he was making a beeline for the Wiccan table. It quickly became apparent why.

He reached across the stacks of brochures and books, grabbed the elbow of a young woman sitting there, and dragged her upright, around the end of the table.

"Daddy!" she screamed, trying to push him away. "*Stop it!*"

"You're coming home right now, Amber," Schaeffer bellowed. "And you're grounded for the summer! No more of this witch nonsense! You're a Methodist, young lady!"

While folks stood around, slack-jawed, the plump, brown-haired girl tried to get loose from her old man, but was no match for him. Now he was manhandling her back the way he had come, through the crowd, toward what sounded like a long and dismal summer.

Out of nowhere, Trudi popped up in the path of the pissed-off parent.

"What's going on here?" she snapped.

Andy had never seen his friend look so incensed.

"I'm sorry, Trudi," the girl bawled. "I'm really so very, very—"

"Shut up, Amber!" her father spat.

The crowd gasped. Andy knew that Schaeffer was hard-nosed. But now word would get out: he was also a first-class asshole.

"My sixteen-year-old daughter is here, at this devil-worshipping festival, without my approval, Ms. Bock," Schaeffer growled. "She snuck out of the house this morning and I just found out where she was. I am exercising my parental prerogative to control and discipline her, and direct her religious practice as I see fit. No more witches or warlocks or magical crystals or herbal remedies for Amber Schaeffer."

The assistant principal was clenching and unclenching his free fist, as if to pop somebody with it. Andy thought that he should go over and insert himself between Schaeffer and Trudi, before anything happened.

"Just so we're clear, Ms. Bock," Schaeffer continued, "I don't want to hear that Amber has spoken a word to you ever again, let alone set foot in that damned shop of yours. If I do, I'll be coming here to set things straight. Even if it means burning your store down to ashes. As for the books you sold Amber, I'll be burning those as soon as I get home."

"Daddy, no!" the girl wailed. Her face was red as a beet, her eyes swimming with tears.

"She's sixteen, Mr. Schaeffer," Trudi said with commendable composure. "That's when kids start really exploring who they are, what they want to become. In two years she'll be able to do what she wants."

"True enough," Schaeffer agreed. "But until then, *I own her*. And in the meantime, I'd suggest that you take a hike on out of New Bergen. You're a corrupting influence on this community and it's time for you to go."

Practically dragging his whimpering daughter along, the assistant principal plowed back out to the sidewalk, disappearing from sight.

Chapter Seventeen

"I think I would have handled that a little differently," someone announced from behind Andy. It was the voice of a battle-hardened mom and grandmom.

"Aunt Bev! How you doin'? You snuck up on me."

Aunt Bev peered up at Andy. She had on lavender jeans and a navy blue sweatshirt decorated with elaborate rosemaling. She even wore a smear of bright red lipstick. The woman had the glow of someone who had just gotten married and won the Ultra Lottery all on the same day.

"The girl shouldn't have disobeyed her father by coming here," Aunt Bev said, shaking her head. "But that man's gonna pay a price for what he just did. Mark my words. Take ordinary teenage embarrassment and multiply it by a million. That's what he did to her."

Andy was unqualified to comment on matters of child-rearing, so he changed the subject. "You must be awful excited, seeing your magnum opus make its debut."

"Oh, I am indeed. This is the high point of my rosemaling career. I hope people like it, though. I know Trudi does, because she gave me a bonus. A hundred extra dollars. And when she was looking at it, before Gus put up the tarp, she had tears in her eyes. She really did. Said I'd caught the spirit of Adonis just about perfectly."

"Well, holy cow, that's excellent, Aunt Bev. Are Uncle Frank and the boys here?"

Bev pointed to the far end of the parking lot, where Frank Engebretson and Andy's two cousins were yakking with a couple of men. They were holding their hands up, apparently comparing the sizes of the fish they had caught the weekend before. Nearby, on the little rental stage, a pair of Indian dancers was gyrating sinuously to sitar and tabla music played over the PA system. Frank, his sons, and the others were studiously avoiding any expansion of their cultural horizons.

"Listen, Anders," said Aunt Bev, "I have to go say hi to my bowling team over there. They said they'd be here and by garsh they are. See you later."

Andy went back to Ansel's trailer and had Troy whip him up a smoked salmon sandwich. Then, noshing away, he meandered around Trudi's mini-festival. There were a good seventy or eighty folks in attendance. And more arrived all the time. Kirsten was certainly going to clear a good profit today. And so would Trudi, who seemed to be selling lots of stuff inside and out. The sky was mostly sunny, the temperature a fairly balmy seventy-two degrees.

It was as if Dick Schaeffer's little outburst had not even happened.

Right at that moment, Andy looked out on Skjegstad Street and his good mood plummeted like a honker hit by a twelve-gauge blast.

Mrs. Runestrand had arrived with her troop of elderly protesters.

Out on the sidewalk in front of Trudi's store and parking lot, she and her dour old acolytes had re-established their picket line. One of them used a walker and another was being wheeled back and forth by Mrs. Runestrand herself. They were all dressed up in their Sunday church finery and carried homemade signs with messages of protest.

Satanic Rituals in New Bergen? NO!

Trudi Bock, go home!

Don't corrupt our precious children!

Andy thought the scene possessed a certain equilibrium. Those enjoying the festivities mostly regarded Mrs. Runestrand's bunch with amusement or bemusement. The paragons of religiosity looked at the revelers with a certain disdain. That would have been fine, until Charlie Adams came charging through the crowd. In a cartoon, she would have had steam shooting out of her ears.

She came right up to Mrs. Runestrand and stood nose-to-nose with her. Charlie's face was flushed with anger and contorted in a scowl. "Get out of here, you old witch," she snarled.

Mrs. Runestrand let go of the wheelchair and scowled right back. "Who are *you* calling a witch, you abomination of femininity?"

Andy found it rather ironic that a little bit ago, a kid wanting to be a witch was busted by her dad. Now, a real witch apparently resented being called what she so clearly was. Anyway, Charlie outweighed Mrs. Runestrand by a good thirty pounds, and should it come to fisticuffs, would have a decided advantage. But Mrs. Runestrand appeared uncowed, standing right up to the taller, stronger young woman.

"You've been persecuting Trudi ever since she opened the store!" shouted Charlie. "She's never done you any harm. But you keep on with this rotten shit."

The church ladies gasped at the s-word.

"And I wouldn't be the least bit surprised if it turned out people from your effing church—"

There was another communal gasp, louder this time.

"—were responsible for murdering Trudi's pet iguana!"

Mrs. Runestrand held her ground, straightening her backbone and pulling back her shoulders.

"We have every right to picket this establishment," she said with steeliness. "The law gives that to us. But a higher law requires that we fight Satan wherever he may appear. We owe it to this community to attempt to clean up the filth wherever it may—"

It astonished Andy how quickly everything happened. Couldn't have been more than a few seconds. There had barely been time for a crowd to gather around the two belligerents.

At the word "filth," Charlie utterly lost it. Grabbing Mrs. Runestrand by the coat lapels, for a brief few seconds Charlie didn't seem to know what to do with the sour old lady. Punch her out? Knock her down? Shake her like a dog shakes a rat?

She never got the chance to decide.

Someone burst out of the crowd and threw himself on Charlie, ramming her hard against the side of a Land Rover parked at the curb.

Charlie was too stunned to defend herself, as the young man pummeled her about the face and shoulders.

Her assailant shouted as he slugged. "Leave. My. Grandmother. Alone."

Andy understood that Charlie had put herself into a whole heap of trouble grabbing Mrs. Runestrand like that. But she surely didn't deserve the beating that Zeke Haugen was giving her.

Bellowing "Excuse me," Andy bulled his way toward the dose of whoop-ass that was being administered, and hauled young Zeke off Charlie.

Zeke tried to slip out of Andy's bear hug, but only succeeded in tramping on his foot and whacking him in the ribs with his elbow. Andy was prepared to restrain Zeke as long as it took, but Mrs. Runestrand came to the rescue.

"Ezekiel Haugen, you stop that right now," the old lady commanded. There was a bit of biblical fury in her voice. "You stop fighting with Mr. Skyberg."

The teenager went limp in Andy's arms, his anger drained out instantly. Andy loosened his grip, but held onto one of Zeke's arms. As he did, he noticed that the miscreant was wearing an old Buzz Saw Ballerina T-shirt in Day-Glo orange. Andy had been a fan of the all-girl punk band back in the '80s.

For her part, Charlie looked dazed. There was a big shiner blossoming around her right eye, and a nasty contusion decorating her left cheek. She also seemed to be bleeding from her nose.

Zeke twisted around, blinking at his grandmother. "Grandma, I was just trying to—"

"Shut it, Ezekiel," snapped Mrs. Runestrand.

That's about when Andy heard the two loud *whoops* from the police cruiser that double-parked next to the Land Rover. Andy hoped it would be Ed Vandegraff. But it was Cass Conlin who swaggered onto the scene. She surveyed the situation, then made brief eye contact with Andy. He raised his eyebrows, hoping for a friendly acknowledgement. But all he noted was an irritated sniff.

"Okay, then," said the sheriff's deputy, hands on hips. "What the heck just happened here?"

* * *

Andy really had to admire his Aunt Bev.

Even though the incident involving Charlie, Mrs. Runestrand, and Zeke Haugen—not to mention the abrupt removal of poor Amber Schaeffer—had cast a certain pall over the unveiling, Aunt Bev insisted on making the most of her fifteen minutes of fame. Along with Trudi, she stood proudly next to the blue tarp, as Gus, up on the roof, released it.

The thing crinkled and crumbled down onto the blacktop. There was a brief moment of silence. Then came a growing wave of applause, and *oohs* and *aahs*, and a smattering of shouted calls of approbation.

Andy himself bellowed, "You rock, Aunt Bev!"

Uncle Frank, standing next to Andy, commented, "My old gal has something on the ball, hasn't she?"

Something, indeed, thought Andy.

About twenty-five feet wide by ten feet tall, the artwork was a cornucopia of color. Rosemaled flowers of every shade and size cascading everywhere. Bits of greenery that had to be aromatic and therapeutic herbs. Portraits of Eleanor Roosevelt and Eleanor of Aquitaine in opposite corners. Though given Aunt Bev's skills as a portraitist, Mrs. Roosevelt strongly resembled Humphrey Bogart with a woman's dowdy hairdo.

And pride of place in the center of the piece belonged to Adonis the Iguana—green, handsome, and now immortalized.

With her fellow Eleanorians standing at the front of the crowd, Trudi gave a rambling oration about our connection with the world of natural healing and spirituality and an iguana's place in it. Then she introduced Beverly Engebretsen.

It looked to Andy as if Aunt Bev were about to accept a Nobel Prize or at least an Oscar. "First," she said, "I want to thank my mother and father…"

Chapter Eighteen

It took a couple of mournful woofs to rouse the boss early the next morning. He appeared in the rear vestibule and let King Harald out into the backyard. The dog did his business and was just about ready to woof for re-entry when he noticed that something seemed amiss.

The boss, or someone else, had left the alley gate ajar.

Harald growled deep in his throat. The alley gate was hardly ever left open. Very suspicious. Could some nefarious activity be afoot?

Harald growled a bit more. But before long, it became apparent that this wasn't a security breach, but a golden opportunity. A chance for an amble, without the necessity of that tiring leap over the fence.

Harald approached the gate, delicately nudged it, and skittered back a few steps.

Nothing happened.

No sneak attack by deadly assassins.

Harald stuck his nose in the gap between gate and post, and pulled the thing open. The alleyway beckoned.

The dog's dilemma was this: he was hungry and his food was inside the house. But a nice ramble wasn't anything to be sniffed at. The choice was an easy one.

Harald's first stop was by a creek that ran through a hilly section of New Bergen, out in the direction of Elbow Lake. He splashed around in the chilly water, primarily so he could enjoy the shivery delight of shaking it all off. Sheets of water erupted from his coat. It just felt wonderful in all his muscles and bones and ligaments. It loosened up everything.

He was headed back the way he had come, when an unlucky red squirrel crossed his path.

Harald knew as well as anyone that pursuing a red squirrel was a nearly hopeless job. They were smaller, quicker, wilier, and meaner than their larger gray cousins. But the principle of the thing still mattered. Any squirrel that he encountered had earned itself a good, damn-the-torpedoes chase. Never mind that Harald had no professional competencies related to tree climbing. Just not in his job description.

The hunt was predictably brief.

After about thirteen seconds of mad scrambling, the reddish rodent ascended the trunk of a large ash tree with dazzling rapidity. It sat panting on a branch about thirty feet up. Then the bushy-tailed critter began to chitter and hiss all manner of squirrelly profanity down on the head of the woofing canine. Harald was exceedingly lucky to not speak a lick of red squirrel—or his big, pointy ears would have burned.

Next up on the dog's itinerary was the alley behind Chet's Burger Bonanza, out by the dumpster.

Usually the garbage hygiene at Chet's was up to snuff. Bagged refuse—often full of unfinished burgers, fries, and other victuals—normally made it safely into the big dumpster. But on a couple of occasions, Harald had found overflowing black plastic sacks lying on the pavement. It had been an easy matter to tear them open and go digging for chow. Harald couldn't have known that yesterday's throngs of Syttende Mai goers had helped Chet's sell a boatload of burgers and other snacks, the remnants of which sat in bags in the alley.

Harald hit pay dirt, so to speak, wolfing down half of a double Chet Cheeseburger, several partial fish sticks, broken cookies, and an almost totally intact pizza hoagie. He was about to dig deeper into the black bag when the back door of Chet's swung open and a tall woman emerged. She yelped in surprise. "Harald!" she snapped. "Just what in the heck do you think you're doin'?"

Harald was baffled at her displeasure. How could doing something that felt so right be wrong? But on such occasions, he had the sense to look at least somewhat abashed.

The woman came over, grabbed his collar, and hauled him down to the near end of the alley. "Now you get on home, you dumb old mutt," she said. She launched him up the sidewalk, in the general direction of the boss's house.

Harald himself had concluded that it was time to head back. He'd accomplished a lot. A cold bath, a well-chased red squirrel, and a tummy full of tasty grub.

But it so happened that his route took him right past the house that belonged to his friend Charlie. He had actually stayed here a couple of times, when the boss couldn't take him along somewhere. Charlie hadn't seemed real friendly lately, but Harald decided to say hello anyway.

He went up to the front door and woofed a few times.

Nothing happened.

He went around to the back door and tried again.

But Charlie didn't answer.

That's about when Harald's exquisitely sensitive beezer caught a whiff of something. Something tangy and interesting. Something worthy of his attention.

Sniffing as he went, the ginger mutt stalked over toward Charlie's garage, bending his path leftward. Whatever it was that smelled intriguing had to be hidden in the narrow, shadowy space between this garage and the one next door.

Harald poked his head into the confined, darkly shaded gap, but had a hard time seeing anything until his pupils dilated. For a brief moment he whimpered happily and set his tail wagging.

It was Charlie.

Lying on her back. In a bent, crooked posture. Staring at Harald upside down—her face bruised and swollen and covered with clotted blood. Eyes wide open, unblinking. A large, bloody dent showing in the side of her head.

Harald licked her hand, which seemed to be trying to reach out of the deep shadows.

But Charlie didn't move. And didn't seem to be asleep.

Harald backed away and began to howl.

Chapter Nineteen

Andy was still dozing when the pounding on the front door hauled him out of his delicious dream. It had involved him and Cass and a white sand beach and a blanket under a palm and no clothing whatsoever.

His first thought was that Harald must have learned to knock on the door. But that seemed pretty unlikely. Whoever it was, they were awfully damn rude to wake him so early after his late night out. He had worked a long, hard day in Ansel's food trailer in Trudi's parking lot, and had spent the evening barhopping around Hobartville with Troy and J. J. Hadn't gotten home until two.

Andy tossed on his bathrobe and stumbled out to the front door. He opened it, ready to deliver a lecture on how inconsiderate it was to wake up a fellow early on a Sunday morning, when he saw Ed Vandegraff grimly standing there. Regarding the assistant sheriff, Andy opened the screen door. This cannot be good, he thought.

"Uh, hi, Ed."

The peace officer furrowed his brow. "Morning, Andy."

"What's up?"

"It's about Harald."

Andy sucked in a slug of air. Wasn't Harald in the backyard? "Is he hurt? Is he okay?"

"He's okay, but we want you to come and get him. I'll tell you what happened on the way."

"Give me a couple minutes to get dressed, Ed." And Andy hurried back to his bedroom.

* * *

When they pulled up in front of Charlie Adams's little one-bedroom house, Andy was amazed at all the emergency vehicles jamming the street. In addition to several units from the Beaver Tail County Sheriff's office, there was an ambulance, the crime lab unit that three adjoining counties shared, two fire trucks, a state patrol squad car, and Doc Hilgenberg's big old black Cadillac. With all those red and blue flashers going, it looked like a psychedelic light show.

Andy could hardly believe what Ed had told him on the short drive over.

Charlie Adams. Dead.

Apparently murdered. Discovered by Harald on one of his rambles.

How in Hades had that dog picked up such a knack of arriving in the wrong place at the wrong time? Until recently, he had been a perfectly ordinary canine with little interest in criminal investigations.

"C'mon, Andy," Ed said, heaving his bulk out of the driver's seat.

They walked right past Carter LaPorte and the two-person crew from Hobartville's only TV station.

"Anything to say about your dog's discovery, Andy?" Carter asked, a narrow reporter's notebook and pen in hand.

Andy shook his head. "Sorry, Carter. Maybe later." He also waved off the TV reporters. Heck, he wouldn't even know what to say.

The backyard was littered with the full panoply of crime-scene paraphernalia—just like on TV. Plastic sheeting obscuring things that the public shouldn't see. Utility lights up on stands. Yellow "CRIME SCENE DO NOT CROSS" tape strung around. A police photographer, snapping pictures of every corner of the yard. Doc Hilgenberg dictating into a little digital recorder. The ambulance crew and their gurney, waiting for Charlie. Sheriff's deputies and other law officers whom Andy didn't recognize.

And in a far corner, roped to the clothesline post, sat Harald, looking gloomier than Andy had ever seen him. The dog spotted his master and began to whimper.

Andy turned to Ed Vandegraff. "Any idea yet who did this to Charlie?"

The assistant sheriff shrugged. "Well, no. Not officially. But we sent Cass over to pick up a certain juvenile subject—I can't say who—as soon as we became aware of what happened to Miss Adams. Unfortunately, this individual vanished during the night. He is the subject of a search at this time."

Zeke Haugen, thought Andy. They let him go with his

grandmother after yesterday's altercation, instead of sticking him in juvie up in Hobartville. Big mistake. And the miserable little sociopath had come in the night for Charlie.

"Have Charlie's folks been told?" Andy said. "They live out in the country near Malden."

"We sent a gal out there, a deputy sheriff, who's good at that sort of thing," Ed explained.

Doesn't sound like Cass, thought Andy. That girl's about as subtle as a jackhammer.

"Not a fun job," Ed continued.

"Anyone informed Trudi Bock yet?"

Ed shook his head. "We're not obligated to contact employers, Andy. Why don't you go tell her? You two are old pals, aren't you?" The cop winked at Andy.

Andy chuckled nervously. He didn't especially want the job. But it was definitely the decent thing to do.

"Yeah, I can go out to her place," he sighed. "I hope Harald wasn't too much trouble."

"Like I told you in the squad, I was the first officer on the scene, after the neighbor called. And that big old mutt of yours wouldn't budge. I expect he figured he was protecting Miss Adams. Fortunately, Cass was next to arrive and she tied him up over there."

There was some heavy activity behind the plastic sheeting that covered the space between the two ramshackle garages. One of the EMT guys backed through the gap in the plastic, pulling the fold-up gurney over the bumpy ground. Another guy was pushing on the opposite end, followed by Doc Hilgenberg—who was the associate county medical examiner, in addition to being a local family physician. On the gurney, shrouded in a heavy, white cloth, was no doubt what remained of Charlie Adams.

As Doc Hilgenberg shuffled by, Andy asked him how Charlie had died.

"Well, her face was pretty beat up," the doctor said. "But some of that could be from the scrape she got into yesterday. I shouldn't be telling you, but I'm thinking the cause of death was blunt force trauma to the side of the head. I can't say for sure until I get her on the table. And I'm asking you to keep this on the q.t., Andy."

As the gloomy procession rattled around the side of the house, Andy went and untied Harald, who positively gyrated with delight at being liberated. He attempted to jump up on Andy and lick his face. But Andy gently removed the dog's front paws and set him back on the ground. "C'mon, big guy," Andy said. "We have a condolence call to make."

* * *

Nearly a dozen roomy tents were scattered on the lawn around Trudi's house. A portable toilet stood off to the side. And at least a few of the Eleanorians had not yet departed, judging by the various cars parked on the grass.

As soon as Andy pulled up, the back door of the house swung open and Trudi emerged. She was followed by three women whom Andy had seen the day before dressed as either the former first lady or the former queen of England. And Carmine Bongiovanni brought up the rear, looking considerably better as a man than an elongated Eleanor Roosevelt.

Andy climbed down from his Silverado and Harald followed. The dog made a beeline for Trudi. She bent over and gave him an energetic hug. He attempted to lick her face, and she allowed him one slurp.

"What a delightful surprise to see you, Anders," Trudi bubbled. "I was just about to make some eggs Benedict for my friends here and I'd love to have you join us." She looked back down at Harald. "And for you I have a big milk bone."

"Hi, Trud," Andy replied. And at that point, he was at an utter loss for words. Never before had he been the bearer of such dismal, worrying news. He suddenly had a lot of respect for the deputy sheriff out at the Adams place.

"I don't like the look of your aura, Anders," Trudi said, instantly serious. Her four friends, standing behind her, nodded in agreement. "You're usually a nice, healthy orange-yellow. But you're muddying to gray. You have a blockage of some kind."

"Yes, gray," said Carmine, his long face suddenly grim.

"Something's wrong, isn't it?" said a thin, pale woman.

Andy had always thought that the New Age stuff was a bunch of hokum, but this posse had his number for sure.

"Yeah, something is wrong," Andy said. He again

struggled to find the words.

"Anders," said Trudi, "out with it now."

He took a deep breath. "Trud, Charlie Adams is dead."

Trudi blinked at him and tilted her head sideways, as if to say, come again?

"She apparently was murdered," Andy continued, wishing he were anywhere but here. "Sometime last night. Harald here found her out by her garage."

Trudi blinked a few more times. Then she wobbled, her knees buckling. Andy's reflexes took over. He caught her under the arms as Carmine steadied her from behind. They eased her down onto a lawn chair and the skinny, pale Eleanorian gently whacked her about the cheeks.

Trudi revived and blinked at Andy. "She's passed? She's gone to a higher plane?"

Andy didn't know anything about higher planes. But he knew for sure that Charlie Adams had truly kicked the bucket. Bought the farm. Augered in. "I'm afraid so, Trud."

Trudi's face quivered for a brief moment just before she burst out bawling and blubbering. Carmine pulled Trudi to her feet and escorted her into the house, along with the others.

Andy looked down at Harald. "Well, that went well, don't you think? Guess we better get going."

The dog seemed a little distraught himself, as if this might all be his fault.

Twenty minutes later, Andy was ensconced in his

easy chair with a tall bottle of Biberschwanz Pilsner and Harald at his side. He'd fired up the forty-two-inch plasma screen and tuned into ESPN. They were broadcasting a tennis tournament from Italy, and that was fine with Andy. It was unusual for him to start drinking at ten in the a.m. But it seemed the right thing to do. In fact, it was his intention to sip his way through the day. With occasional pauses for sustenance and releases of Harald into the backyard. Just blot it out. What a hellacious morning.

* * *

The last thing Andy remembered was watching a spectacular crash during some stock car race out of Alabama. He was foggy on the details. But someone may even have gotten killed.

It was the bonging of the doorbell that roused him out of his Biberschwanz-induced slumber in front of the big-screen TV. That, and Harald nudging his knee.

"Just a minute," he bellowed, hauling himself up. It was dark outside. He must have dozed through most of the afternoon and early evening. His head throbbed and he groaned under his breath. These days, just a few beers were all it took. He used to have more endurance. He went over to the door and opened it.

There stood Trudi, looking red-eyed and puffy in the face.

"Hey, Trud, how you doin'?" Andy said, while simultaneously thinking, *Uh-oh*.

"Hi, Anders," she replied. "Okay if I come in?"

"Sure," he said, pushing open the screen door. "But

how come you're here, Trud?"

She walked into his living room, looking surprised that he had apparently been watching a sumo wrestling tournament on his plasma screen.

"The Eleanorians all left this morning and Mom just went home," she said. "But the truth is, Anders, I don't want to be alone. You don't mind, do you?"

An honest answer to that question was clearly not in order, so Andy said, "Not in the least. Would you like a Biberschwanz?"

Chapter Twenty

Andy stumbled out of the bedroom and down the hallway, into the bathroom. The only light on in the house was the night-light above the toilet—welcome illumination for a fellow whose aim might be off after guzzling beer all day. His head was throbbing, as if someone were thumping it with a rubber mallet. Out in the kitchen, he built himself half a peanut butter and jelly sandwich, washing it down with OJ straight from the carton. Then he took a couple of aspirins. He checked on Harald. The big dog was snoozing soundly in the shadows, on his doggie bed in the back vestibule. At least *he* didn't seem to be having nightmares about poor Charlie.

Standing at the kitchen counter, continuing to sip on the juice, Andy marveled at how things had gone absolutely bonkers in New Bergen.

Bitter controversy over something that seemed pretty harmless. Vitriolic accusations. Heavy-handed political machinations. An old leftie who turns out not to be paranoid after all—the police state actually having it in for him. A romantic breakup out of left field. Brawls in the street. Father-and-daughter confrontation. A murdered lizard. Now a murdered woman. And his own beloved mutt somehow having developed a nose for black deeds.

Andy didn't believe much in deep, dark nights of the soul. But this sure felt a lot like one.

Here he was, almost forty, and he was still puttering along like some kid just out of college. No wife and now no girlfriend. A low-paying food service job with little future. Living in a boring house that he rented, between two elderly sisters, in a safe little town. Well, formerly a safe town.

His dream vocation of painting could never seem to break out of the rut it was stuck in. He'd sell a canvas now and then, but it was pretty trivial stuff. Life in the Cities sure hadn't worked out. And now his retreat to New Bergen was feeling iffy, too. He didn't have any idea of what to do next, where to go.

Well, at least he didn't have it as rough as Trud…

Trud?

Andy slapped the OJ carton down on the counter and rummaged through his brain.

Trudi had come. They had talked about Charlie and the whole big mess, and talked and talked and talked. Called out for a pizza. They drank many bottles of Biberschwanz Pilsner. At least Andy had. That's where the memories went fuzzy.

"Oh, shit," he muttered.

Putting the OJ in the fridge, Andy went back to his bedroom. It was pitch black in there. He listened carefully and didn't hear anything. But then the very faintest scent of patchouli graced his nostrils. Andy *did not* wear patchouli.

And just at that moment, someone on the far side of his big bed rolled over and mumbled a few incoherent words.

Man, oh man, Andy thought. *What have I done?*

That indeed was the question. Because Andy couldn't recall a damn thing about how Trudi had gotten into his bed. Not to mention what they may—or may not have—done there.

What to do?

He couldn't kick Trudi out, not now. But in case something had happened, he didn't want it to happen again. He was exhausted and his head was still throbbing. What the heck time was it?

Back in the kitchen, he looked up at the clock over the breakfast nook. Five o'clock. He sure didn't want to get back in bed, so he might as well stay up. After tiptoeing into the bedroom for his clothes, Andy dressed in the bathroom. A short time later, he brewed a pot full of coffee and toasted an English muffin. The very last morsel of muffin with blueberry jam was about to vanish when Trudi appeared in the hallway door, wearing nothing but a radiant smile.

"Well, aren't we an early riser," she pronounced coyly.

Andy put down the fragment of muffin and stared.

Well, one thing a guy had to say about Trudi was that for a woman of about forty without a stitch of clothing on, she looked remarkably fit and firm. And voluptuous. And bounteously curvy in all the right places. A female whose knickers any straight guy would not object to getting into. Except for Andy.

She made a mock little-girl frown at him. "I said, 'Aren't we up early?'"

Andy put what he hoped looked like a sincere smile on his face. "Yeah, I don't usually sleep in that often. Um, aren't you cold?"

"No, I'm just fine. We Bocks are pretty warm-blooded for a bunch of Germans."

There was a slightly cumbersome pause, before Trudi spoke up again.

"I just want to say, Anders, that you were wonderful. Simply wonderful. Like I remember from our good old times at the university. After that terrible day yesterday, you made me feel warm and safe and—"

Andy jumped up. Because all of a sudden, he heard the front door of his house click open.

He did the terrible calculus. Only three other people had the key. His sister Kirsten. One of his neighbors. And…

Cass!

"Trud," he gasped. "Stay here and I'll be right back."

"Were you expecting visitors?" she asked, looking surprised to have her soliloquy interrupted.

"Nope," he said, brushing past her, while trying not to touch any of that exposed flesh.

He trotted into the living room to find his worst

nightmare realized.

Cass, dressed for duty, was headed for the kitchen.

"Uh, hi," Andy said, blocking the hallway door.

"Hi, Andy," she replied.

"Umm, how are you doing?"

"Well, fine, I guess."

"You haven't been returning my calls."

Cass shrugged. "I get a little hot under the collar once in a while and I need time to cool off. You oughta know that by now."

Andy sensed that Cass might be trying to offer an olive branch. He could be wrong, but he didn't think so.

"If you don't mind my saying so," he said, "seems like kind of an odd time for a visit."

The law officer shrugged again. "Thought it would be better to come in person. Hope that's okay."

She smiled at Andy, a little flirtatiously.

This was looking good. Maybe there was a chance to patch it up with Cass, if they could get past the problems of Thor and, well, the naked woman in the kitchen.

"The reason I stopped by," Cass said, "is because the sheriff wants to know more about when Harald might have gotten loose yesterday. The timing of it. Where you think he may have gone before he got to Charlie's place."

"Could we do it later, Cassie?" Andy pleaded. "I'll meet you at the sheriff's station, say ten or ten thirty?"

Cass gave him a quizzical look, but nodded. "Sure, ten would be fine."

Andy grinned nervously, wishing Cass back out the

door and down the steps.

Then the wheels all fell off.

"Anders," Trudi's voice trilled from down the hall-way, "who is it?"

If Andy hadn't been caught in the middle, he would have found Cass's expression well worth a chuckle. Eyes popping open. Mouth gaping in amazement. Skin flush-ing. But there he was, between the devil and the deep blue sea. And holy cow, was it not funny.

He turned and blinked at Trudi, as she came into the living room.

At least she'd put on a bath towel.

Right behind her was Harald, looking bright and chipper.

"Well, hello, Deputy," Trudi said, padding up next to Andy. "Nice to see you. Anders, maybe the deputy would like a cup of coffee. I know I would."

Harald, for some mysterious reason, started to lick Trudi's knee.

"No, thank you," the deputy replied icily.

Andy knew that the figure of speech was "staring daggers." But Cass looked more like she was staring hollow-point, nine-millimeter slugs.

"I'll see you at ten, *Mr. Skyberg*," Cass said with unnerving evenness. She turned and marched out the door.

Mr. Skyberg? Andy thought. Kiss of death.

For all of Cass's pronouncements on their freedom to "see other people," Andy was sure that her philosophy applied pretty exclusively to her. Hypocrisy, thy name is Cassandra. Oh well, it couldn't have lasted.

"Did I say something wrong?" asked Trudi, wearing an innocent look.

Andy hadn't appreciated her sneakiness. She'd been presented with a tactical opportunity and had used it to take out her opponent. Pretty darn smooth, for sure. But it didn't change a thing regarding the way Andy felt about her.

Trudi was a nice, attractive, unconventional woman who would drive Andy absolutely batty if he should choose to hook up with her again. That's why he had broken it off all those years ago in college.

Now that there was a possibility that, after nearly twenty years, he had again done the deed with her... Well, there was nothing wrong with a one-night stand, he supposed. He just hoped he had enjoyed it.

"Anders, are you okay?" Trudi said, as Harald licked her other knee. She at least had the decency to look a little guilty. "Cass is practically a child, you know. Not right for you at all."

True enough, he thought with irritation. *And neither are you.*

Chapter Twenty-One

Andy had a pretty good idea of why Thor had been so danged hot for him to come out to the farm after the lunch shift two days later. The old geezer said that Andy could expect a good laugh. But he didn't say why and wouldn't answer when Andy asked if it had anything to do with the white panel truck.

Andy felt kind of uneasy. But a nagging touch of curiosity pulled at him. And if he could prevent Thor from doing anything illegal, that would be a best-buddy type of good deed to do.

He pulled up in front of the Hofdahl house just before two o'clock and hopped out of the truck. Goats in a near-by pen bleated their enthusiastic greetings. It was a little windy that afternoon and Andy pulled his maroon-and-gold university baseball cap down tight.

The instant Thor came out of the house, Andy said, "Okay. Enough with the big mystery. What kind of hare-brained scheme are you getting me sucked into?"

Without speaking, Thor handed Andy his beloved Russian spotting scope. "Take a look at the ridge up there." He pointed. "To the right of the tree line."

"That's Trollhaugen Road," Andy said.

"Your sense of navigation is impressive. Now look." Thor took off his glasses and began to wipe them with his handkerchief.

Andy peered through the hefty piece of Soviet optics, searching a bit from side to side. Then he spotted it. The white panel truck that Thor had been fulminating about. He handed the scope back to his friend. "So what about it? You showed it to me before. It's still there. Old news."

"I aim to have a little fun with 'em, Andy. And if you don't want to come with, I'll understand. But I could use some moral support."

"What are you planning to do, Thor?"

"Come along and you'll see."

At that, Thor walked around the side of his house and returned a moment later with a cinderblock. He set it in the bed of his battered Jeep pickup. He repeated the process three more times.

Now Andy felt a little queasy. "You're going to block their tires, aren't you?"

"Yup," answered Thor. "At least until they tell me what they're up to."

"They could call for backup. You could get arrested."

"Andy, I was busted at Berkeley in '67 and Chicago in '68, and a few other times as well. I was a hardcore old peacenik hippie, you know. The pigs don't scare me in the least." He climbed into his Jeep. "You coming?"

"Oh, bull feathers," Andy muttered, joining him in the cab.

"Been meaning to ask, how're things with you and Cass," Thor queried, as the two of them drove off in the Jeep. "After all, my commotion here was the reason why you argued with her."

"There's more to it than that," Andy groaned, telling Thor about the disaster of Monday morning. Of Cass showing up unannounced at his house. Of Trudi emerging wearing only a bath towel. Of the meeting at the sheriff's station with Ed and a very hostile Cass.

Thor started to chuckle, but had the decency to put a lid on it.

A few minutes later, Thor pulled his Jeep up behind the white panel truck. No one was in sight.

Both men climbed out of the old Jeep and Thor advanced on the van. He looked in the mirrored porthole that faced his farmstead, much like a little kid gazing in through a toy store window. Andy preferred to hang back.

"Hello," Thor bellowed. "Anyone in there?"

No one answered.

Thor hammered on the side of the van with a closed fist and hollered, "Wakey, wakey, time to get up."

Andy grimaced as Thor returned to his Jeep for the first cinderblock. Andy pondered what he'd have to tell Thor's wife, Sonny, when she came to bail out her highly combustible husband. Maybe something like, "Thor had an awful Haight-Ashbury flashback, and I just couldn't stop him." Or maybe something as simple as, "His obstreperous, screw-the-establishment Norwegian gene got activated."

Thor tucked the cinderblock in front of one of the van's rear tires. He looked up at Andy. "You gonna help or what?"

Andy shook his head. "Just as soon not get tossed in the hoosegow, Thor. Thanks very much."

Thor snorted and went back for another cinderblock. In a couple of minutes the van's rear tires were fully hemmed in. Trollhaugen Road was muddy from last night's rain, so any effort to dislodge the blocks by going forward or backward would likely dig the tires into a mire. Andy had to admit that his pal had these people by the cojones. If they were in there, they'd have to come out and move the blocks—and face the terrible wrath of Thor Hofdahl. That was the whole idea of this exercise.

"Now we sit," Thor said, grabbing two folding lawn chairs out of the back of the Jeep. He had definitely come prepared.

Thor didn't have much to say and neither did Andy. So while Thor read the crumpled copy of *The Atlantic* that he'd pulled from his back pocket, the younger man simply sprawled in the lawn chair and stared out over the nearby fields. Normally, he would have been admiring the beautiful afternoon—pleasant breeze, blue sky with puffy white clouds, and all. But his mind kept going back to the scene in his living room with Trudi and Cass. It seemed that everything that had been happening the last few weeks was conspiring against him.

He'd been ruminating for a good ten minutes when he

heard someone tramping through the woods off to his right.

"Incoming," Andy announced to Thor. They both hopped to their feet.

This was state forestland, and the underbrush grew densely. So the two men had no idea whom to expect. They simply couldn't see until their visitors popped out of the greenery.

And it was hard to say who looked more astonished.

Andy, gaping at Cass.

Or Cass, gaping at Andy.

That didn't last long, though, as Andy noticed the tall, ruggedly handsome man with a blond crewcut, who was trailing after Cass. Moreover, the guy seemed to be tightening his belt, as if his jeans had recently been somewhere rather lower than around his waist.

Andy was hardly surprised. Cass was a good-looking woman, back on the market again. But with a fellow law officer? Out in the woods?

Only Thor had the sense to say anything. "Nice day, isn't it, Cass? Gonna introduce us to your friend?"

That's when the back doors of the van opened and another stranger came into the scene. He was middle-aged, a bit portly, and balding with a comb-over. It was the bozo Andy had seen tromping through the trilliums a couple of weeks earlier. The man shot a gimlet stare at Thor, then Andy, then took a peek under his van.

"You know," the comb-over guy said, "this is a public road. Sticking cement blocks under a person's vehicle that could damage that vehicle might, in some circles, be considered an act of criminal vandalism."

As Cass and her friend came down onto the road, Thor approached the comb-over guy.

"Who are you people and why are you spying on me?" he asked.

Andy was impressed at how unruffled Thor sounded. But, of course, his friend—before he had been a hippie peacenik—had done a year as a grunt in Vietnam. He could be pretty darned steely. "I came up here the other day and knocked on your door," Thor said, "and you were too chicken to answer."

The trillium-squashing, comb-over guy seemed unsure how to respond. He simply shook his head, turned, and grabbed one cinderblock, then another, setting them in the weeds by the shoulder of the road. Repeating the process, tall, blond, and handsome guy strode over and snatched up the blocks under the other side of the van.

As Cass brushed by Andy, he spoke up. "Who are these people, Cassie? What's this all about?"

She pivoted and glared. "*Mr. Skyberg*, I seem to recall that our relationship has entered a terminal phase. As in dead. So, not to put too fine a point on things, *it's none of your effing business*."

Then the tall, blond man approached.

Andy didn't know what came over him, but he blocked the guy and stared him in the face.

"At least have the decency to tell us what's going on here," Andy demanded. "Thor hasn't done anything to deserve this kind of treatment."

"I am sorry," the man said, "but I cannot tell you anything. Now please get out of my way."

The guy had some kind of lilting accent. Maybe Swedish or Norwegian. What was a fellow like that doing in what Andy assumed was a federal investigation? This certainly thickened the plot.

"Sir," the blond man said, "out of my way. Please."

Feeling suddenly stubborn, Andy shook his head.

Before Andy could utter a peep, the guy took his arm, gave it a gentle twist, and shunted him off to the side—as easily as if he'd manhandled a five-year-old. Andy yipped in surprise as his arm went numb.

A moment later, Cass and her new friends roared away.

Thor turned and clapped Andy on the shoulder. Andy winced.

"Hey, pal," said Thor, "at least we didn't get busted. Though you were trying awfully hard with Cass's new boyfriend."

Chapter Twenty-Two

Andy had enjoyed driving big Lincolns around the Cities. He'd chauffeured hundreds of celebrities, sports stars, and CEOs—as well as oodles of ordinary folks on their special days. He could count among his acquaintances rock stars, bestselling authors, and titans of industry. At first, he drove as an employee. Then he bought his own Town Car and subcontracted. He liked being his own boss and he thought everything was going great. Until his last couple of years in the business.

That's when the big limo services began to squeeze out the little guys like him. The contracts they offered would lead him to lose, not make, money. And the alternative was disagreeable: come back and be an employee.

For some reason, though, he couldn't stand to give up his Lincoln Town Car. The thing was paid for and was in great shape. He loved that car to pieces. So when he moved home to New Bergen, the Lincoln came with him.

And this May, his sister Kirsten had come up with a special use for it.

It seemed that Elbow Lake Lutheran Church had raised money for kids who normally couldn't have afforded to go to prom. The donations would cover gowns, hairdos, rental tuxes, corsages, boutonnieres—the whole nine yards. Kirsten chipped in four dinners at Ansel's. She asked Andy to chauffeur the two young couples in his Lincoln.

He was actually kind of excited to be able to take the Black Beast, as he called it, out again, with real clients. It would be just like the old days. It would be fun.

"Now, one thing," Kirsten had added. "I want you dressed up classy. Go up to Hobartville and rent a proper tux. I'll pay for it. And I want you to have a small sunflower in your lapel. You know, because of the Vincent van Gogh theme that they're having. You can get one at the florist."

It was just like his sister to insist on something like a tux with a sunflower. She always had some niggling little thing that needed to be done. But he supposed that her attention to detail helped make her so successful out in San Jose.

Being her brother, though, Andy couldn't help but think that this was a pretty ridiculous request.

"What's wrong with my black suit?" he sputtered.

"Well," Kirsten replied, "it's about ten years old. The seat is shiny. And it doesn't quite fit you anymore."

"Whadaya mean?"

They were standing right outside Kirsten's little office at the back of the restaurant. She rolled her eyes, then reached across and briefly pinched both sides of Andy's spare tire.

Andy groaned. Point taken.

So, the day before the prom—beguilingly christened "Starry Night in New Bergen"—Andy visited both of Hobartville's rental formalwear shops. The only tux left that would fit him was robin's-egg blue, with broad, dark-blue sequined trim.

"But I'll look like a circus clown," he lamented to the skinny girl behind the counter.

"Sorry," she said, working hard not to burst out laughing. "You should have come sooner. You're lucky to get this one. After all, it's prom season."

So much for "classy."

Andy picked up a single dwarf sunflower at the florist shop in Hobartville. Then he had one final task to carry out.

He stopped by the walk-up apartment of a lady named Mrs. Hokkanson, whom Aunt Bev had told him about. She might have some ideas about the celebrated ebelskiver recipe. The old dear seemed delighted to have a gentleman caller, and managed to produce the names and numbers of two elderly Herkimer County residents who, she said, might possibly lead Andy to the recipe.

* * *

Per Kirsten's instructions, Andy set out at about five on Saturday afternoon to pick up the pair of young couples. Two of the kids lived in town and the other two out in the country. Even in his clown suit, Andy was enjoying being back in the saddle, so to speak. He felt like a million bucks, piloting his Black Beast around town.

Andy and his charges arrived at Ansel's at six sharp, and he dropped the kids off. He killed the dinner hour up in his studio, munching on a sandwich and listening to a ballgame. About ninety minutes later, the phone on his hip dingdonged and he went downstairs to load the youngsters back into the Beast. Next stop, New Bergen High School gymnasium.

After depositing his charges into the hands of prom chaperones, Andy wandered around the high school parking lot, visiting with folks who had just dropped off their own kids. Andy had gone to high school with many of the parents. The evening soon became half high school reunion and half tailgating party. There was food, drink, and plenty of 1980s and '90s hits blaring out of car and truck stereo systems.

Andy was feeling pleasantly nostalgic, when a red Prius zoomed into the parking lot, seemingly heading right for his Lincoln. It zipped up next to the Black Beast. And who should emerge but Trudi Bock and a young man in white tie and tails. It was the first time Andy had seen Trudi since her semi-naked, early-morning encounter with Cass.

Looking very pleased with himself, Michael Muelhoff promptly planted a top hat on his head, at a jaunty angle. Trudi was clad in a cream-colored gown with voluminous sleeves and pearl trim. Some kind of medieval costume, probably an Eleanor of Aquitaine thing, Andy thought. Her auburn hair was done up in beautiful, jeweled combs. She really did look fine.

"Hey, Trud," Andy said, "what's goin' on?"

Young Mr. Muelhoff walked up beside his boss and she took his arm.

Trudi grinned at Andy. "I'm going to the prom."

Andy desperately wanted to say, *why would you do such a thing if you didn't have to?*

As if reading Andy's mind, Michael Muelhoff spoke up. "I was having a hard time finding a date. And Trudi said why didn't I ask *her*."

The reasons for Michael's inability to snag a teenaged girl were plain to see. Short, skinny, receding chin, braces on the teeth, bad posture, grating laugh. Maybe the kid would mature into an impressive specimen. And who was to say he wouldn't make a billion bucks in Silicon Valley. But for the moment he was a disaster. Trudi was doing humanitarian work here, bless her heart.

"But," Andy said, genuinely surprised, "can an adult go to prom with a kid?"

"I'm eighteen, sir," Michael announced proudly, "so I'm legally an adult. Furthermore, the rules don't stipulate the age of a date for a student who goes to prom. So yeah, Trudi is allowed to come."

"I am proud to go with Michael," Trudi proclaimed, clearly meaning it.

A small crowd had gathered round—some of them looking amused, some of them appalled. One of the women suddenly whispered, "Look out, Trudi. Trouble on the way."

It was Dick Schaeffer, approaching at flank speed.

"What is this?" the pugnacious educator snapped. "What are you doing here, Ms. Bock?"

"I'm going to prom with Michael, Mr. Schaeffer," Trudi said sweetly.

"You can't do that," Schaeffer growled.

"Sure she can," Michael announced. "I researched the rules. I'm eighteen, so I'm good for going out with an older lady."

Andy saw the kid make very subtle goo-goo eyes at his date, who was several inches taller than him. Michael definitely had a crush going. Andy understood perfectly. He could remember a couple of older ladies whom he had had things for as a teenager. Not that anything happened, of course. No reenactments of certain scenes from *The Graduate*, alas.

"Furthermore, Mr. Schaeffer," Michael continued, "nothing states that a student's date has to be below a certain age. My dad's an attorney and he checked it out."

Schaeffer looked as if he were about to blow at any moment. The kid's comments had only made his face redder, his expression more truculent. But the assistant principal somehow managed to dial it down a notch with a spot of deep breathing.

"I cannot prevent you from attending tonight, Ms. Bock. But I still aim to stop your interference in my daughter's life. You keep away from her," he hissed. "Or mark my words, you will pay the price."

With a snort, Schaeffer turned on his heel and marched back into the high school. Trudi and her date followed at a safe distance.

Just before the mismatched couple strolled out of earshot, Andy heard Trudi say, "This one's for you, Amber."

And man, did Andy have a change of heart about Michael Muelhoff. That kid wasn't going to become a Silicon Valley mogul. He was headed for a big law firm in Manhattan, then on to the Supreme Court.

* * *

After taking the four kids home sometime after midnight, Andy ended up at Ansel's for a nightcap with Kirsten, her daughter Aurora, and Aurora's boyfriend Travis.

Rory was dressed up for the prom in a kind of Morticia Addams gown—but without the black tendrils trailing along on the floor. Her lipstick was purple, as were her fingernails. Her long, blond hair was combed out straight, down her shoulders and back. Travis, for his part, had on a plain black suit, with black shirt and black tie.

They were huddled over at a window table, sipping on a pair of chai lattés, nibbling on edamames that Kirsten had steamed for them, and whispering intently to each other. Knowing unsentimental Rory, Andy figured it was unlikely that they were muttering sweet nothings to each other. More likely, they were comparing the latest nerdcore hip-hop tracks that they'd recently downloaded from the Internet.

Rory was a great kid. Andy thought it was kind of sweet that she had been appalled when her mom made Andy wear that inexcusable tux. She offered her uncle a

bit of sage advice: "You gotta stand up to Mom sometimes, Andy. Otherwise, she'll walk all over you."

As if he hadn't known that. For about forty years.

He sat with his sister at the wine bar. Kirsten sipped
on a cool fumé blanc, Andy a decaf cappuccino.

"Went well, didn't it?" Kirsten said. "Do it again next
year?"

"Sure," Andy answered. "Why not? It was a kick."

"Had an e-mail from Mom this morning."

"Where are they?"

"Saint George, Utah."

"So they're hiking Zion again?"

"Yeah. Some of the easier trails."

When his parents had retired a couple of years earlier,
they sold the house in New Bergen, bought a big Airstream and three-quarter ton GMC, and hit the road. They
came home every now and then, and stayed in Kirsten's
guesthouse.

"When will they be back?"

"They don't know yet. Maybe not till after Labor
Day. You know how Mom loves autumn at home."

They sat a few moments in silence.

"You heard from Karl lately?" queried Kirsten.

The number-crunching, results-oriented Kirsten had
long since given up direct communications with the
ne'er-do-well little brother. She let Andy handle that.

"Not since Christmas," Andy said. "So I guess he's
still in Tahoe dealing blackjack and dodging his alimony
payments."

"Any news on the ebelskiver front?"

"Talked yesterday to an old lady in Hobartville name of Hokkanson. Aunt Bev tipped me to her. She had a couple of leads who live in Herkimer County. Give me some time off, and I'll check 'em out."

"Why don't you just call them?"

Andy shrugged. "I suppose I could do that. But some of these old gals are getting up in years and can't hear that well on the phone. And they really do like a visitor now and again. Look at it this way, I'm creating some good karma for you and Ansel's."

Kirsten rolled her eyes. "Now you're starting to sound like Trudi. But okay. Day after Memorial Day's slow, so go Tuesday. Kill two birds. Take your tux back and check things out in Herkimer. I'll put you down for your regular hours."

"And buy me a tank of gas?"

"You drive a hard bargain, Anders Skyberg," Kirsten said, nodding, "but okay."

They both sipped from their drinks, lost in thought.

Kirsten cleared her throat.

"Yeah?" said Andy.

"I owe you an apology," sighed Kirsten.

"What for?"

Andy was a little taken aback. Apologies from Kirsten were few and far between.

She sighed again. "Your black suit really would have been better than that crime against couture that you're wearing."

"And I always thought baby blue was my color," Andy said with a perfect poker face.

Kirsten grinned, then swished some wine around in her mouth, savoring it. "And you said that Dick Schaeffer made another scene."

"That he did. But I think he's met his match in Trudi Bock." Andy chuckled. "I don't know how she manages to ruffle everyone's feathers the way she does."

Kirsten sniffed and shook her head. "It's no mystery, Andy. Trudi loves this kind of drama, loves to wave the red flag in front of the bull. She's a provocateur. She's gotten in Schaeffer's face and in Dittbrenner's and Brenda Erickson's and Mrs. Runestrand's. That's no accident."

Andy hadn't thought about it that way, but Kirsten's theory of Trudi made sense. She always did like to stand up for whatever was the *cause célèbre* of the day. Nothing much deterred her.

"Even so," Andy said, after a long sip of cappuccino, "I sometimes wonder if maybe the two dead Eleanors aren't keeping an eye out for her. Because she always seems to come out smelling like a rose."

Chapter Twenty-Three

The same skinny girl was smirking behind the counter when Andy arrived at Buck's Tuxes in Hobartville the following Tuesday. She asked how the blue tux had worked out, and Andy replied that only two or three people had made funny cracks. That was fewer than average, she said.

"Next year," Andy said, "I'm reserving my tux a month ahead."

"That would be smart," the girl agreed.

After dispensing with the unfortunate item of formalwear, Andy and King Harald rolled eastward into Herkimer County, whose catchy slogan was "Historical Sites and More."

Their first stop was in the town of Pinetop, just about where the state's deciduous woodlands gave way to evergreen forest. Pinetop's biggest employer was a pulp mill that produced the cheap paper used in throwaway advertising flyers. The plant emitted a certain sulfurous scent that could tweak the nose miles downwind. But Pinetop remained unoffended, happy to tolerate the aroma in return for 400-plus good-paying jobs.

It was lunchtime, so dog and man stopped at a bustling burger joint on the edge of downtown Pinetop. Harald, of course, remained in the truck. Andy ordered a triple-burger with nothing on it for the dog and a bacon cheeseburger for himself, with *everything* on it. Plus chips and a diet cola. All to go.

He was heading out the door when he spotted someone familiar in one of the tall booths back in the dining room. He instantly recognized that square, ruddy face. Jerry Dittbrenner. The pork professional who was suing Trudi Bock. This time the guy had on proper farmer's duds—jeans and a blue work shirt, with a green tractor cap.

He was talking earnestly with someone whom Andy couldn't see. Clearly a woman. Because a small hand with fingernails of neon green reached across the table and held Dittbrenner's forearm, in an oddly affectionate way.

Andy was suddenly very curious. He knew Dittbrenner had a wife and kids, although the marriage was rumored to be on shaky ground.

Who was the farmer's companion?

Gripping his bag of chow in one hand and his soda in the other, Andy made a sortie toward the restrooms in the back of the place. He didn't even glance in Dittbrenner's direction, hoping he wouldn't be spotted. He popped into the men's room, waited a couple of minutes, and came back out.

From this angle, he could see the farmer's friend.

He almost dropped his jumbo soda when he did.

Sitting there, still holding onto Dittbrenner's arm, was Lauren Kastner, Trudi's employee. She wore an expression of genuine fondness.

They were truly an odd couple. He, a stodgy, middle-aged hog farmer. She, a twenty-something with piercings and tattoos and spiky, short blond hair.

What in heck, Andy wondered, was she doing with a guy who was suing her boss? And why were they acting so darned cozy?

Andy scurried out of the burger joint, pretty sure the two of them hadn't seen him. He and Harald drove to a town park and had their lunch. But Andy ate like a robot, hardly noticing the bacon cheeseburger as he chomped and chewed and gulped.

When he finished, he pulled the phone off his belt and punched in Trudi's number. He got her voicemail and started talking.

* * *

Mrs. Antonia Brovald lived right across the street from the paper mill on the outskirts of Pinetop, and had dealt with the ubiquitous odor by filling her little house with all manner of scents. Potpourris. Incense. Air fresheners. An electronic device that spit out a mist of perfume. The hodgepodge of sweet and floral and spicy and piney and vanilla that mixed with the mill smell almost made Andy's stomach do flip-flops. But he managed to keep it together. Other than that, it seemed like a pretty typical old-lady kind of house. Neat as a button, with every piece of upholstered furniture covered in plastic. Andy crinkled down on the sofa with his cup of weak instant coffee.

"So you're after that famous ebelskiver recipe?" Mrs. Brovald asked. Her short hair was dyed black, and she had black eyebrows drawn rather too enthusiastically over her rheumy eyes. Tall, thin, and stoop-shouldered, she resembled a dyspeptic vulture. But Andy soon was charmed by her gracious manner.

"That's right," he said, his mind still fixated on Lauren and Jerry. "My sister runs Ansel's in New Bergen, and I—"

"Oooh," exclaimed the old lady, her generously lined face brightening. "My daughter took me there for my birthday lunch last year. The most wonderful trout almondine. And the cheesecake? Positively yummy."

"I'll tell Kirsten how much you liked it. Anyway, she needs that ebelskiver recipe for Elbow Lake Days this August. And Mrs. Hokkanson over in Hobartville said you might have an idea of where to find it."

"Like I said on the phone, Andy, I certainly do remember those ebelskivers. It was Reverend Peder Nielsen's wife who made them. Her name was Dagmar and she was a full-blooded Dane, you know. Worked part-time as a cook at St. Magnus Prep for a few years. A very generous, dear woman but she kept that recipe so secret that no one else was ever able to copy it. She'd mix up the batter at home and bring it with her." She shook her head, as if still amazed at such culinary cloak-and-dagger. "I had Dagmar's ebelskivers myself a few times. Light as a cloud and delectable, too. Put on some butter, maple syrup, strawberry preserves—just divine."

"You wouldn't know where to find Mrs. Nielsen, would you?"

"Heavens, no. We weren't that close. I haven't heard of her in years. Don't know if she's alive or passed on."

After bidding Mrs. Brovald and her aromatic smash-up a cordial farewell, Andy rejoined Harald in the Silverado and headed to their second and final stop in Herkimer County.

Capitola "Cappy" Briggs had been a high school teacher in Pinetop and had retired many years ago to her log cabin in the piney woods of northeastern Herkimer. She was a bundle of energy—a sinewy little woman, with a close-cropped head of pure white hair.

"Oh, you betcha, I remember those ebelskivers," she said, sitting across from Andy in her knotty pine breakfast nook, with Harald lying next to her on the floor. She attempted to push the plate of cookies at Andy one more time, but he put up his hand. "They were just basically pancakes, of course, but awful good. The whole deal with them was because of a couple of special ingredients that Mrs. Nielsen put in them. Did something to them kind of magical."

"Mrs. Brovald told me that Mrs. Nielsen kept that recipe top secret."

"That's absolutely right. If she had revealed what was in the recipe, she would have had to kill you." Cappy hooted at her joke.

"You wouldn't know if Mrs. Nielsen is still alive, would you?"

"No, I sure don't. But tell you what I'll do. I'll ask around a little bit, do a little detective work, and see what I can find out. Now how about you and me and that sweet pooch of yours have a hike. You know, I have a gorgeous two-mile path through the woods."

Andy almost said no, but it was awfully pretty out there. "I think Harald would enjoy that," he said.

* * *

Andy knew it had been a mistake, drinking all that coffee those two old dears had thrust at him. So there he was, lying awake in bed after one a.m., staring at the ceiling. He thought about Cappy's invitation to come back anytime to paint on her 400 acres. The land offered gorgeous vistas of pine and birch, and rolling fields full of native flowers. Andy's caffeine-fueled brain couldn't stop imagining the canvasses he would create.

Then his mind went back to the unforeseen sighting of Jerry Dittbrenner and Lauren Kastner. Were they having a fling? If not, why the rendezvous up in Herkimer County? In any event, this didn't look good. Something shady was going on.

Andy's noggin was racing its engine, like a muscle car wanting to drag. And when that happened, the only thing for it was to get up and move around. A walk sounded awfully good.

He dressed, slipped on his Nikes, and tiptoed out

through the kitchen. Down in the back vestibule Harald seemed asleep. But just as Andy unlocked the back door, the dog snorted awake and raised his head.

"Sorry, Harald," Andy said. "Didn't mean to wake you up."

He grabbed Harald's lead from the hook on the wall, waved it around, and asked, "Wanna take a walk, big guy?"

Harald suddenly perked up, his tail gyrating.

From Andy's point of view, it looked like an affirmative. He clipped the lead on Harald's collar, and off they went.

Under a lovely, starry sky—as lovely as anything Van Gogh painted—the man and the canine first made a probe in the direction of Elbow Lake. But Harald balked after a few blocks, and tried to haul Andy back in the direction of downtown New Bergen. Andy resisted briefly but finally let the dog have his way. After all, Harald had behaved himself beautifully all day long—waiting patiently in the Silverado, sitting politely in Cappy Briggs's kitchen, and pretending to be disinterested in squirrels on their hike through the woods. What the heck, Andy thought, let Harald choose the route tonight.

Andy was no Peeping Tom, but he loved being out like this when almost everyone in town was dozing. The lit windows they passed—and there were a few of them—caused him to wonder, what was it that made someone a night owl, apart from simple insomnia.

Maybe a book they were itching to finish. Or a terrific

show on TV. Or midnight oil that had to be burned. Or the rheumatism that wouldn't let them sleep.

Almost before Andy knew it, Harald had hauled him down Muskie Avenue onto Skjegstad Street. They took a left toward the business district.

Andy and Harald walked by antique store after antique store, the shoe store, one of New Bergen's several chiropractors, and Ansel's. Andy put on the brakes, and Harald obliged by sitting down. They'd been marching along for about half an hour, and the hike home would make it an hour-long perambulation. That ought to tire a fellow enough to fall asleep properly—for at least a few hours.

"Come on, Harald, let's go home," Andy said, starting to turn back the way they'd come.

But without any warning, Harald charged off in the opposite direction, almost yanking Andy's right arm out of the socket.

Andy yelled for the big dog to stop.

King Harald, though, had other ideas, hauling Andy across Skjegstad Street and down the block.

Then the dog took a sharp right turn into the parking lot of the Karma Kubbyhole, at which point he lurched to a halt and started to bark frantically.

Andy was absolutely baffled by Harald's bizarre behavior, until he looked up.

He couldn't believe it.

Someone had taken what must have been gallons of red paint and heaved them up onto Aunt Bev's mural.

Half of the artwork was covered with big splashes of pigment. Or so it seemed under the light of the nearby streetlamp.

Somewhere out of sight, back in the alley, an engine rumbled to life.

"Let's move, Harald!" Andy barked.

The man and the dog sprinted around the back of Trudi's store just in time to nearly get run over by an old, dark-colored Dodge pickup.

They sprawled back against the brick wall as the truck roared by.

Andy had no time—not to mention very little light— to see either the driver or the plate number.

But there was some luminosity coming from inside the Karma Kubbyhole.

In fact, the door into the store's back room was wide open. And a cheerful, flickering orange glow could be seen in there.

Andy peeked through the doorframe.

The place was on fire.

And Andy didn't have his cell phone.

Chapter Twenty-Four

Andy and King Harald trotted the six blocks to the sheriff's station. The New Bergen fire hall was too far away, on the other side of town. It took about five minutes, though the dog could have made it in two. Gotta start working out, Andy thought, huffing and puffing.

All the lights were on inside the sheriff's station and a black-and-white was parked in the reserved spot. But Andy didn't see anyone through the locked glass door. He pounded on it with the heel of his hand. Where was a cop when you needed one?

He was almost ready to give up and head for the all-night truck stop out by the Interstate—the only other place he could think of to make a phone call in the middle of the night—when the restroom door inside swung open. And out stepped Cass Conlin.

Andy pounded on the glass again and Cass recognized her late night visitor.

An angry scowl came over her face.

"Trudi's store's on fire!" Andy shouted through the glass.

Andy could tell that Cass said something profane in

his direction—something that began with an "m" and ended with an "r."

She tramped over, still scowling, and unlocked the door.

Before Andy could utter a word, she snarled, "If this is some kind of pitiful effort to make up for your rotten behavior—"

"Cassie, will you shut the heck up!" Andy snapped. "The Karma Kubbyhole's on fire! I saw the arsonist drive away. Almost ran over me and Harald."

Cass suddenly looked conflicted. Loathe to give up her rant in mid-invective, but excited to have a potential arson flare up while she was the duty officer. She quickly called in the report to the fire station, Ed Vandegraff at home, and sheriff's headquarters in Hobartville.

After a white-knuckle ride with siren blaring, the former couple peeled into a spot in front of the store. Piling out of the black-and-white, leaving Harald in the back seat, they regarded the burning Karma Kubbyhole with astonishment. Then Cass peered briefly at Andy and nodded. He translated that to mean: "Okay, so you weren't lying."

Not half a moment later, the big red pumper truck roared up, siren blaring. The crew tumbled out and started to unreel the hose that they would hook up to the fire hydrant.

Flames and smoke poured out of the building, both back and front. It had been less than ten minutes since Andy and Harald had discovered the fire, but Andy was pretty certain the building would be a total loss. He wondered if the arsonist had set fires in multiple spots inside the store. Why would it otherwise burn so fast?

As the fire crew began to blast water into the flames, New Bergen's second fire engine pulled up.

Standing by the squad car, Andy figured the most important thing now was to prevent the conflagration from taking out the whole block. Two doors away from Trudi's place was a shop devoted to antique toys and gizmos, known around the world among collectors. And it would be a damn shame if that burned. Fortunately, Doug Esbensen's insurance agency sat in-between. At least Doug would probably have plenty of good coverage.

Cass was doing what Cass did best—ordering people around. That is, getting the gawkers who'd arrived to back off to a safer distance.

Now the fire crews had the second hose snaked around the rear of the Karma Kubbyhole, shooting the torrent of water through the back door. But the fire still burned so fiercely that Andy wondered how they could control it in time to save the block. He didn't like the look of things.

Still, it was a mesmerizing sight. Watching a fire report on TV didn't hold a candle—so to speak—to the real thing.

For some mysterious canine reason, Harald decided that now was the moment to raise a ruckus. From the back seat of Cass's police cruiser, he started to howl like a timber wolf.

Was there something Andy should know about? Or was Harald a little slow to take note of an emergency situation?

It didn't matter. No one else seemed to notice in the furor of the roaring flames.

As the tons of water gushed into and onto Trudi's little domain, more and more people began showing up, bleary-eyed but enthralled. Cass had Ed Vandegraff with her and they had their hands full pushing the spectators back. Pretty soon, reinforcements arrived from Hobart-ville. Sheriff Mandsager himself, along with more deputies. Another fire truck. The mayor of New Bergen and most of the city council regarded the scene with horror.

After an hour or so, the firefighters had the blaze pretty much under control. The rest of the block apparent-ly had dodged disaster. But the fire crews kept shooting two streams of water into the ruined, smoking Karma Kubbyhole. Just to be safe, Andy supposed.

Harald had calmed down by then. Andy, figuring it was time to spring his dog from the cop cruiser, ap-proached Cass, who was threatening some overeager shutterbug with instant incarceration.

"Hey, Cass," he said. "I'd like to get Harald and go home now."

The sheriff's deputy turned around. "I'll open the door for you. But before you vamoose, you're going to need to talk to Ed or Sheriff Mandsager. You're the only witness, and they'll want to ask some questions."

After Andy extracted Harald from the cop car, he

went over to Ed Vandegraff and told him about every-thing he'd seen. Ed took notes as Andy recounted the evening's events. The old, dark-colored Dodge pickup. A D150, Andy guessed—1992, give or take. The fire inside the back room. The heart-straining jog to the sheriff's station. The inferno he and Cass discovered.

"I think Sheriff Mandsager would like to know how it is your dog always seems to find himself at the scene of the crime," Ed said, putting his little notebook away.

Andy chuckled nervously. "Yeah, weird, huh?"

If he didn't know any better, he might have thought that Ed was a little suspicious of King Harald's master. Didn't they always say that arsonists and other criminals liked to hang around to see the results of their handi-work? What did the murders of an iguana and a woman and a serious case of arson all have in common? King Harald. And who was the boss of King Harald? Andy Skyberg.

Ed nodded. "Yeah, weird. I'd suggest you call his office and set up an appointment. ASAP." Then he turned and sauntered off to help Cass with crowd control.

Well *there's* something to look forward to, thought Andy, a little bit shocked. His first police interrogation.

The man and dog trudged homeward, around the corner by Ansel's and halfway up the block on Perch Avenue. Suddenly, a red Prius came barreling down Perch and screeched to a halt close to them.

For a few beats, Andy didn't recognize the car. When he did, he gulped, "Uh-oh."

The Prius's door whammed open, and out of it burst Trudi. She had on an oversized sweatshirt and jeans. Her bounteous auburn hair was a tangled fright wig. And her face was the very picture of shock and dismay.

"Anders," she wailed, dashing over and hurling herself at him. "Is it true? Is it true?"

Reluctantly, Andy gave her a long squeeze, then disengaged, as Harald kept trying to jump up on her.

"Oh, man, Trud," Andy groaned. "Afraid so. Harald and I were out on a ramble and spotted the fire. It's pretty bad."

It positively broke Andy's heart to look at Trudi, who had tried so hard to make a place for herself in New Bergen. She had plenty of money. She could have stayed in the Cities or moved to Paris or Bali. She didn't have to move to boring old New Bergen to try to convert the natives to the wonders of the Brave New Age. Whoever was doing this to her deserved to be hung, if you asked Andy.

"Will you come with me, Anders?" Trudi pleaded. Her voice quivered and she blinked back tears.

From where they were standing on Perch Avenue, they couldn't see the ruins of the Karma Kubbyhole. So Trudi had no precise idea of what she was walking into. She shouldn't have to witness this all alone.

"Sure, Trud," Andy said. "Glad to."

"I promise you," she said, sucking in some air, "that I won't lose it."

"I know this is terrible timing," Andy said. "But I

have to ask you a quick question."

Trudi looked anxious to go, but nodded.

"Did you get my message?"

"Yes, I did."

"Have any theories about Lauren and Dittbrenner?"

"Yes, Anders, I do. But right now I have to see my Kubbyhole."

* * *

Trudi blinked in shock at her first sight of the drenched, blackened ruin of her dream. But she was good to her word, for a little while, and didn't start blubbering. New Bergen's fire chief began to tell her how they had done everything they could, but the building was too far gone. He said they had been lucky to save the rest of the block.

Then a look came across Trudi's face that genuinely scared Andy. Her features went white, like something he'd imagine on a person having a stroke. "Trud, are you all—"

"Gus," she gasped. "Gus!"

She turned to the fire chief, then back to Andy, and back to the chief.

"Gus sleeps in the basement," she said, panic vibrating in her voice. "Do you think—"

That's when Trudi lost it.

Doing the right thing, Andy threw an arm around her and let her bawl on his shoulder. He caught sight of Cass giving him the evil eye, and, by gosh, he just didn't care anymore.

"How soon can you see if Gus is in there?" Andy asked the chief, as Trudi sobbed away.

"Not until we know it's safe to go in," the chief answered grimly. He was a rail-thin man of about fifty, with a trim, salt-and-pepper beard. He'd been hired away from a town in Nebraska. "Maybe later today. Hopefully, the gentleman didn't stay there last night."

Andy didn't have the heart to disagree, what with Trudi still being plastered to his side. But he had seen Gus's orange VW minibus parked on Skjegstad Street before he and Harald had spotted the fire.

He was very much afraid that Gus Johnson had surfed his last pipeline.

Chapter Twenty-Five

It was about 6 a.m. when Andy drove Trudi home in her Prius, Harald riding shotgun in the back seat. She immediately phoned her mom, who promised to come right away. Then Andy persuaded her to down a couple stiff belts of brandy and try to take a nap. She sur-prised him by complacently following his suggestions—kind of zombie-like.

He supposed she had something resembling shell-shock or post-traumatic stress. Heck, this woman had practically had a bull's-eye on her back for weeks now.

After Trudi crashed on her big, full-tester bed, Andy phoned Thor for a ride home. With Harald happily inhal-ing a stiff breeze in the back of the Jeep, Andy and his friend dissected all the dreadful events of the past weeks and tried to make sense of them.

"We have an assassinated iguana," Andy began, as they pulled out of Trudi's driveway onto the blacktop. "We have poison-pen notes sent to Trud. Mrs. R and her holy rollers are on the warpath. Her grandson gets in a brawl with Charlie Adams and goes missing. I personally get kind of sucked in, not merely because Harald finds the defunct lizard, but mysteriously a letter bearing my name appears in the paper, which opens the way for the city council to scotch Trud's Eleanorian bash."

"Meanwhile," Thor said, taking up the thread of general weirdness that had infected Beaver Tail County, "the harmless old coot with socialistic opinions finds himself under surveillance by some kind of government authority. For reasons that are perfectly obscure. A 1960s flashback? Something that Thor Hofdahl did back in Berkeley? Or has something more recent aroused the all-seeing eye of Big Brother?"

"And don't forget the all-seeing eye of Cass Conlin," Andy put in. "She just about implied that to hang with you was tantamount to joining the anarcho-nihilist-jihadis."

Thor shook his head as they zoomed past the New Bergen grain elevator. "Some people would say any guy who sides with an opinionated old geezer instead of a very well-put-together, blonde birdie has a few screws loose in his head."

"You know, no one's ever accused me of displaying much common sense," said Andy.

"Anyway," Thor continued, "thanks for supporting me on this. I know half of New Bergen thinks I'm a geriatric whack-job, so I really appreciate you sticking your neck out for me."

Andy never had possessed the knack of taking compliments graciously. However well-deserved, they made him uncomfortable. He blamed it on that awful

Norwegian instinct for self-deprecation. To acknowledge praise meant you agreed with it. Which signified that you had a swelled-up head.

"Well," he finally answered, "you'd have done the same."

Thor raised his eyebrows. "Don't be so sure."

They both laughed as Thor steered his Jeep into the Java Shack on the outskirts of New Bergen. After Andy secured Harald's lead to the inside of the truck bed, the two men went inside for a pick-me-up. An espresso for Thor and a grande cappuccino for Andy. They sat in a corner booth.

"So anyway," Andy said after that first delectable sip, "things ramp up when Zeke Haugen attacks Charlie."

"Who is murdered that very night," Thor observed. "Casting a strong suspicion on young Zeke."

"And don't forget Trud's encounters with Dick Schaeffer."

"That prejudiced puritan prick," said Thor.

"In addition, we have Brenda Erickson's very public campaign to shame Trud into selling her back the Fundingsland farm. And now this. Trudi Bock's store burned nearly to the ground. If Gus Johnson was in there, well…"

Andy knew that Thor liked Gus. Both had California in their backgrounds. Both had lived pretty liberated lifestyles—albeit in different eras. It wasn't until Gus showed up—with his shortboard still in the back of his VW—that Andy learned Thor had surfed away a year or two of his younger life.

"Awful way for a guy like Gus to go," Thor said. "Better to buy it on your board."

"Amen to that," Andy agreed somberly.

Andy felt just awful about Gus. He'd been a fine new eccentric to add to the New Bergen collection. Maybe a miracle would happen and he'd turn up safe and sound. But Andy doubted it.

"And then there's Jerry Dittbrenner," Andy continued.

"I'd forgotten about him. Trudi and her humane society pals have made it very hot for that guy, with their accusations of animal abuse. But he's suing her, right? Why would he need to resort to violence?"

"There's more to it than that," Andy said. He recounted his weird sighting of Jerry Dittbrenner and Lauren Kastner in the Pinetop burger joint.

Thor whistled. "Wow, a genuine fifth columnist in Trudi's store? Probably spying or sabotaging or whatnot. This whole deal is just fascinating, isn't it?"

"Not if you're Trud," sighed Andy. "Not if you're me."

"Okay then, our suspects are pretty clear," Thor said. "Mrs. R and her minions. Including that juvenile delinquent grandson of hers. Dick Schaeffer. Your old girlfriend."

"Huh?" Andy said.

"The former Brenda Fundingsland."

Andy made a cross with his two index fingers, as if to

fend off an approaching vampire. "No girlfriend of mine, Thor. Never was. Date from hell."

"And finally, we have those improbable lovebirds, Jerry Dittbrenner and Lauren Kastner." Thor took off his glasses and rubbed his eyes. "If it were me, though, I'd put money on Mrs. R's bunch. With that Zeke Haugen kid doing the dirty work. They got some real brambles in their knickers about protecting Beaver Tail County from the malarkey and voodoo that Trudi Bock sells."

Andy sighed. "You forgot another suspect, Thor."

"Who's that?"

"Anders Skyberg."

Thor looked dumbfounded.

"Ed Vandegraff just this morning wondered how it is that King Harald unerringly sniffs out crime scenes before anyone else."

"Hate to say it, Andy, but he makes a fair point. You aren't a serial killer, are you?"

"About as much as you're a Tea Party libertarian."

"Have you figured out if you have alibis?"

"No, pretty much I don't. I could have gone to Trud's place and cut Adonis's neck. I could have bonked Charlie Adams on the head. I could have set that fire."

Andy sipped some more on his cappuccino. "What I don't have is motive. Why would I do all this nasty stuff to Trud?"

"You have no reason at all," Thor agreed. "And another thing that stumps me, Andy, is that the crimes seem way out of proportion to any possible provocation.

Not worth killing a lizard for, let alone a woman and a poor bozo caught napping in the wrong basement at the wrong time."

"What an unholy mess," Andy groaned, shaking his head.

"The thing is this, old scout. The oligarchs, the pluto-crats, all the servants of the one percent. They don't want free thinkers out there like me. Like Trudi Bock. They just want happy, little robots who'll do their work for less and less money, with less and less freedom. Hollow out the middle class until there's nothing left. Until we're all practically slaves in chains. This whole business of perse-cuting Trudi and me is just a tiny little part of the campaign to scare the drones. The rest of the people see what happens to Trudi and me, they'll behave them-selves."

Andy nodded, although he didn't really believe that Wall Street had it in personally for Thor and Trudi. But someone sure did.

* * *

With the very center of Skjegstad Street closed off for the post-fire clean-up, Kirsten decided to shut Ansel's down for the day. She and J. J., though, whipped up sandwiches and drinks for the fire crews, police, and reporters. Andy delivered the food up and down the street. Free and on the house. The biggest excitement downtown that morning was when two news copters from the Cities warily circled each other up above the devastated Karma Kubbyhole—*whump-whump-whump-*

ing away.

Carter LaPorte had managed to buttonhole Andy as soon as he returned to the scene of the crime.

"Will you give me an exclusive, Andy?" the editor asked just outside Ansel's. "The *Chronicle* would be grateful. Your personal account of what you saw and what you think happened. You're the only witness to the actual event, other than the perp."

"I don't know if that's the right thing to do, Carter," Andy replied. "The other reporters have to make a living, too."

"At least let me have the first interview then. As a personal favor? I know the *Chronicle* messed you up with the fake letter to the editor. But shouldn't you give your old hometown paper the first shot at the story? You can talk to the guys and gals from the Cities later, huh?"

Andy had never been at the center of a media frenzy, but he supposed he did owe it to the readers of Beaver Tail County. He shrugged and nodded. "Yeah, okay, Carter. Let's go inside Ansel's and I'll give you the scoop."

The two men sat at the wine bar and Andy recounted the whole nocturnal misadventure, from the moment he arrived back in New Bergen after his ebelskiver quest. The late night ramble with Harald. The dog's insistence on visiting the Karma Kubbyhole. The awful defacement of Aunt Bev's mural. The close call with the Dodge pick-up. The fire. All of it.

Carter scribbled notes furiously, interrupting to throw in questions and comments.

"How's Harald sniffing out these crimes?"

"Do you think the arsonist tried to run you down?"

"What do you know about Gus Johnson?"

"Any chance he might have been elsewhere?"

"What do you think Trudi's done to deserve this kind of persecution? Any theories?"

Andy answered everything as well as he could. It turned out his visit with Carter was good practice for his interviews with the other reporters—two from TV, and two from the big metropolitan dailies. As the interviews went along, Andy honed his answers down to the bare essentials. He wasn't enjoying himself and wanted it all to be over.

After his fifteen minutes of fame with members of the media, Andy joined Kirsten and J. J. in the kitchen to help throw together another passel of sandwiches for the emergency crews out on the street. Andy was halfway through slicing a spiral-cut ham when he heard an agitated shout of "Anders! Kirsten!"

He made eye contact with his sister and that rare magic of telepathic communication between the twins occurred.

Andy could almost hear Kirsten's brain mutter "Uh-oh," just as his was blurting out exactly the same thing.

Aunt Bev had arrived.

The brother and sister put down their work and headed out into the dining room.

Aunt Bev was standing there by the host's lectern at the front of the restaurant, looking depressed and shrunken. Obviously, she had just seen the fate of her grand artistic composition.

She looked from Andy to Kirsten and back, blinking through the tears. "They splashed my mural with red paint. Then they burned it down. It was good. It was the best thing I ever painted. People liked it."

Kirsten, being a hardboiled software executive, wasn't given to crying or hugging or getting sentimental about almost anything. Oddly enough, Andy had always been better at comforting the grief-stricken. And it fell to him again, as he stepped over to Aunt Bev and enveloped her in a hug. He felt genuinely sorry that her magnum opus had come to such a catastrophic end. He'd actually gotten used to the thing and didn't mind it—in a primitive-artsy sort of way.

"If Trud rebuilds," he said, rocking his aunt as if she were an agitated five-year-old, "I'm sure she'll have you re-do it. Betcha the insurance will cover the cost."

"You think so, Anders?" Aunt Bev sniffled.

"Oh, yeah, sure," Kirsten put in, patting her aunt on the shoulder.

That's when Andy saw Ed Vandegraff approaching Ansel's, looking as grim as he had ever seen the burly lawman look. Andy gently let loose of Aunt Bev and nodded at Kirsten, who had also seen the assistant sheriff. Another vibe went between the twins: *This doesn't look good.*

Ed pulled open the door and stepped in.

Clearing his throat, he said, "Afraid I have bad news.

We sent a firefighter in and she found a body in the basement. We've sent somebody over to Doc Swanstrom's office, to secure Mr. Johnson's dental records. We'll need those to make a positive ID."

"But it could be someone else," Aunt Bev said, grasping for a straw.

Andy knew that Gus had charmed a lot of the ladies of the town—his aunt apparently among them.

"I suppose that's possible," Ed said. "But not very likely."

Chapter Twenty-Six

As Andy drove up to Hobartville the next morning, he didn't know quite what to expect from the police interview. But it didn't take him long to figure out what Sheriff Mandsager was after.

The lawman, sitting steely-eyed across from Andy in the interview room, clearly wanted to trip him up. Find some nefarious reason why King Harald had been the first to arrive at every significant crime scene in the last month. Uncover some motive that would have compelled Andy to persecute Trudi Bock—beyond Andy's frank admission that he didn't want to date the woman.

But the jowly, growly sheriff got no satisfaction from the lanky restaurant worker.

Throughout the questioning, Andy tried his best to keep an even keel. And he thought he was doing a pretty good job, though he was blinking and licking his lips a lot.

But holy cow! Underneath he felt like a nervous wreck, afraid his mouth would mess up somehow and land him in the clink for eighteen years. Because even though he was totally innocent of any wrongdoing, the law, in its awful majesty, sometimes overlooked such piddling little details. Anyway, sitting in this chair was way harder than it looked in a cop show on TV.

"One more thing," the sheriff muttered, as Andy stood up to leave.

"Yeah?" Andy said warily.

"Your friend, Thorstein Hofdahl."

"You mean the guy Cass Conlin and those feds were surveilling?" After everything that had happened, Andy couldn't help but be a little snippy.

"You know perfectly well who I'm talking about, Mr. Skyberg."

"What about him?"

"Could you possibly talk some sense into Mr. Hofdahl and persuade him to stop picketing the sheriff's office?"

Andy could barely stifle a grin. So Thor had gotten under Mandsager's skin after all. And he had only been protesting for a few days, just a few hours a day. Andy had helped him make the sign, which proclaimed: "No more police state tactics! Ask Sheriff Mandsager about Thor Hofdahl!"

"And why should I?" Andy queried pointedly. "You people spied on Thor. The guys in the van and even Cass. Thor actually found a bug in his phone. And the last thing he did that was even remotely illegal was smoke some weed back during the Carter administration. Whatever you think Thor is guilty of, you have the wrong guy. And I'm betting you know it. 'Cause that surveillance truck and those two cowboys have disappeared."

Mandsager didn't say a word, but his jowls were quivering with frustration.

"Am I right?" Andy said. "Or am I right?"

The sheriff ran his tongue around behind his stubbly upper lip. "What does Mr. Hofdahl want?"

Now Andy allowed a smile. "I can't say for sure. But my guess is that he wants an explanation, an apology, and a promise that it won't happen again."

"I don't know that I can get him all that," the sheriff grumbled. "But I'll see what I can do."

"I'll mention it to Thor," Andy said.

He was about to step out of the room, when another thought occurred to him. "Sheriff, have you had any leads on Zeke Haugen?"

Sheriff Mandsager shook his head. "Nothing new. The young man hasn't been seen since Cass dropped him off at home the day of the altercation with Miss Adams."

"In other words, the night Charlie was murdered."

"Correct. We have a bulletin out for Mr. Haugen nationwide, but nothing so far. He could be anywhere by now."

"Do you think he did it?"

"He's a person of interest, Mr. Skyberg," the sheriff said coldly. "Just like you."

* * *

A week later, Skjegstad Street had returned to a semblance of normalcy. The summer vacation season had officially begun and every day, hundreds of tourists—

most of them wielding AARP discount cards—ambled up and down its length, snagging antiques and crafts and assorted geegaws. Ansel's and other downtown eateries bustled.

The only visible reminder of the recent unpleasantness was the charred chasm that had once been the Karma Kubbyhole, now surrounded by orange hazard fencing. The ruined metaphysical shop garnered only a handful of gawkers and curiosity-seekers. But underneath, everyone who worked on Skjegstad Street or had patronized the Kubbyhole felt a pall of gloom.

Word had come back two days after the fire that the body found in the store's basement was indeed that of Jonathan "Gus" Johnson.

Andy was putting in extra hours at Ansel's, hosting and bussing as needed. While he felt a certain obligation to keep an eye on Trudi after the fresh trauma of Gus's death, his schedule didn't allow for any babysitting. But it turned out he wasn't needed. In the wake of the tragedy, various relatives, friends, and neighbors clustered around her.

Her mom came back for an extended stay. Trudi's other employees, now without jobs in a tough economy, visited frequently in an effort to boost her spirits. New Age pals journeyed to New Bergen to wrangle Trudi through healing bouts of crystal therapy, reflexology, reiki, sweat lodge, and green tea enemas. Trudi's six-foot-six attorney friend Carmine Bongiovanni—that most striking of Eleanor Roosevelt impersonators—came up to help with legal matters. Praying that there were no hard feelings, several members of Mrs. Runestrand's band of merry pranksters, as Andy sometimes called them, turned up with hot dishes and Christian sympathy. After all, they had merely wanted to shut down the Kubbyhole, not burn it to a crisp.

Not least, Carter LaPorte had taken Trudi out on a couple of dates.

Andy couldn't have been happier. The newspaperman seemed like a good match for her.

Aunt Bev had been in touch with Trudi regarding a repeat rosemaling engagement—that is, should the Karma Kubbyhole be rebuilt. With her insurance money and her own substantial slush fund, Trudi had the means to start again. What no one around New Bergen knew was if she had the will.

"You know, Andy," Kirsten said, late one evening as they were closing up, "this whole deal with the arson at Trudi's store has an upside."

Andy was a little baffled. It seemed entirely downside to him. "What do you mean?"

"Trudi has plenty of people fussing over her. Her mom is keeping an eye on her. And Carter LaPorte is becoming an attentive companion. The lady doesn't really need you anymore. You're off the hook as a potential suitor."

Andy knew very well that his sister thought Trudi wasn't the match for him. And she'd been right.

But Kirsten *did* believe that, with a bit of luck and a

lot of hard work, anyone could find the ideal mate.

She approached her relationship with her husband, Alan Vanska, with her typical discipline. She had insisted they take personality inventory tests when they first started talking about marriage. Then they negotiated an iron-clad pre-nup. Even Alan's work as a mergers-and-acquisitions consultant, which had him on the road three weeks a month, was considered an advantage. The couple thought that too much time together—for such a pair of Type A brainiacs—might lead to friction. And darned if it hadn't all worked out pretty well.

"I wonder if Trud's going to rebuild," Andy finally said.

"Well, if she doesn't," Kirsten replied, "I might like to buy that property.

Andy was surprised. He had no idea that Kirsten had an interest in owning more real estate in downtown New Bergen. "What for?" he asked.

"New Bergen has one decent coffee café. But it's behind the times. I'd like to set up an operation where we roast our own beans. Only the best quality. Custom one-cup drips. French press. Mocha pot. Espresso, of course. I want the best coffee in the state, outside of the Cities. And I'm toying with the notion of creating a genuine Scandinavian deli."

"Sounds ambitious."

"That's not all. It's going to have an art gallery."

"A gallery?" Andy perked up.

"Not frivolous, touristy stuff. But serious work. Like

your winter landscapes. I mean, Andy, your pieces deserve to be better known. And I'd like to help. And of course you'd have to scout out other artists who have the right stuff. If it happens, I'd like you to run the operation."

Andy was slack-jawed with amazement. "Where do I sign up, Sis?"

* * *

When he strolled out of Ansel's that evening, on toward midnight, Andy was still walking on air, visualizing his great new project with Kirsten. There were only a few people on the sidewalks, gathered in clumps outside a pizza place and a couple of bars south down Skjegstad Street. Two Harleys rumbled to life in front of one of the bars and came rolling majestically down the blacktop—a heavy, black-jacketed man on one, his husky, black-jacketed female friend on the other. Right past Andy.

He turned to watch them go, not a little envious. Sometimes he regretted that he'd never had the experience of riding a powerful, Milwaukee-made machine.

Well, it was never too late. Maybe some day.

That's when he noticed someone standing in front of the hazard fencing that still surrounded the former Karma Kubbyhole. It was a man, and he was looking in at the charred ruins.

Now there'd been plenty of curiosity seekers who'd come for a look, but this guy seemed a bit different—arms crossed, rocking back and forth on his heels.

Andy walked down the block for a better look and that's when he recognized the fellow.

It was *him*, in jeans and workshirt and green tractor cap. The same outfit he'd worn in Pinetop, when he was having his *tête-à-tête* with Lauren Kastner.

Andy debated simply turning around and leaving. But he couldn't resist confronting the hog farmer.

"Excuse me," he said, striding across the street. "Aren't you Jerry Dittbrenner?"

The man turned around and regarded Andy with that ruddy, pugnacious mug. "Yeah. What of it?"

"You're suing Trudi Bock," Andy said.

"Yeah, I am. And the humane society. The woman defamed my hog operation in the paper, on the radio, on the TV. It's already cost me quite a few bucks and I aim to get that back, plus damages. It's been a huge pain in the butt. And why should you care?"

"I'm a friend of Trud's, and I'd think that after this…" Andy gestured at the ruined Kubbyhole. "…you'd maybe back off a little."

"Did you ever think the Karma Kubbyhole might have picked up some bad karma because of what Trudi Bock did to me?" Dittbrenner gave Andy a penetrating glare. "I'm sorry that guy died in the fire. But look, that woman nearly destroyed my business. And I have a wife and three kids to support."

And a mistress, too, thought Andy.

"Maybe Trudi got what was coming to her," Dittbrenner continued. "Did that ever occur to you?"

He stuck his hands in his pockets and tramped away, without another word.

As much as Andy hated to admit it, the guy had a point. Trudi's proclivity for sticking her nose in where it didn't belong was her biggest weakness. And sometimes there could be unpleasant consequences.

Chapter Twenty-Seven

Andy had worked ten days in a row and was getting a little frazzled. In addition to his normal duties, he had to pick up the slack while Kirsten and J. J. trained in the college and high school kids who worked at Ansel's through the summer. Finally, on a glorious Monday morning, he had a day of rest and recreation in front of him. The plan was for a fishing expedition with Thor to Rose Lake, then some burgers and a few beers somewhere on Skjegstad Street.

Rather than haul out his dad's Alumacraft, Andy decided it would be easier to fish from the shore. There was a lovely, wooded spit of land that reached out into the lake. It rose a few feet above the water and provided a fine spot for casting. This corner of the lake was noted for its feisty, small-mouth bass.

On the short drive out, Andy asked Thor about Sheriff Mandsager's half-assed peace offering. Andy hadn't talked with Thor in over a week.

"To tell you the God's honest truth, Andy," the old curmudgeon said, "I was kind of enjoying the whole deal. I haven't walked a picket line in so many years that I

can't remember when. I haven't felt this alive and en-
thused in ages. People would drive by and shout, 'Hey,
you commie pinko fascist, go back to where you came
from.'"

"That would be New Bergen," Andy observed, as he
steered the Silverado onto the dirt road that led into Rose
Lake.

"True," Thor agreed. "But they were probably thinking more like Norway. Anyhoo, it felt pretty good to get
insulted by those pinheaded rednecks. And then there
were the folks who stopped by and asked why I was
picketing and what I thought was going on. And we
would have a good conversation about government surveillance and the right to privacy and so on. There are a
lot of decent, right-thinking folks in Hobartville, Andy."

"And you didn't want the party to end." Andy wondered where this story was going.

"Basically. I wanted to push Mandsager hard as I
could. See what happened. Old geezers don't often get
opportunities to raise some honest hell."

"So you're keeping me in suspenders here, Thor.
What happened?"

"I called up to Mandsager's office and said I'd be
interested in hearing what he had to say. The fact is,
Sonny really wanted me to knock it off. She was worried
I'd get roughed up or some ridiculous thing. Anyway, the
next morning I get a call from Cass Conlin, asking if she
can come and talk."

"She told you what that surveillance was all about?"

Thor nodded.

"So spill it."

"You know that one of my personal projects is making a new English translation of *Skjorfjeld's Retreat from Vinland.*"

Andy did indeed know about it. Thor never tired of telling him about the old Viking saga. But Andy was too polite to say that the subject bored him utterly to death.

"Yup, Thor," Andy said. "I've heard tell."

"Well, Andy, I managed to secure some of the key missing vellums, made by medieval Norwegian monks. Copies of the original missing manuscript that Ole Skjorfjeld himself commissioned in the 1050s. Copies that fill in blanks. On loan from a private party who shares my passion for Skjorfjeld. A Norwegian hedge fund manager. I have to return them by the end of the month. They're insured up the wazoo, I can tell you. I even had to buy that fireproof safe to keep them in."

"And these things are kosher, so to speak?" asked Andy. "Relics that are legal for private parties to own?"

"Absolutely. My friend has the paperwork from the Norwegian authorities."

"And why does this guy entrust such valuable material to an old fart from rural Beaver Tail County?"

Thor looked a little hurt, then puffed himself up. "You'd have no way of knowing, Andy, because clearly the subject matter bores you."

Uh-oh, thought Andy. Busted.

"But I'm actually considered something of a legit

Skjorfjeld scholar. I go down to the university every fall to give a talk for the Scandinavian Studies program. And I'll tell you, there's just no substitute for having the original documents in hand. Photocopies, computer scans just don't cut it."

"Okay, Thor, I tip my hat to you. But what does this have to do with the feds busting your chops?"

"Other Skjorfjeld vellums were stolen from a university archive in Oslo five or six months ago. The authorities over there managed to keep it on the quiet. So when I started posting my new translations and essays on my Skjorfjeld blog, three, four months ago, the Norwegian national cops caught wind of it. Because the stolen material was similar to what I received from my private collector friend, the officials over there couldn't be sure whether or not I had the hot vellums taken from the archive.

"I'm guessing they had no other leads at the time, so they got on the horn with the feds here. Check out this Thor Hofdahl character. They had no idea that someone had legally shipped authentic Skjorfjeld vellums across the Atlantic."

Andy scratched his head. This was getting confusing. "So the Norwegian cops thought you were the thief? And they brought in the FBI?"

Thor nodded. "That fellow Cass was out in the woods with? Remember him?"

Andy could hardly forget the guy. Tall, athletic, rock-hard, ruggedly handsome. He also remembered that certain glow on Cass's cheeks when she emerged from the woods with him.

"Cass wouldn't say," Thor continued. "But my guess is, he's Norwegian national police. The upshot of the whole deal is that they caught the actual guy who did it, who had the stolen goods. He was trying to sell them to some high-end collector in Las Vegas."

"And thus the panel truck and comb-over guy and big Lars—or whatever his name is—all disappear," Andy said.

"Yup. And a back-door apology comes from Mand-sager, via Cass Conlin. No regrets from the feds, of course."

"You ought to tell Carter LaPorte. Be a heckuva story."

"Naw," said Thor. "I promised Cass to not spill the beans. I have my answers. That's good enough. I'm not supposed to tell anyone. I shouldn't be telling you. Anyway, in the end, whatever makes Sonny happy…"

Andy grinned. "…makes Thor happy."

"Exactly. Mama ain't happy, ain't nobody happy."

"Well, I'm glad you can put the whole sorry affair to rest."

Moments later, they arrived at the fishing spot at Rose Lake. They extracted themselves from the Silverado and Andy gave Harald the okay to go exploring. The ginger-colored hound hopped down onto the ground, and loped into the undergrowth.

Five minutes later, Andy and Thor were casting into

about eight feet of opaque, green water. Andy was bouncing a jig around, and Thor was casting a squiggly, neon-green plastic worm. Their respective angling methods had worked a treat here before. They were both enthroned in folding lawn chairs, atop a muddy, four-foot embankment.

A few minutes after Andy's first strike—probably a small-mouth bass, which promptly spit out the hook—Thor cleared his throat rather dramatically.

Reeling his line in, not looking at his friend off to the left, Andy said, "Yeah, Thor, what is it?"

"Ummm, as far as you know, Andy," Thor began, "has Harald been imbibing any holy water?"

As he pulled his red-and-white jig out of the drink, Andy chuckled. He figured Thor had some really silly punch line for him. "Well, Thor, this priest, this rabbi, and this Lutheran pastor walk into a dog house and—"

"Ummm, Andy, look over there." Thor pointed left with his index finger.

Andy leaned over and peered around his friend.

Out on the water, about twenty-five feet beyond the end of the point, he saw a dripping-wet Harald.

Standing.

His tail wagging vigorously.

Knee-deep in what ought to have been about ten feet of water.

Shuffling delicately a step or two this way and that.

Possibly a miracle.

But more likely, something else.

"What do you suppose Harald's standing on?" asked Thor, after the two men had reeled in their lines.

"Only one way to find out," Andy replied. He took off his shirt, then his shoes and socks. He emptied his pockets of change, keys, and wallet. He unclipped the phone from his belt. He gave it all to his friend for safekeeping.

"You know, Andy," Thor said, "I bet Mandsager has a diver for this kind of job. You oughtn't to risk your neck."

"It isn't that deep, Thor. I'll just suck in some air, duck down, and see what's what."

Andy lowered himself down the muddy embankment, as close as he could get to his "miracle" dog. Harald, seeing his master ease himself into the murky, green water, started woofing lustily, as if to say: *Come on in, Boss, the water's great.*

Andy, appropriately dogpaddling, drew near to Harald, whose tail was attempting to do the rumba. He swam toward Harald from the side, and grabbed the canine's left front leg. Harald attempted to lick his face, but Andy muttered, "Not now, Harald."

Andy slid his hand down the dog's leg, and felt the sheet metal of some kind of truck or car roof. He couldn't say which. "It's a vehicle, Thor," he bellowed back toward the shore.

Harald thought that Andy was playing with him, and tried again to slobber a lick across his master's face. But Andy treaded water backward to get away from the overly friendly mutt. He gulped in a big breath of air and dived down.

The lake water was murky. Nonetheless, Andy could see ahead for a few feet. And what he saw was a dark-colored, old Dodge pickup truck. Circa 1990s. He was pretty sure he had seen it before. The night of the Karma Kubbyhole fire. The arsonist's get-away vehicle.

He popped back up for another lungful of air, and heard Thor shout, "Whadaya see, Andy? What is it?"

Andy was far too engrossed in his task to holler back an answer. He swam around to the other side of where Harald was standing, and dove again.

This was the part that scared Andy. Not any fear of accidental drowning or other submarine mishap. He'd been on the swim team in high school, and could putter around underwater for minutes at a time. No, Andy was feeling leery of what he might find.

He grabbed the side mirror on the driver's side of the submerged Dodge and pulled himself farther underwater for a good look inside the cab. The window had been rolled down. He saw something in there that seemed anomalous. Kind of splotches of Day-Glo orange and black. He blinked through the murk, trying to make sense of it. Then all of a sudden, he did.

There was someone in the driver's seat, slumped over towards the passenger's side. Andy couldn't make out a face or even a head.

But the Day-Glo orange thing with black splotches clarified itself.

It was a Buzz Saw Ballerina T-shirt. A souvenir from that late '80s, all-girl punk band.

The last time he'd seen one was on the afternoon of the Syttende Mai celebration—on Zeke Haugen, just before he attacked Charlie Adams.

Chapter Twenty-Eight

The expression on Sheriff Mandsager's face seemed clear enough to Andy, there on the banks of Rose Lake: *Why are you and your damned dog tormenting me?*

Andy almost felt sorry for the bull-doggish lawman. Here he was, cruising to an easy re-election, and this bloody mutt and his bloody owner kept uncovering one piece of mayhem after another. Madge Juntenen was positively crucifying Mandsager in the *Chronicle*. *Why no arrests? Why does the wave of murders continue? Why is a big old mutt outperforming the functionaries of the law?*

As soon as Mandsager emerged from his Ford black-and-white, he spotted Andy and signaled for him to come over.

Believing the best defense was a good offense, Andy started to say that if he, Andy Skyberg, had had anything to do with this, or the other incidents, why would he lead the law right to the crime scene? Wouldn't he want it to stay a secret? The sheriff grumbled something unintelligible and told Andy to give a statement to Cass Conlin, who had been the first to arrive on the scene. He did just that, in another frosty encounter with his former girlfriend.

Andy, Thor, and Harald stuck around to watch the sheriff's diver hook up the submerged Dodge to the recovery truck's winch. Slowly, the old black pickup emerged from the murk of Rose Lake. Once it was up on dry land, Mandsager and Doc Hilgenberg approached it and peered into the driver's side window. The sheriff sighed deeply and signaled for his photographer to come over and get some shots.

Cass approached Andy and Thor. "Okay, you two have to go."

She squatted down and patted King Harald on the head. "Hey, big guy, why don't you leave the crime fighting to the professionals, huh?"

He licked her cheek as his tail thumped on the turf.

Cass stood and regarded Andy, then Thor. "Now scram."

* * *

Three mornings after his ill-fated fishing expedition with Thor, Andy stumbled out of his front door, blinking and yawning, and picked up his copy of the *Beaver Tail County Chronicle*. He woke up rather quickly when he saw the top headline on the front page: *Drowning Victim Identified as Suspect in Murder*.

Standing there in his blue bathrobe, Andy scanned the first few paragraphs of Carter LaPorte's story.

So it *had* been Zeke Haugen, slumped over in the driver's seat in his Buzz Saw Ballerina T-shirt. Sheriff

Mandsager was quoted as saying that young Mr. Haugen had apparently been severely intoxicated with alcohol when he drove the Dodge pickup into Rose Lake. Forensic examinations of the truck, its contents, and the crime scene were ongoing.

Noting that Mr. Haugen was a person of interest in the investigation into the Charlene Adams murder, Carter LaPorte asked the sheriff for a comment. The sheriff declined to answer. Might Mr. Haugen have been involved in the arson at the Karma Kubbyhole store in New Bergen? Again, the sheriff said he had nothing further to say at this time.

After Andy let Harald out into the backyard, he sat down to a cup of coffee and a toasted English muffin.

The facts seemed pretty clear: Zeke Haugen had been behind the big crime spree, after all.

Nasty little piece of work that he was, Zeke must have taken his grandma's campaign against Trudi Bock too much to heart. Assassinated Adonis the iguana. Attacked and later murdered Charlie Adams. Set the Karma Kubbyhole on fire. Probably didn't know that Gus Johnson was snoozing in the basement.

Maybe knowing he'd killed an innocent man tipped the kid over the edge into powerful remorse and guilt. He tried to shut off the pain with too much booze, like so many before him. Maybe he even intended to drive the Dodge into Rose Lake. A suicide.

Whatever happened with her delinquent grandson, Andy thought, Mrs. Runestrand didn't deserve the shit storm that just descended on the Runestrand clan.

Andy didn't much care for the old gal, but he had to respect her. She had her principles and firmly stood her ground. And he owed her big time, for saving his scrawny neck when he was only a rug rat.

On the third page of the paper, Andy spotted a story on the defamation lawsuits that Beaver Tail County farmer Jerry Dittbrenner had brought against the humane society and one of its board members, Trudi Bock, owner of the recently burned Karma Kubbyhole store in New Bergen.

Ms. Bock's attorney, Carmine Bongiovanni, had attempted to get the suits dismissed, but the judge allowed the actions to go forward.

The hog farmer's attorney was quoted as saying, "Of course, we're all very saddened that Ms. Bock lost her shop in that terrible arson fire. And we regret the loss of life in that incident. But it has no bearing on the merits of our case against her. She libeled and defamed my client's hog operation, and my client personally, and she must pay the price."

* * *

That afternoon, between his lunch and dinner shifts, Andy drove out to the Haugen place with the wild-rice-and-sausage hot dish he'd whipped up right after breakfast. He'd never thought of it before, but a hot dish really was a better thing to leave with the bereaved than some crummy condolence card or flowers that were tossed in a day or two.

The driveway was full of vehicles, and visitors were filing in and out of the house. Steeling himself for the encounter—but knowing it was the right thing to do— Andy climbed out of his Silverado with the hot dish in a paper bag.

People were milling around the living room. Andy recognized a few of them. The mayor of New Bergen. One of the vice presidents of the Lovely Lena Macaroni Corporation. Several of Mrs. Runestrand's troop of stalwart picketers. Assistant principal Dick Schaeffer.

A particularly tight knot of mourners was clustered around someone Andy couldn't quite see. Someone short. That had to be Mrs. Runestrand. Andy stood in the queue, holding his hot dish before him, like an offering of frankincense and myrrh.

While he was waiting for access to her, Andy couldn't help but eavesdrop on Schaeffer, who was fulminating to the husband of one of Mrs. Runestrand's acolytes. It was hard *not* to hear the guy. He had a voice like a drill sergeant, try as he might to keep the volume down.

"…and with any luck that blasted woman'll just pack up her bags and get out of town. And take her devil-worshipping ways with her. That fire's the best thing that's happened to New Bergen in years."

The old boy Schaeffer was talking with looked taken aback. "But a man died in there, Dick."

"It's too bad about the guy in the basement. But he was just some kind of bum. A worthless scrounger. Probably a pagan himself. No big loss. Just wish I could've been there to see that place burn down."

Andy cringed when he saw the cruel grin spread across Schaeffer's face.

"For the way Trudi Bock messed up my little girl, *corrupted her*, I swear, if nobody else had done it, I would've torched that store myself. Jeannie and I have a big job ahead of us, getting that kid straightened out."

Just then, the line moved and Andy suddenly found himself face to face with Mrs. Runestrand.

There was no grief in her features when she recognized Andy. For someone who had just lost a grandson in rather horrific circumstances, she looked remarkably self-possessed. She would have made a terrific poker player, if only gambling hadn't been a sin. A woman standing next to the old lady gently removed the hot dish from Andy's hands and took it away. Andy believed it was one of Mrs. Runestrand's daughters.

"I just wanted to come and say how sorry I was to hear about Zeke," Andy mumbled.

Mrs. Runestrand regarded him evenly. "You and I, Anders Skyberg," she said, "are somehow joined together when it comes to matters of mortality and water, are we not?"

Andy hadn't thought of it that way, but nodded in agreement.

"I regret that you had to be the one to find Ezekiel. It cannot have been pleasant. But I want you to know that, sinner though he was, my grandson was not a murderer.

He was not a suicide. I know…" She sighed and shook her head, among the rare signs of emotion that Andy had ever seen on her. "I *knew* my Ezekiel well, and though he was violent, and though he was venal, and though he was troubled, he did not have it in him to kill a lizard, let alone a human being."

If it had been any other old lady, Andy would have hugged her and planted a peck on her fuzzy old cheek. But this was Mrs. Runestrand, and you just didn't do that to her. So instead he reached out and lightly touched her on the shoulder.

Back in the truck, Andy started thinking about what she had said: that Zeke wouldn't have killed anyone.

In a way, Andy hoped the old lady was totally wrong on that point. Because if Zeke was innocent of the murders of Charlie, Gus, and Adonis, it meant that the killer was still on the loose.

Chapter Twenty-Nine

Andy decided the moment was right to balance the books on his relationship with Trudi. He wanted, in the parlance of the classic kiss-off, to "just be good friends." He wanted assurance that she was okay. And he had a teeny ulterior motive for visiting her. He wanted to know if she intended to put her prime downtown lot on the market. He and Kirsten were itching for a heads-up.

It was Saturday. Andy had the morning off and took a chance that Trudi might be home. And it so happened she was. They sat at the center island in her gorgeous kitchen, near the spot where poor Adonis had met his fate. She poured some iced tea and found a couple of asiago scones in her fridge.

"You look awfully good, Trud," Andy observed, as his old lover bustled around.

"Now, if you'd said that a month ago," Trudi replied, "I might have felt there was a little bit of hope for us."

Andy thought the best thing to do was keep his trap shut, as Trudi dropped ice cubes in the two crystal tumblers.

"When I came to New Bergen last year, it hadn't

occurred to me that you might be here, too." She climbed up on one of the tall chairs and slid a tumbler of tea in Andy's direction. "But the minute I saw you that first time I walked into Ansel's, my heart skipped a beat."

Uh-oh, this might get emotional, Andy thought. Not good.

"You're a fine looking man, Anders Skyberg. You've hardly changed a bit. And the memories I have of our time back at the university are some of the sweetest that I possess. I don't know how you got away."

Andy recalled that ultimately it had something to do with his reluctance to participate in a weekend of bowel cleansing. The final straw.

"But you did. And when I got another chance to rekindle our relationship... Well, I just had to try. But here we are, a year later. And..."

Some wise fictional character once said that, when confronted with a great emotional difficulty, the best thing to do is to do the thing you *least* want to do. Andy realized that he was facing exactly that kind of moment. He had to do the gnarliest thing possible for a guy like himself: be truthful to a woman about the way he felt. Mostly, he'd had the good fortune to avoid such situations all his life.

"Trud," Andy interrupted.

"Yes, Anders." She looked pleased to have loosened his tongue.

"You're a gorgeous, sexy woman. Always have been, always will be. Smart, funny, kind."

Trudi glowed a little.

"And we had some good times back in college. In and out of the sack."

She nodded.

"Trud," Andy continued, "you're what I think of as a kind of *avant garde* personality."

"That is one of the nicest things anyone has ever said to me, Anders." Trudi beamed.

"But I'm not an *avant garde* kind of guy, Trud," Andy said, as if it hurt him to admit it. "There's the New Age stuff. All the therapies and herbal remedies and séances and chakras and astrology and all that Eleanorian business with visits from two dead women. I just don't believe in any of those things. I couldn't be with anyone for long who took it so seriously. But for you, it's your identity and profession. It's *you*. And I could never ask you to give up something so vital."

She surprised him by giving him a bittersweet grin. "Andy, I've known all that for twenty years. I'd have to have been a total dunce not to notice how ill-at-ease you were with some of my friends and their views. There were times when you looked about as comfortable as a cat at a dog convention. But after I found you again, I was just hoping that maybe you'd changed and expanded and become more open to the universe. I know now that's not to be. Not that you aren't a good and kind person."

Blissful relief flooded Andy's unexpanded brain. He felt as if a huge weight had been lifted right off his shoulders.

"But you know something, Anders?"

Andy shook his head.

"I will always be your true friend. And if you ever need me, for anything, just call."

"And right back at you, Trud," said Andy, reaching over and briefly squeezing her hand.

They sipped their tea silently for a moment, before Andy spoke up again.

"What are you going to do about Lauren Kastner? I mean, the girl must've been spying on you for Jerry Dittbrenner."

Trudi gave him a little Cheshire-cat grin. "Don't you worry about Lauren and that man. I have everything under control."

Andy wondered what that comment meant, but he decided to drop the subject.

There was another moment or two of silence, until Andy felt the urge to fill it in.

"I hear you're spending time with Carter."

Trudi nodded. "We're interested in some of the same things, Carter and I. Like classical music and architecture. We went down to the Cities for a tour of Cass Gilbert buildings. Just fascinating. And we're planning a little jaunt over to Wisconsin to visit Frank Lloyd Wright sites. I'm taking it slow, though, after all I've been through. But right now I have to say I enjoy his company."

Andy was genuinely happy for his friend. But he still had to find out about her plans for the torched downtown property.

"Do you think you'll rebuild the Karma Kubbyhole, Trud? Everyone is dying to know."

"I haven't decided yet, Anders. The place was so special. And Charlie and Gus were such a big part of what made it that way. Could I really catch lightning in a bottle twice?"

"It's going to be hard not to associate a lot of bad stuff with the Kubbyhole." Andy tried to sound neutral, though he knew perfectly well what he wanted to happen. "Maybe you'd be better off starting up somewhere new. I betcha you wouldn't have any trouble finding a buyer for the lot."

"That's for sure," Trudi said, rolling her eyes. "The day after the fire, Brenda Erickson called me, saying she and her husband would take the place off my hands, as a favor to me. Do you believe that?"

Andy made a mental note to tell Kirsten about Brenda's preemptive bid.

They talked a little bit more. About Zeke Haugen and the hammer found in the sunken pickup truck. Both Zeke's fingerprints and tiny hairs from Charlie Adams's head were found on it. And one of Zeke's friends had confessed to being part of the rubber iguana prank with Zeke. He had provided the bottle of catsup.

Trudi might well have displayed a bit of schadenfreude at the fate of Mrs. Runestrand's grandson. She'd earned it. But Andy was impressed to learn that she had paid the old lady a visit of condolence.

"It takes a big person to forgive and forget like that, Trud. Especially after the way Mrs. R treated you."

"Oh, Adeline isn't so bad," Trudi said.

Andy nearly did a double take. How many times had he ever heard anyone call Mrs. Runestrand by her first name? Not too darned often. And to think it was Trudi doing it.

"Once you peel back that armor of hers, she's pretty friendly. I told her that Zeke's light burned too brightly for this world. He's moved on now to a better place."

"She actually bought that?" Andy asked incredulously.

"Well, I believe it myself. I wasn't trying to pull one over on her. And she certainly found some comfort in my words. Keep in mind, Anders, that she's worrying herself sick that Zeke not only murdered someone, but may have killed himself. Double sins of the worst sort."

"A one-way ticket to the torments of hell," Andy said.

"Exactly. But Adeline is strong. I told her that she'd be a lot happier if she didn't keep trying to pound all the round pegs of the world into those little square holes of hers. I doubt if she'll take it to heart, though."

As he was heading out the door, Andy turned and regarded Trudi.

"That night you slept in my bed. I was pretty snockered. I was wondering. Did we really…?"

A coy look came across Trudi's face.

"Now, Anders Skyberg. Nice girls don't kiss and tell."

* * *

Later that day, Andy was in the middle of an encounter with a wine saleswoman who was pushing a new line of Napa Valley varietals, when he saw Thor Hofdahl tramp into Ansel's. The old fart glared at him meaningfully and jabbed an index finger downward: *Get over here pronto so I can talk to you.*

Glaring back, Andy tapped the crystal on his Timex: *You're going to have to wait, old man.*

Thor nodded and allowed J. J. to take him to a seat by the window.

Andy continued to sip the saleswoman's wares at the wine bar and made notes. One of his jobs was to scout wines and report back to Kirsten. He was impressed by the Zinfandel. Ansel's reds could use some beefing up and he thought it would make a great addition to the cellar.

Twenty minutes later he plopped down opposite Thor, who was doing some sipping of his own—on a tall, Biberschwanz Dunkles.

Thor put his elbows on the table and leaned over toward Andy, signaling some kind of whispered confidence. "I have news for you, hot off the presses."

Andy leaned right back at him. "Yeah?"

"You know how Trudi butted heads with Dick Schaeffer over his daughter getting into witchery?"

Andy nodded. "You know, it's called Wicca."

"Of course," whispered Thor. "Wicca. The girl… What's her name?"

"Amber."

"I was out at Hogan's Farm Store getting some stuff that Sonny needed. I was in line and overheard the woman in front of me yakking with the checkout girl. And you won't believe what I heard."

Andy wanted to laugh, but choked it down. Sometimes Thor was a worse gossip than any of the busybodies Andy knew.

"It seems that Amber up and ran off with her boyfriend."

"No kidding?" exclaimed Andy.

"The girl at the cash register said Amber had e-mailed her friends a copy of the note she left her parents, stating that she was going to start a new life at some undisclosed location with the man of her dreams. And she had no intention of ever setting foot in a Methodist church again."

"And any word yet on how that worked out?" Andy asked, full of admiration for the girl's gumption.

"Got as far as the Cities. She left a couple of clues and they were able to pick her up, along with the boy. But I guess Schaeffer went ballistic."

"That guy's got a master's degree in ballistic."

"Anyway," Thor said ominously, "if I were Trudi, I'd watch my back."

Chapter Thirty

Andy was very much afraid that his big landscape of Lake Bonga looked way too much like a Klimt. Not that there was anything wrong with that. In fact, Andy was a fan of the great artist's work. It's just that he wanted those teeming birches to scream *Andy Skyberg*. Not the name of some dead Viennese master. Andy didn't know if he needed to make the monochromatic trees more sinuous, or perhaps change the color palette altogether. But the general composition looked good.

He stood in front of the canvas, in the knee-length mechanic's coat he'd ordered from England. Arms crossed, a filbert rake brush poised in his hand. "I may have to start all over again, Harald," he sighed.

Harald, sprawled on the rug in front of the studio sofa, didn't seem to be listening. His tail flopped from one side to another, then again.

Andy's artistic reverie was broken when the cell phone on his hip ding-donged at him. He lifted the paint-splotched coat and grabbed the gizmo.

"Hullo, Andy Skyberg here," he said.

"Andy," said an old-lady voice, "it's Cappy Briggs up

236

in Herkimer.'"

"Well, hi there, Cappy. How you doin? What's up?"

"I have some good news for you. I managed to track down where Mrs. Nielsen is living."

"I'd almost forgotten about those darned ebelskivers," Andy laughed. "So where will I find her?"

"Before I tell you, Andy, you have to promise me something."

"If I can, sure. What?"

"You have to come up one of these soonest weekends. I'll have homemade venison bratwurst for the grill. My own hand-ground mustard, dark rye bread, potato salad, cole slaw, strawberry shortcake, and, best of all, a case of Biberschwanz Pilsner, chilled to perfection."

"Can I bring a friend or two?"

"Abso-tively, posi-lutely! The more, the merrier."

"Well, then, Cappy, we got a deal. Now where will I find Mrs. Nielsen?"

"She's in an assisted care place down in the Cities. Lutheran outfit, of course. St. Gustav's Residence. Right off one of those pretty lakes they have down there, in the middle of town. I talked to her on the phone. Other than being a little deaf—I almost had to shout—she seemed to still have most of her marbles. She rarely leaves the place. She said she'd find the recipe for you. Just don't drop in at lunch or dinner. She said that's what they live for there, strapping on the old feedbag. A regular stampede.

"Now Andy, what's a good date for you to come up

here for brats and beer?"

* * *

As an MBA and steely-eyed entrepreneur, Kirsten Skyberg wasn't about to let Andy squander a whole day in the Cities solely on a visit with a pastor's ancient widow. She had him stop in to check out a new vendor of back-office and operations systems for restaurants. He listened to the sales pitch and then visited a couple of eateries that used the software and hardware. It was after one when he arrived at St. Gustav's Residence. A receptionist at the information desk directed him up to the fourth floor.

He rapped on the doorframe of room 417—the door being open—and a cheerful, fluttery old voice bade him to come in. He heard the squeak of a wheel as he eased inside what superficially resembled a college dorm room. But instead of there being Katy Perry and Kanye West posters on the wall, there were framed religious scenes and pictures of grandchildren who probably had children of their own by now. And instead of flat-screen computer monitors winking and blinking, there was a decrepit, nineteen-inch RCA that was, in a manner of speaking, *still* a color television—all green. A faded, antediluvian episode of *My Three Sons* was flickering on the screen, with the sound turned up very loud. William Demarest was imparting some piece of wisdom to one of the boys.

The squeaky wheel belonged to a wheelchair that contained a wispy old lady in a floral dress. She blinked expectantly up at Andy through gold-rimmed tri-focals.

Her face wore something like ninety years' worth of wrinkles. But her eyes twinkled and her smile was genuine. She aimed her remote control at the TV and dialed down the sound.

"Mrs. Nielsen?" Andy said.

"What did you say?" asked the old lady.

Andy recalled that Cappy had warned him that she was hard of hearing. "Mrs. Nielsen?" he asked, rather more loudly.

"You've come to the right place," she answered brightly. "And you must be young Mr. Skyberg."

No one had called Andy "young" in a long time. "None other," he answered at full volume. "And please call me Andy."

"Now, Andy, I understand from Cappy Briggs that you've been searching high and low for my old ebelskiver recipe."

"That's right, ma'am."

"Well, after she called, I asked some of the folks here to help me go through my boxes that I'm allowed to keep in storage. Even though I don't need them, I hung onto my favorite cookbooks and recipe boxes. As you stagger on toward ninety and a hundred, they take so much of your stuff away from you. But I had to keep some things. I've been in here for eleven years, you know, and…"

Andy had spent enough time with old dears to know that there was no rushing them. By and by, Mrs. Nielsen would come to a full stop. It proved to be about half an hour later.

"Now I think Cappy told you that my sister Kirsten runs a restaurant in New Bergen called Ansel's," Andy said. "And in early August, we're having the annual Elbow Lake Days. As a special treat for the occasion, Kirsten wants to make people your famous ebelskivers."

"You know, Andy, a friend of mine in Hobartville sends me packets of clippings from the *Beaver Tail County Chronicle*."

Here we go again, thought Andy.

"I've been reading about the murders up there. What in the world do you think is going on? You know, when Pastor Nielsen and I lived in Beaver Tail County, there'd be the occasional crime or scandal. But murder? Hardly ever. And not targeting one poor, unfortunate woman. Miss Bock, I believe her name is. And from what I read, your pooch has been right in the thick of it."

As the ebelskiver recipe receded further from his grasp, Andy recounted King Harald's recent checkered career, while Mrs. Nielsen listened raptly.

"The only thing I can recall from my earlier life that even approached the seriousness of what you're describing," she said, "was when I was a part-time cook at St. Magnus Prep. Pastors never made much money back then. We could barely get by on my husband's income, what with five youngsters to feed. So during the school year I'd earn a few extra dollars in the kitchen at the prep school. Four hours a day, six days a week. It really helped." She paused and pursed her desiccated lips. "I'm veering off-track, aren't I?"

Andy politely said, "No, no, your story is very interesting."

"As I was saying, Andy, only one event I can think of from back then could be compared to what's happening in Beaver Tail County now. It was, in a way, a *kind* of murder. But in slow-motion, don't you know."

"I don't understand what you mean," Andy said, "by 'a kind of murder.'"

Mrs. Nielsen rolled closer to the overstuffed wingchair that Andy was sitting in. She leaned toward him as if she wanted to be sure that no one would eavesdrop on the conversation. Which was a flawed notion on her part, given how loudly Andy had to speak.

"Nowadays the headlines are full of news about the misuse of children by men—and by a few women—who claim to be Christians. You know what I'm talking about."

Andy nodded. The old lady couldn't quite bring herself to say the phrase *sexual abuse*.

"We had just such a thing happen at St. Magnus Prep when I was there. It's a good half century ago now, so I can speak about it. But at the time, nothing got out. It wasn't a topic that any newspaper would touch, even if someone had told them everything. You didn't talk in public about—" She paused for the right words. "—*that* subject. You never impugned the reputation of a pastor or priest. They were above reproach, immune. Which is why the bad ones could do so much to the children."

"So what happened at St. Magnus?" Andy asked.

"Why did you call it a 'kind of murder'?"

"This pastor, who led the choir and taught Christian studies, tutored a number of the boys in his apartment. Oh, he was proper at first. Then, gradually..."

Andy nodded. He got the picture.

"Most of the boys kept it quiet," she continued. "Imagine how embarrassing it would have been for them, poor dears. But one of them, having had a worrying change of personality, told his father everything. And his father was chairman of the St. Magnus College Board. The pastor's punishment was not trial and imprisonment, as he deserved, but instant banishment from the prep school."

Andy knew not to get frustrated with the old lady. "But what about the murder?" he gently asked.

"Effectively a murder, really. A suicide actually. One of the boys killed himself a year or two later. They found him hanging in the chapel. Terrible, terrible thing. The other boys had managed to, as they say, tough it out. For whatever reasons, this youngster wasn't strong enough. He couldn't stand to go on."

"What was the name of the pastor?"

Mrs. Nielsen sighed. "It was so very long ago. But give me a moment."

Andy could almost see the wheels turning in the old lady's head. She really was trying hard to haul up that memory from half a century ago. After a moment, she fixed Andy squarely in the eye, and nodded.

"It's Tremmel," she said grimly. "Reverend

Tremmel."

She paused and pursed her lips, looking as if she was laboring for another word, but couldn't find it.

"I'm sorry, I can't remember his first name. They just moved him up to North Dakota, practically in the middle of the night. We heard he was working as a chaplain in a nursing home. Of course, they wanted to get him away from the children as quickly as possible. He died a few years after the incidents at St. Magnus. He was drunk, they say, and he drove off the road into a big tree.

"Now the name of the boy. The name of the boy." She rubbed her chin and briefly ruminated. "I cannot for the life of me remember his name."

Andy reached over and patted her knee. "Don't worry about it, Mrs. Nielsen. It's not really important. I'm impressed that you recalled who that minister was. I mean, I can barely remember names of people I met last week."

Andy and Mrs. Nielsen yakked for another twenty minutes about the weather and fishing and how the tourist business was going in New Bergen. Then Andy stood and said good-bye. He was almost ten feet down the hallway when he heard the squeak of the wheelchair and an urgent call.

"Andy! Mr. Skyberg!"

He pivoted around and Mrs. Nielsen rolled out through her door, almost running into the coffee trolley that a teenaged aide was pushing along.

"What is it, Mrs. Nielsen?"

"We got to chitchatting so much," the old lady said

breathlessly, "that I forgot to give you this." She reached into her cardigan pocket and extracted a folded piece of pink paper.

Andy hooted. "The ebelskiver recipe?"

"Indeed it is. Complete with the secret ingredient."

With a hearty thanks, Andy took it from her, then bent over and kissed her fuzzy, old cheek.

"Wait till I tell the girls that I got bussed by a handsome young man," Mrs. Nielsen laughed. "They'll all be jealous."

Andy made it about twenty-five feet this time.

"Andy! Andy!"

He sighed and turned around, trotting back to his new friend. The old ladies, they sure did like to prolong a visit.

"I remembered," she said, with a proud smile. "The boy's name. It was Lyle. Lyle LaPorte."

Chapter Thirty-One

In his chauffeuring days, Andy had driven the upscale residential streets around St. Gustav's many a time. He could practically navigate them blindfolded. That was a good thing, because as he drove out of the senior residence's parking lot, he barely realized where he was going.

Mrs. Nielsen had thrown him a curve.

He kept turning it over and over in his head.

Half a century ago, a boy named Lyle LaPorte had tied a rope around his neck and died.

Fast forward to present-day Beaver Tail County, where a man named Carter LaPorte had moved into the area and gone to work at the local newspaper. Coincidence? It could be. Andy figured there must be thousands of LaPortes in the world.

Why shouldn't one of them turn up in Hobartville?

Right?

Right?

Suddenly, Andy realized that he was tooling north on the Interstate, right through suburban frontage-road land. How the hell had he gotten here?

Punching in the cruise control for 70 miles per hour, Andy tried to remember what Carter had told him about his past. Grew up in the Cities. Parents dead. Lengthy stint in the military. Brief marriage. A second career as a newspaper man. Another brief marriage. But nothing about any previous connection to Beaver Tail County. Or about a relative named Lyle who might have killed himself.

Andy drove a bit farther, and pulled over into a sprawling truck stop. He detached the phone from his hip and searched the directory for Trudi's cell number.

What would he say when she answered?

He ruminated a moment, then came up with a pretext for calling.

Trud, I was gonna ask if you needed someone to keep an eye on your place while you're on your trip with Carter—if you should end up going.

He selected Trudi's number and punched the button.

For all her ditziness, Trudi did have an uncanny ability to read people. She claimed she could see their auras—how they were feeling and what they were like. She had been spending a lot of time with Carter lately. But she wouldn't go off alone on a trip with a guy who might have an iffy aura, would she?

Trudi's phone rang four times and the voicemail picked up.

"You have reached Trudi Bock, proprietor of the Karma Kubbyhole," her disembodied voice cheerfully chirped. "I can't take your call right now, so please leave your message at the sound of the temple bells. I'll get back to you as soon as I can. May the spirits keep you well."

As promised, there came a bong-bing, and Andy made his offer to watch Trudi's place. He asked her to give him a call.

The rest of the way home, Andy mulled over the history that Mrs. Nielsen had revealed. The relief of finally tracking down that damned ebelskiver recipe had been supplanted with a tickle of queasy foreboding in the pit of his stomach.

* * *

The first person Andy saw when he walked into Ansel's was his sister. She peered at him with raised eyebrows: *Mission accomplished?*

Andy nodded and pulled out the folded sheet of pink paper. He walked over and handed it to Kirsten.

Without saying a word, she unfolded it and read. Slowly, a smile came over her face. "So that's what she did. Makes perfect sense." She beamed at her brother. "Good job, little bro."

In the wake of Mrs. Nielsen's disclosure, Andy hadn't even bothered to look at the recipe. He was about to ask Kirsten to hand it back, so he could read it, when he noticed someone sitting at the wine bar, noshing on a cracker-crust pizza with a glass of white wine, reading a paperback novel of some sort. It was Trudi's mom, Toots Strassberger, attired in a gaudy sort of sack dress. He hoped earnestly that she could put his fears to rest.

"Oh, hello, Anders," Toots said cheerfully, as he sat on the stool next to her.

"Hi Toots, how you doing?" Andy replied. "I didn't know you were still in town."

"Trudi had me come back to watch the farm while she and Carter do their Frank Lloyd Wright tour," Toots said.

"They've left already?" Andy squeaked.

"Uh-huh. They headed out bright and early this morning. They're driving Trudi's Prius. So much nicer than that rusty old Taurus that Carter has. It's a long drive and they wanted to get to the resort by mid-afternoon."

Not what I wanted to hear, Andy thought. What to do? He wasn't great at thinking on his feet in situations like this. And he didn't want to scare the sap out of Toots. But he knew he had to ask her a couple of questions. And boy-oh-boy, he sure hoped he got the right answers.

"Toots," Andy said, "you grew up in these parts. Can you remember anything about a student at St. Magnus Prep committing suicide years ago? Back in the Sixties?"

She looked a little puzzled by the sudden change of subject, but attempted to address it. "You know, Andy, that sort of thing has been happening forever. Kids get to that adolescent stage and some of them just can't seem to handle what the world is dishing out. I'm sure it's even worse at a prep boarding school, where the kids don't have their families with them. And youngsters that age can be really mean to each other."

Andy only had to remember Brenda Fundingsland to agree with her assessment.

"And I know for a fact that there was always a bit of hostility between the rich kids who attended the school and the scholarship students. When my brother worked there, he was always having to mediate disputes between the two groups. Why, I remember—"

"The famous Uncle Herb worked at St. Magnus?"

"Yes. He taught there. I think I mentioned him to you. He was a pastor."

"Reverend Strassberger?"

"No, no. He was my older stepbrother. My widowed mom married his widowed dad. My stepbrother was quite a bit older than me and he was a saint. I just adored him. He led the choir at the prep school, and one of his ensembles won a state choral competition."

Andy felt a shiver of apprehension tingle up his spine.

"So what was his last name, your stepbrother?"

"Tremmel. Herbie Tremmel. Such a sweet man."

Oh hell, thought Andy.

"Herbie stayed at St. Magnus for four years, I think. He enjoyed the young students quite a lot."

I bet he did, Andy thought darkly.

"But suddenly he felt a calling to minister to the elderly and infirm. We were very surprised, but it was just so much like him to suddenly pick up and go to where he was needed most. Up to North Dakota. He attended to two or three nursing homes, and died in an automobile accident while driving between them. He was only about forty.

"Trudi never knew him, of course. She was born a

few years after he passed away. But I know for a certainty that Herbie's deep faith and love for the people he served influenced her choice of careers. She's quick to give him credit for her spirituality. At least in part."

Andy rummaged around in his memory. "Didn't Trud meet Carter for the first time when he interviewed her for the *Chronicle?*"

Toots pursed her lips. "Yes, I think that's right, Anders. When she opened the store, she bought some ads in the paper, and they sent Carter down to do a story."

"Do you think she mentioned her uncle in the article?"

"It wouldn't surprise me. All these years later, everyone in the family is still proud of Herbie Tremmel. I know I repeat myself, but the man was practically a saint."

The gears whizzed and turned in Andy's head. He needed to talk to Trudi. Everything might be perfectly okay. Or she could be in some very deep doo-doo indeed.

"Listen, Toots," Andy said. "Do you know the name of the hotel that Trud and Carter are staying at? I really would like to talk with her."

"What in the world for?" asked Toots. She smiled a tiny smile. "Are we perhaps a little jealous?"

"No, Toots, it's not that," Andy said with utter honesty. Then he lied his ass off. "Trud commissioned me to do a painting of the poor old Karma Kubbyhole, and the frame I want to order for it goes for a lot more than I thought it would. I just want to get her okay for the extra cost."

Toots looked a little puzzled. "I'm sure she'd be fine with that. But can't it wait until she gets back?"

"Actually, no," Andy dissembled. "My framing shop tells me that style is almost out of stock. I have to get my order in pronto. It's perfect for the painting. I really need to get her approval right now. Do you know where she and Carter are staying?"

Toots dug around in her purse, and found the name and number of the hotel. "Trudi said this is one of the most elegant inns in the area. It's nearly impossible to get reservations, but Carter pulled a few strings, and booked them in for a couple nights. It's right in the heart of Frank Lloyd Wright country."

Andy jotted the information down, said good-bye, and trotted out to his truck.

Leaning against the driver side door, he punched the number of the hotel into his smartphone.

"River Bend Resort," answered an older woman's voice.

"Hi there," Andy said. "I wanted to get in touch with one of your guests."

"Of course. The name, please."

"Trudi Bock."

"Just a moment, please."

Andy heard a keyboard clacking, then a brief pause.

"I'm sorry, sir, we don't have anyone here under that name."

"How about Carter LaPorte?"

There was more keyboard racket, then the voice came back. "No one by that name, either, sir."

Andy thanked the woman and cut the connection.

Okay, Monsieur Poirot, Andy thought. *Now what?*

There could be a perfectly sensible reason why Trudi had gone off the grid, failing to pick up or return her calls. A sensible reason why she and Carter weren't where they were supposed to be, at the River Bend Resort.

But there seemed to be just too many coincidences. This situation smelled, and smelled badly. Andy jumped into the Silverado, and two minutes later pulled up in front of the sheriff's station. He found Ed Vandegraff inside, sucking on some of that foul java they made there.

"Andy," the beefy lawman said. "What's up?"

And Andy told him. Everything that he'd learned that day from Mrs. Nielsen and Toots Strassberger. About Herbie Tremmel and Lyle LaPorte. And about his own feverish speculations.

Ed sat there stolidly, betraying no response whatsoever. He waited for Andy to run out of steam. Then he spoke.

"Sheriff Mandsager has closed the case, Andy. Zeke Haugen was clearly behind the spate of attacks and killings related to Ms. Bock and her store. Now the ostensible connection between Mr. LaPorte and Ms. Bock's uncle is certainly unusual, but it's no proof that she's in danger. Besides, there's no evidence that anyone's missing. Those two are on a romantic getaway, I gather, and I bet they simply changed their plans.

"Andy, go home, have a couple of beers, and calm the heck down."

Chapter Thirty-Two

It was about 6 p.m. when Andy parked his truck in the driveway and trotted over to Elsie Bjorklund's place to pick up Harald. The elderly widow was happy to take care of the big mutt when Andy didn't want to leave him unsupervised. Fortunately, Elsie had a date to go to a church choir concert, and didn't offer to show Andy—for the umpteenth time—her semi-legendary, mint-condition, and nearly complete collection of *National Geographic*s that no one was allowed to touch.

Back home, Andy nearly took Ed Vandegraff's advice. Pop the tops off a couple of Biberschwanzes, build a bologna sandwich, and settle in for the ballgame.

After all, performing stealth investigations and heroic deeds weren't exactly in Andy's job description. Let Ed Vandegraff worry about Trudi Bock's situation—whatever that might mean.

And *that* was the problem. Ed *wasn't* worried. He, like Sheriff Mandsager, seemed convinced that Zeke Haugen had been behind the recent mayhem in Beaver Tail County. So he had no interest in some obscure suicide from half a century ago.

But Trudi and Carter were out there somewhere. *Not* where they were supposed to be. Maybe they *had* gone off the grid for some innocent reason. Say, they had changed their minds about staying at the River Bend Resort and were improvising.

Or maybe Carter was not at all who he seemed to be. Maybe Lyle LaPorte had been someone close to Carter. Maybe the newspaperman wanted revenge for what Trudi's uncle had done.

Carter had gained Trudi's trust and affection. She probably wouldn't have objected if he suggested a detour on their way out of town. And then, by the time they ended up somewhere remote, it would be too late for her.

Suddenly Andy remembered that, at their seafood gumbo dinner a month earlier, Carter had mentioned he was renting a lake cabin. But he didn't say which lake.

Problem was, there were about seventy lakes of any size in Beaver Tail County, and at least that many in each adjoining county.

If Andy could figure out where the cabin was, he could at least go and check it out.

His only shot, though, was talking to someone at the *Chronicle* who might happen to know where Carter's rental was.

Andy needed to lie his ass off one more time. He thought a moment, then came up with what he hoped would be a good story.

He went out into the kitchen, Harald right on his heels, and found the newspaper's phone number in that morning's edition. Punching the buttons of his phone, he got through to a woman at the switchboard, who said, "Good evening, *Beaver Tail County Chronicle*."

"Could I have the editorial department, please?"

"Certainly," the woman said, and Andy heard the phone ringing.

"Hi," said another female voice. "Editorial."

"Oh, hi," Andy said. "Is this Madge Juntenen?"

"It is. To whom am I speaking?"

"Andy Skyberg, Madge."

"Oh my gosh, Andy. I've been meaning to call you about that awful mix-up with the bogus letter, but things have been so darn hectic here that—"

"Don't you worry about it, Madge," Andy laughed. "All is forgiven."

"Well, I'm the editor of this publication, and I'm ashamed that we screwed up like that."

"Madge, don't sweat it. But you could help me with one little thing."

"You just name it."

"Carter LaPorte borrowed a couple of books from me for a piece that he's writing on Horace Frenchman, and I wanted to get them back."

"Well, Carter's on vacation, but he'll be back next week."

"Yeah, I knew that, Madge. He left me a message before he took off. Said he'd stuck the books in the screen door of some cabin that he's renting. So I didn't have to drive all the way up to Hobartville. But the darn message cut off before I could get the location. I wonder if someone there knows where the cabin is."

Madge chuckled. "Yup, I do. It's my cousin Don Cooper's fishing shack on Mud Lake. 'Cabin' does it more justice than it deserves. Don had hip replacement surgery and decided to skip the angling this summer. Not feeling up to snuff yet. I hooked him up with Carter. Anyway, you get to it by the south entrance road off County 101. Take a left. Look for the name Cooper on a driveway sign on the lake road. It's about a quarter mile from the turn."

Andy thanked the newspaper editor and quickly whipped up that bologna sandwich for himself, and a bowl of doggie chow for Harald. Ten minutes later, they were rolling north, with a couple of good hours of daylight left for discreet snooping. It was a beautiful June evening—sunny, clear, and warm. Andy, though, could feel chills deep down in his bones.

* * *

Though he didn't normally like using the cell phone while he was driving, Andy made an exception this time, dialing Cass Conlin's personal cell number. He got her voicemail and repeated everything he had learned that day—up to and including Ed Vandegraff's dismissal of his worries. He gave the location of Carter's cabin and said he was heading up there to check it out. He just wanted someone in law enforcement to know what he was up to and where he was going. Hopefully, Cass would take him seriously.

It was about a twenty-minute drive to Mud Lake and Andy had no trouble finding it. Aunt Bev and Uncle Frank had rented a cabin on the north end of the lake for several summers when Andy was a kid. He had fond memories of swimming and canoeing there, in water that was as clear as crystal and, ironically, unmuddy.

Andy pulled the Silverado into the weeds just beyond the crooked, weather-worn Cooper sign. He cranked the windows down so his dog would have plenty of air.

"Now, Harald," he said, peering into the canine's big brown eyes, "you just wait here. I'll be back in a little while. You *stay*, okay?"

The dog seemed to understand the verb "stay," and slumped down in the passenger seat. But he whimpered when Andy climbed out of the pickup and slammed the door shut.

Harald, Andy figured, would probably spot a squirrel and let loose with a chorus of barks. Not what your average busybody needed while skulking around potentially hostile territory.

Andy crept down the edge of the muddy, rutty track that led into Don Cooper's cabin. It was barely wide enough for a Model T, let alone something like the Silverado. It went on and on, several blocks at least, through thick woods. But finally, a decrepit fishing shack hove into view, as the dirt track opened up into a small clearing. Mud Lake glittered and glinted a short distance beyond it.

Andy paused in the deep shade at the end of the

entrance track, scoping out the situation. The shack didn't look much bigger than one room and the cheap vinyl siding that it had been sheathed in failed to do much for its appearance. Off to the side was an outhouse. And right next to it sat a vehicle of some sort, hunkered down under a shiny, bright blue tarp.

Staying just inside the weeds and shrubbery at the edge of the clearing, Andy made his way over to the outhouse, then nipped around to the other side to check out what was under the tarp. Squatting down, he lifted a corner of the blue material—slowly, so it wouldn't make any loud, crinkling noises.

"Oh, shit," he muttered under his breath. "Oh, shit."

A red Prius.

A red Prius with a bumper sticker that said, "I brake for Wiccans."

Trudi's red Prius.

A red Prius that ought to have been tooling around central Wisconsin at this very moment.

Andy lowered the corner of the tarp back down to the ground and eased himself behind the outhouse, ripely odoriferous and queasying, as privies often are. He slipped back into the margin of the woods. At least he shouldn't be too visible here. When he figured he had moved back a safe distance, he stopped to collect his wits.

He supposed he ought to go check out the shack. But that didn't seem very appealing or very smart. Trudi might have bought the farm already, rendering heroism moot. And if she was still alive, who was to say he'd be able to get her out? Carter could be in there, with a gun to her head.

There was a third possibility, Andy supposed. Maybe Trudi and Carter were in there, having mad, passionate sex.

Then Andy peered at Don Cooper's dilapidated fishing shack and sighed. There is no reason in the world, he thought, for any sane couple to have a romantic interlude here rather than at a gorgeous deluxe resort in the lovely, rolling Wisconsin countryside.

What Andy needed to do was get hold of Cass. Even she'd have to admit that the presence of Trudi's Prius under a tarp out in the woods smelled awfully fishy. And if she came and saw the situation, she'd call Ed Vandegraff and the rest of the cavalry.

Ring up Cass again. That'll do it.

Andy pulled out his phone and blinked at the screen in disbelief.

"Crap on a stick!" he swore.

There was no signal here!

Nothing.

Zero.

Zippo.

He had to get somewhere where the bleeping phone would work.

Andy found his way back to the dirt entrance track and strode as quickly as he could, trying not to make any noise.

He came around a bend, peering down at the dirt. He didn't need to twist an ankle in one of the numerous ruts.

"Hey there, Andy."

He looked up and gasped.

There stood Carter LaPorte. In military camo. Pointing what looked to be a .45 semi-automatic at Andy's chest.

Andy, usually the most cordial of people, didn't know what to say.

"I'm really, *really* sorry that you're here," Carter said. "You seem like a nice guy. I don't want to hurt you. But I don't see how I can avoid it."

Andy said the first thing that popped into his head.

"Was it your brother? Your cousin?"

Carter grinned. "Holy cow, you've been doing your homework, haven't you?"

"Which is it?"

"Lyle was my big brother. Died when he was thirteen. I was ten."

"Trudi didn't kill him, Carter."

"It's not as simple as that." Carter gestured with the handgun. "How about you turn around and head back to the cabin. I had this all figured out, but now we have to improvise."

"What do you mean," Andy said, feeling almost nauseous.

"You're going to have to dig a second grave, my friend. Now get moving."

Chapter Thirty-Three

Inside the fishing shack were a couple of swayback single beds. On one of them lay Trudi Bock, on her side—bound foot, hand, and mouth with duct tape.

Her eyes popped open when she saw Andy clump through the door. She tried urgently to say something, but all that emerged through the tape was incoherent mumbling.

Andy started to say hi to his long-ago squeeze, but realized it was pointless. If ever there was a time when small talk seemed inappropriate, this was it.

"Andy," Carter said, following his new captive inside at a safe distance, "I want you to lie facedown on the floor, with your hands and feet splayed out. If you try to move from that posture, I *will* shoot you."

Andy did as he was told, arranging himself at an angle where he could just see Carter, who stood inside the doorframe with his .45.

"I was telling Andy here," Carter said, clearly addressing the duct-taped New Age retailer, "that it was most unfortunate he figured out my back story. Because if he hadn't, I don't know why he would have turned up here. Took a little detective work, huh, Andy?"

"Whatever," Andy groaned.

"Anyone else know?"

"I told Ed Vandegraff," Andy replied truthfully, "but he thinks I'm a loon. Said I should go home and have a beer. I shoulda listened."

"You should have, indeed," Carter said. "I genuinely regret having to put you in the ground. But I can't have you spouting off. Especially after Trudi and I fail to return from our architectural outing in Wisconsin."

"Can I ask a question, Carter?" Andy said.

Carter nodded.

"Have you been holding this grudge for half a century?"

"Have I been holding a grudge?" Carter repeated. "For over fifty years? A year and a half ago I probably would have said no. But thanks to this lady here, I had to reconsider. I thought I'd put it behind me. But the very first time I met our Trudi—when I interviewed her for the *Chronicle*—she lit a fuse inside me. Didn't know she'd done it, of course. But she did."

Some more desperate mumbling sounds came from Trudi's direction, but Andy had no better luck interpreting them than he had before.

"I've already explained this to Trudi, Andy. So I hope she'll forgive me if I repeat myself. But as I recall it, at the very first opportunity, she brought up her sainted uncle, who had taught at St. Magnus Prep. He was so kind and so generous and so sweet and so cuddly and so close to God. And the boys just loved him to pieces. Isn't that right, Trudi? You mentioned him more than once."

As a daddy longlegs skittered past his nose, Andy calculated that Carter was about ten feet away from him. No way could he lurch to his feet without taking a .45 slug.

"Now I thought, Andy, that maybe she was just, well, clueless. Maybe her family never got the memo on dear ol' Uncle Herb. So next time I saw her, I made up a story about checking with some old-timers. Who said Herb Tremmel left St. Magnus in a hurry, suspected of diddling the little lads. Know what our Trudi said?"

Assuming it not to be a rhetorical question, Andy muttered, "No, what?"

"She said the family had heard about those terrible lies. Nothing but slander. Didn't believe a word of them. Herb Tremmel would never do such nasty things to his dear little boys. Herb Tremmel was a saint."

Carter went silent and Andy bent his head up for a better look—not easy to do in his prone posture. "I take it," he said, "that this was some kind of turning point."

"You take it right, Andy," Carter confirmed. "At first, all I thought about was how stupid this woman was. Then, gradually, over the course of the winter, I began to have a few ideas for punishing her. Because she did need to suffer some pain for denying the truth. For denying the torture that my brother and those other boys went through.

"So I began rather small. It was ridiculously easy to

do. I knew when she would be in town working. I waited for a nice day, and drove out to her place in that old Dodge pickup. Walked in and defaced her intimate apparel. Then I grabbed the lizard, and slashed its neck with one of the kitchen knives."

Trudi whimpered and sobbed from behind Andy.

"Hung it in one of those pretty little trees. Then I saw your mutt coming along, Andy. So I vamoosed out of there."

"And I suppose," Andy sighed, "you wrote the poison pen letters. And the fake letter that shut down Trudi's Eleanorian shindig."

Carter laughed. "Guilty as charged. Nothing personal against you, Andy. I put your name on that letter to the editor because you were the first New Bergenite I could think of. Basically, all I wanted to do was make Trudi's life a little more miserable."

"Why did you have to kill Charlie Adams?" Andy asked. "You did kill her. Right? It wasn't Zeke Haugen?"

"No, it wasn't young Mr. Haugen."

Andy could hear Trudi sobbing uncontrollably now.

"One of the nice things about living in small rural communities," Carter said, "is that there's a deep inter-connectedness among people. A deep sense of history."

"So?" said Andy, who wanted to also say: *Cut the shit.*

"Turned out that one of Charlie's uncles was in my brother's class at St. Magnus. She knew the story. Recognized my name and put the pieces together. Told me to lay off Trudi or else. Well, I'd gone too far to turn back. And when Zeke got in that very public brawl with her at the Karma Kubbyhole, all the cards just fell into place. If Charlie should happen to get killed, all eyes would turn to Zeke.

"What I hadn't counted on was that Zeke was hanging around Charlie's house later that night. I don't know what he planned to do. Something unpleasant, no doubt. Anyway, he saw me do the deed out in the backyard. He popped out of nowhere and, believe it or not, tried to blackmail me right then and there! One thing you have to say about the kid, he had a lot of brass."

Andy groaned. "Guess he'd never watched any mystery shows on TV. Everyone knows how that usually ends up."

"I am going to miss you, Andy," Carter said with a smile. "I really am. But quite correct. It's dangerous to blackmail a murderer. I convinced Zeke that I had ten thousand dollars squirreled away out here. Like a little lamb, he climbed right into the truck and came with me. When I got him out here, I offered him a screwdriver, heavy on the vodka. Then another and another. Said I'd pay up when we were done and drive him back to town. He was a pretty cheap drunk and he passed out quickly. I wiped the hammer I used on Charlie and put his prints on it. Then I dragged him out into the lake here and drowned him. He struggled a little, but it wasn't hard."

There was something that Andy couldn't figure out, and as long as Carter was in a chatty mood, he might as well ask. Talking was way better than shooting.

"But one thing I don't understand, Carter," Andy said, trying to subdue the quaver in his voice. "You killed Zeke the night of the Kubbyhole Block Party and put his body in the Dodge pickup in Rose Lake. But I know I saw your pickup a week and a half later, when you set the Kubbyhole on fire."

"Good catch, Andy. See that old Maytag fridge there in the corner? Strip out the shelves, and there's plenty of room for one juvenile delinquent. I put the setting down as low as possible. Kept Zeke nice and fresh." He chuckled at his little joke. "I wasn't sure what to do with the body. It had been a really long night and I was exhausted. I was making it up on the fly, you know. As long as Zeke was chilling, I just ended up procrastinating. You know how that goes."

"No, I don't know how that goes," Andy observed with a bite of sarcasm. "I always dispose of my murder victims immediately."

"Oooo," chuckled Carter. "Ouch."

Andy glared up at him, but held his tongue this time.

"Anyway," Carter continued, "the night of the fire, what seemed to have been the bad break of you seeing my truck turned into a sweet opportunity. I could pin both the murder and the arson on Zeke. I put him in the Dodge and sent it into Rose Lake, into the shallows there. With the murder weapon. Where they were bound to be discovered, when some yahoo drove his boat over the truck. I hadn't figured on your dog finding it first."

"And what about Gus Johnson?" Andy asked grimly.

"Well, for that I'm genuinely sorry. If I'd known he was in the basement, I wouldn't have torched the place. Just splattered that asinine mural outside with paint."

"And for the grand finale, there's Trud and me."

"The end of this Jacobean drama, my friend."

"So what happens now?" Andy didn't really want to know, figuring all his options to be unappealing. But he had to keep Carter monologing.

"While I follow at a safe distance, you're going to carry dear Trudi out into the woods, where I've dug a single grave. You can either dig a second hole, or dig the existing grave a bit deeper, should you care to spend eternity together with her. Your call."

Andy was almost at his wit's end. Not since his tumble into Gaasedelen Creek as a three-year-old had he felt the cold breath of the Grim Reaper flickering so closely to his neck. This really could be the big one, and he had no idea how to prevent it. Carter seemed pretty comfortable with that .45. And Andy had no doubt that traditional heroics would end badly.

"It doesn't have to be this way, Carter," he said. "Just tie me up like Trud and drive away. You'll have plenty of time to make an escape, and get to Costa Rica, or wherever the hell it is you're planning to go."

"Seeing as how I've murdered two people—I'm not counting Gus—you two don't make much more of a difference. Trudi has to die. Sadly, Andy, because you stuck your nose in, you do too."

"But that house of yours," Andy said, trying to buy yet more time. "It's gorgeous. How could you throw it away? You'll never be able to live there again."

Carter was silent for a moment. Then he spoke, quietly and intently.

"That's the thing I regret most, Andy. I put my heart into that place. But some things are more important."

"So you're going to let ancient history ruin another life," Andy said. "I'm talking about yours, Carter."

The murderer sighed an exaggerated sigh. "You just don't get it, do you, Andy? Think about what Herb Tremmel did to my brother those dozens of times. What he did to my family by tearing the heart out of it. My mom disappeared one day and never came back. My dad drank himself to death, when he wasn't beating the crap out of me. So you see, Andy, we all paid a price for dear Uncle Herb's sins."

Carter paused for a second. "And you know what's really ironic? Lyle was at St. Magnus on a scholarship. He won it because he was such a sharp kid. If he hadn't gone... Well, most of his old classmates from Polk Elementary are probably still alive. They went on to have families and careers. They're enjoying their grandkids by now."

"Let it go," Andy begged. "Please let it go."

"After all these years, I have the chance to make it right. Or as right as I possibly can. And killing this woman is the only way I know how. The only way I know how to get back at Herb Tremmel. I'm doing this for

Lyle, for Mom and Dad, for me. I'd be a coward if I bailed out now."

It seemed to Andy that Carter wasn't blowing any smoke here. He looked utterly determined to carry out his mission of justice—at least as he saw it. There was no doubt that he'd pull the trigger. And Andy's demise would be nothing but collateral damage. Unfortunate and unfair. But there you have it.

"Now we still have a little daylight left, Andy. So I'd like you to slowly stand and pick up Trudi."

Keeping an eye on the .45, Andy clambered to his feet and, without a word, bent over and hoisted Trudi up in his arms. She kept mumbling through the duct tape, her desperate eyes flaring. Andy still couldn't understand a damned word.

"Good," said Carter, backing out the door. "Now come outside with her."

When Andy and Trudi emerged into the lovely evening air—darkening blue sky above, birds twittering all around—Carter gestured with his gun.

"See that little gap in the bushes?" he said. "Deer path. You're going down there. I'll be right behind. No funny business, Andy."

Andy kind of juggled Trudi—she was a heckuva load—and trod into the woods, down the deer path. It was cool and damp and dark, and mosquitoes started to feast on them. Andy would have given anything to be able to slap at the miserable little bloodsuckers. He could hear Carter tramping behind.

It took a slow five minutes to get to their destination—a spot sloppily cleared out at the edge of the path. There was a ragged hole in the loamy soil, about six feet long by two wide by three deep. A shovel leaned against a basswood tree, and a couple of lantern flashlights hung from a branch.

"Put her down," Carter ordered. With a grunt, Andy complied, grounding Trudi as gently as he could.

"Now, Andy," Carter said, "you need to decide something. Is it a king size for you and Trudi? Or twin beds?"

Andy pondered the question seriously. It would take a while to dig a second hole, which gave him and Trudi a chance to survive a bit longer.

"I want my own grave," he said.

Carter nodded. "I don't blame you. Now get the shovel there and start digging next to Trudi's spot. Keep your back to me. If you swing around with that shovel, I'll shoot you. And trust me, Andy. A .45 slug makes a big, nasty hole."

Chapter Thirty-Four

King Harald fidgeted in the cab of the Chev Silverado, going from one open window to the other. Back and forth and back and forth. Sticking his head out, sniffing and watching.

The first thing that happened after the boss left him was the arrival of another vehicle. Someone got out of it whom Harald recognized. It was the human who had given him those tasty little meat sticks. A very *nice* human.

But the human didn't even say hello when the big mutt let out a polite, subdued woof. He just briefly looked at Harald and walked down the dirt track, into the woods, out of sight. The dog didn't worry about it. Maybe there'd be meat sticks later.

It had been Harald's intention to *stay*. As ordered. The boss had said so, and so it would be. Absolutely, positively, definitely.

If not for one small thing.

Well, actually, not as small as a squirrel. Somewhat bigger, in fact. But just about the same shade of gray. And sort of plump. With really big eyes. And very long ears. And a fluffy white tail.

If not for this small thing that hopped across the road, Harald *would have stayed*. He really would have.

But the rabbit did hop across the road. And looked like a fat, fluffy, vaguely squirrelly sort of thing that deserved to be chased and caught.

Not a single thought passed through Harald's brain as he heaved himself out of the open window and tumbled helter-skelter onto the weeds at the side of the road.

It was pure reflex.

A jumble of long legs and flapping tail, Harald quickly reoriented himself toward the rabbit and—not too brightly—barked at it. The sound gave the little gray critter the heads-up that it needed to beat a speedy retreat, if it was going to avoid an early, violent demise.

Its ears shot up like rockets and its head swiveled to take in the rapidly oncoming canine. Like an Olympic sprinter, the rabbit took off down the trail toward the lake, with King Harald in hot pursuit.

Just at those instants when Harald thought he was getting within range of the rabbit, it cut practically sideways—with an agility a big gawky dog could not equal. Harald wheeled in the new direction, and kept up the chase.

The life-and-death contest unfolded partly on the dirt track, and partly amid the trees.

Had the rabbit been a squirrel, things would have ended rather quickly, with Harald chalking up another loss. But rabbits—fortunately, for a dog—do not climb trees.

So the hunter and hunted followed a frenetic, zig-zag course down toward the lake.

The dog and his would-be prize tore out of the woods into the clearing that contained the decrepit shack, Harald lagging behind by about fifteen feet. They orbited the little building twice. Then the rabbit darted right, into a gap in the woods. Once again, Harald overshot, but was soon hot on the trail.

Predator and prey blasted down the path, zigzagging as they had since the start of the chase.

Harald nearly lost the bunny at one point, when it seemed to simply disappear. But by means of some urgent scampering around among the weeds, he managed to flush the long-eared critter out into the open again. And off they went.

The big mutt was grimly silent throughout the whole pursuit. Utterly intent on obtaining the thing he wanted above all else: getting the small and furry thing in between his jaws and crunching it. Beyond that, he hadn't thought very much about what he would do with a small, furry, dead thing.

Following the course of least resistance, the rabbit sprinted down the path at breakneck speed—showing no sign of running out of steam. Then, with the agility that comes of being a small, furry thing that bigger, furry things would like to kill, it cut neatly to the right and vanished into some undergrowth. Just as the path began to curve left, past a clump of obscuring trees and bushes.

Harald kept barreling on.

Right into a human standing in the middle of the path.

Knocking the human over.

Sending his canine self tumbling tail over teakettle.

Out of the corner of his eye, Harald saw the boss standing there, holding some kind of big stick in his hands.

Chapter Thirty-Five

Andy was leaning on the shovel, panting from exhaustion, when Harald blasted around the bend in the deer path, galloping flat out. Without any warning whatsoever.

Andy saw every little detail in slow motion.

Harald plowed into Carter's derriere, tumbling the double murderer face first into the loamy soil.

Carter grunted as his gray .45 automatic cartwheeled into the air and landed with a thud, practically at Andy's feet. Andy stared at the object, amazed that it, and apparently his and Trudi's salvation, had arrived so unexpectedly. Then he snatched it up. He knew enough about handguns to realize there was a bullet in the chamber, the weapon ready to fire.

As Carter stumbled to his feet, Harald—who had recovered more quickly from the collision—attempted to jump up on the man and lick his face.

But instead of a friendly greeting, Harald got a hard backhand across the snout. He yelped and hopped backward, shocked at the discourtesy.

"You really are an asshole, aren't you, Carter?" Andy

growled, aiming the automatic at the newsman's chest. "You murder and kidnap people. And now you abuse dogs. I am sorry about your brother. I really am. *But get the hell over it!"*

Harald slunk over to Andy, then pivoted and started barking at Carter.

"That's the thing, Andy," Carter said, brushing himself off and sidling up the path. "You never do get the hell over it."

"Stay where you are or I'll shoot," Andy threatened, gripping the .45 two-handed, like he'd seen on TV.

Carter kept shuffling forward, never breaking eye contact with Andy. "Will you, now?" the killer said very quietly, stooping to pick up the shovel Andy had tossed aside.

"Put it down," Andy ordered. "I mean it."

The dog was still barking. "Harald, shut up!" Andy snapped.

His command made no impression on Harald, who kept at it hot and heavy.

Carter came closer by a few inches. "You know, Andy, I thought it was pretty sharp of you to guess that I might be going to Costa Rica. Actually, it's Belize. *Was* Belize. I'm thinking now that swaying palms and pristine Central American beaches may be off the program."

Andy was near panic. Carter was getting closer and closer to Trudi. And it seemed dreadfully obvious what he intended to do: smash her brains in with the shovel. Andy might really have to shoot.

"Last time, Carter," he said, his voice a little wobbly. "Put down the shovel and take that tape off of Trudi."

The tempo of Harald's barking increased, as if to underline his master's increasing panic.

"Andy," Carter replied, unruffled, "I've known people like you all my life. And people like you just don't have it in them to shoot other people. Nothing to be ashamed of. That's just the way it is."

"Carter, for heaven's sake, you're a writer!"

The man with the shovel laughed. "And writers don't kill people? Before I was a reporter, I was in the Army. Know what I did there?"

Andy shook his head. At least Carter had stopped moving. But Harald was still barking at Carter and it was driving Andy up the wall.

"What I was, Andy, was a sniper. I've killed people. Some of those people that I saw through my scope, I gave them the name Herb Tremmel. It made killing them easier."

"I will stop you, Carter."

"Andy, you just don't have what it takes to shoot a man," Carter said, as he stepped toward Trudi, shovel raised for a killing blow.

"But I do!" a woman's voice snarled.

Both Andy's and Carter's heads swiveled.

There at the bend in the path stood Cass Conlin, Glock 9 in two hands. In a wide-legged shooting stance. In an utterly incongruous short, red cocktail dress. Behind her, looking as astonished as anyone, was her studly blond Norwegian cop.

Carter turned back in Trudi's direction and started to swing the shovel.

The Glock barked once and Andy could see Carter's upper arm explode in a spray of blood. The shovel went flying, landing just a few feet beyond Trudi's head. Her eyes were as wide as saucers.

Carter collapsed in a heap, howling in agony.

And Harald went ballistic. In addition to barking, he was now jumping around like a lunatic.

Andy stood frozen in the spot, mouth agape, as Cass darted up to the wounded newspaperman, Glock aimed down at him.

"You stay right there, Mr. LaPorte," she ordered. "We'll try and get some medical attention for you ASAP. But if you attempt anything funny, I will shoot you dead, understand?"

Whimpering in pain, Carter nodded and slumped closer to the ground.

"Andy," Cass continued, "give Lars that .45."

Amazing, thought Andy. The guy really was named Lars.

"Then I want you to get back out on County 101 and phone this in on the 9-1-1."

"But there's no signal here, Cassie," Andy sputtered.

"Not here there isn't. But there is out on the highway. Tell 'em what happened. Tell 'em I responded to your call. Tell 'em we need an EMT unit here stat. Tell 'em we have a wounded perp and one vic."

"How'd you find us out here?"

"Heard Harald barking."

"What about Trudi?"

The duct-taped New Age maven was again mumbling and now wiggling wildly.

"Lars'll take care of her."

That's when Andy noticed that Cass had no shoes on. "Cassie," he asked, baffled, "where are your shoes?"

She looked at him as if he were incredibly dense. "Andy, are you frickin' nuts? You think I'm wearing my Manolo Blahniks in here? Now you and Harald *go!"*

As he and Harald loped away, Andy could hear Cass begin to read Carter his rights.

* * *

Andy and Harald led Sheriff Mandsager, several deputies, and the EMT crew in from the south lake road by flashlight. It was a dark, moonless night. The mosquitoes were now out in squadrons and everyone was slapping at them.

When they arrived at the scene of the crime, they found Cass patiently guarding Carter, who held a red-stained handkerchief against his wounded arm, applying pressure. Trudi was sitting on the log with Lars, looking dazed.

The moment she saw Andy and Harald, she struggled to her feet and stumbled over to them.

"Oh, Anders," she blurted, enveloping him in a weak embrace. *"You saved my life."*

Andy couldn't help but notice that she had an angry

red rash across her mouth and cheeks where the duct tape had been.

"Well, you know, Trud," Andy mumbled, "anyone would have done it."

He gently pried himself loose, and patted her on the shoulder. Then Trudi bent over and accepted a slobbery lick from Harald.

Andy could hear her when she whispered in the dog's ear. "You're a hero, too, King Harald. How did you find us?"

In response, Harald, ever modest, licked her again.

It was a weird scene, out there in the woods in the pitch black, with battery lanterns hanging from trees and flashlights dancing around. The EMT guys field-dressed the wound of a deflated, defeated Carter LaPorte and, with two deputies escorting, slowly walked him away. The crime scene photographer arrived, and started taking dozens and dozens of pictures. Sheriff Mandsager himself jotted down a statement from Andy.

Finally, on toward midnight, a deputy encircled the site with yellow crime-scene tape.

Andy, Cass, and Harald started walking back down the narrow deer track toward Don Cooper's decrepit fishing shack—Cass in front, wielding the flashlight. Andy had to admit, she looked awfully fine in that tight, short cocktail dress—barefoot or not.

"Cass," Andy muttered, "I just wanted to say something."

"Yeah, Andy, what?"

"You came and saved my life. Trudi's life, too. And I know how pissed off you are at me. So thanks."

She stood there stolidly, still incongruous in her little red dress.

"I don't know what it was, Andy, but the vibe I got from your call just didn't sit well. I'm thinking, there at Chez Louie, right as I'm tucking into my *coq au vin*, that Ed told you not to worry. Ed knows his stuff. But something just nags at me. I tell Lars what I'm thinking. He says, 'Cass, follow your gut.' And my gut says, 'What if Ed's wrong, and Andy's walking into something nasty.' I can't let that happen. Can't take the chance."

"That shot of yours," Andy said. "Amazing that you managed to wing him like that."

A dark scowl came over the deputy sheriff's face. "I was aiming for a kill shot, Andy. And I missed."

"Oh," Andy replied, happy that he hadn't been standing closer to Carter.

"And by the way, I'm heading out to D.C."

"D.C.?" Andy squeaked.

"I was offered a job at the FBI." She grinned broadly. "Desk agent, to start. But I'm shooting for field agent some day."

Well, Andy thought, I guess there'll be no reconciliation.

"Hey, Cassie, congrats. A big step up."

"There are only two things I'm really going to miss about Beaver Tail County," she said.

"What are those?" Andy asked, wondering if one of

them would be a certain ex-boyfriend.

"Biberschwanz Pilsner. And Harald."

Chapter Thirty-Six

Normally Kirsten didn't let dogs into her restaurant. But on a slow Tuesday afternoon, in the midst of a mid-July heat wave, she gave King Harald the hero a one-day pass. He had to wear a lead, though, and the lead had to be tied to Andy's chair. The dog sat attentively, as if honored to be allowed into the inner sanctum.

Andy and Kirsten and Thor and Thor's wife, Sonny, and Aunt Bev were sitting expectantly at one of the big tables at the front of the joint, awaiting the end result of the great ebelskiver adventure. Back in the kitchen, Troy was making the first batch of ebelskivers, using the batter Kirsten had whipped up from Mrs. Nielsen's recipe. The tension was palpable—or at least as tense as waiting for glorified pancakes could get.

"I've been picking up old ebelskiver pans ever since I came back," Kirsten said, sipping on a black coffee. "Always thought it would be fun to have them on the menu for Sunday brunch. But I wanted something special for a recipe."

"If not for Mrs. Nielsen's ebelskiver, Trud would have bought the big one," Andy observed, handing Harald half a Slim Jim. Ever since that close call out in the woods by Mud Lake, Andy had regularly given his dog the treat—now that he knew how much Harald liked the meaty confection.

"If I hadn't visited with Mrs. Nielsen, I wouldn't have heard of Lyle LaPorte and gone looking for Trud at Mud Lake," he continued.

"And you wouldn't have almost gotten your own bucket kicked," Thor added.

Sonny—a tanned, blond, trim sixty-year-old, who still ran in half marathons—jabbed her husband in the ribs with an elbow. "Heavens, Thor, it ended up okay."

Andy laughed. "He's right though, Sonny. It was bone-headed of me to blunder out there all alone. But awfully good that I did. I would have felt terrible if Carter had killed Trud."

"Actually," put in Thor, "the both of them would've just vanished from the face of the earth. We never would've known what happened to Trudi."

"Well, speak of the devil," Sonny announced. She gestured toward the door with a tilt of her head.

Everyone turned to look.

In marched Trudi Bock and her tall Eleanorian friend and attorney, Carmine Bongiovanni.

The former New Bergen retailer—in crisp, white linen trousers and a gorgeous aloha-style blouse, cascading with dazzling hibiscus blossoms—waved jauntily and steered Carmine toward the table.

"Everyone's here," she bubbled. "How wonderful. I

just wanted to come and say good-bye one last time."

She still had a few red blemishes from her encounter with the duct tape, Andy noticed, but otherwise looked fully recovered from the unpleasantness at Mud Lake three weeks earlier. It seemed like good old Trud back in form.

"Will you join us, Trudi, Carmine?" Kirsten said. "It's the rollout of the famous ebelskiver recipe."

Tail gyrating, Harald gave a little woof.

Trudi tousled the bristly fur on his head.

"We were going to have a bite anyway, before we left," said Carmine. "Thanks for asking us."

They squeezed into the last two chairs at the table and proceeded to explain that, after the sale of the downtown property to Kirsten was completed, the two of them planned to travel to the Mediterranean to retrace the steps of Eleanor of Aquitaine's crusade of the mid-twelfth century. Nothing anti-Muslim was intended. The couple merely wanted to take in the spiritual dimension of the old queen's quest. And could Kirsten and her attorney come down to the Cities next week, say on Tuesday or Wednesday, for the closing?

Kirsten said that Wednesday afternoon would be great. She could do double duty and bring Aurora along. They were checking out colleges for her. Kirsten would find out if her lawyer was available, too.

"I hate to ask, Trud," said Andy, "but won't you have to come back for the trial on that stupid Dittbrenner thing."

Both Trudi and Carmine smiled.

"Jerry will be withdrawing his action against the humane society and me in a few days," Trudi explained. "In return I'll be making a public apology for what I said, and so will the society. Also, I'll be paying his legal expenses. For his part, Jerry's promised to use more humane methods to deal with sick and injured animals. I still don't agree with even that. But there's the real world for you."

"How'd this get put together, Trud?" asked Andy. "Last I heard, you were still sounding pretty militant."

"It was Lauren," she said.

"What do you mean?" Andy said.

"You saw her with Jerry up in Pinetop, Anders," said Trudi, "and I think you got the wrong impression. They were not, as you suspected, having an affair. Lauren wasn't any spy or secret agent. She and Jerry are members of the same alcoholics' support group. Improbable as this may seem, considering the way they look, they're just good friends who try to keep each other on the straight and narrow."

"I don't understand," said Sonny. "What happened?"

"Lauren was our go-between," explained Trudi. "She helped us negotiate a truce. It upset her that two of her friends were at each other's throats. Anyway, I was tired of the whole business. And this was a chance to get it over with."

"And another thing," said Carmine, looking as though he'd just won a big case in court.

"Yah, what's that, Carmine?" Aunt Bev asked.

"Brenda Fundingsland Erickson has given up her harassment of Trudi. We got her off our backs. Finally."

"Well, that's great," said Andy. "How'd you do it?"

Trudi picked up the thread. "We didn't do a thing. It seems that she and her husband were about to lose a big financial backer they had from down in the Cities."

"They had to use his money or lose it," Carmine explained. "So they managed to find a farm property on the other side of town that works nearly as well for their McMansions and golf course."

"So, *hasta la vista*, Brenda," bubbled Trudi.

"And I heard Dick Schaeffer had the wind taken right out of his sails," Aunt Bev said with a satisfied look. "After Amber ran away, and they got her back, his wife Jeannie read him the riot act. Go easier on that girl, or else. And if there's one person in the world that man's afraid of, it's Jeannie. At least that's what Doris Schattenheimer tells me. She and Jeannie are in the same Zumba class."

"Well, I hope good karma catches up with Amber," said Trudi. "She's a great kid. And maybe her dad will finally reach a higher level of enlightenment."

"Here they come," J. J. bellowed, striding across the dining room, holding a big tray loaded with ebelskivers. She banged down four plates in front of Kirsten, Thor, Sonny, and Aunt Bev, then returned to the kitchen for more.

Andy didn't mind not getting his ebelskivers right

away. After all, this was his sister's baby, so to speak. He knew how much she wanted to knock it out of the ballpark for Elbow Lake Days.

Andy watched Kirsten pour a drizzle of pure maple syrup onto the spherical pancakes. She cut a piece with her fork, speared it, and rubbed it around in some more syrup. The fork headed for her mouth. She tentatively bit off an ebelskiver fragment and began to chew.

Everyone was on tenterhooks, awaiting her judgment.

It was the look of the serious professional at work—objectively assaying the flavors and textures rolling around inside her mouth. Right after she swallowed, there came a radiant smile.

"No wonder these ebelskivers were famous," she said, nodding.

Everyone started to breathe again.

Thor did his own sampling and beamed. "Best ebelskiver I ever tasted. What are those flavors?"

"I don't know from ebelskivers," said Sonny, "but wow!"

Aunt Bev nodded after her first bite, and said, "Good one, honey." And she patted Kirsten on the shoulder.

A couple of minutes later, J. J. arrived with three more plates of ebelskivers.

Andy was impressed by the rich texture and subtle flavor. There was definitely a hint of something familiar, but he just couldn't place it.

"What *is* the secret, Kirsten?" asked Trudi.

Kirsten put her fork down and took another sip of

coffee. "You know, I phoned Mrs. Nielsen after Andy brought the recipe back and she explained why it was she had kept it secret all those years."

"Okay, I'll bite," said Thor. "Why did she keep it under lock and key?"

"Well, people certainly tried to pry it out of her. But when she'd stumbled across these ebelskivers back during the war…"

Andy smiled. For folks of Mrs. Nielsen's generation, and even a bit for their kids, "the war" meant only one thing. The big WWII.

"…The old lady who made them picked Mrs. Nielsen—who was still a single woman at that time—to be the bearer of the flame, so to speak. She had to promise to never tell a soul how the things were made."

Trudi sniffed. "I'm sorry, Kirsten, but that just seems silly. It's only a recipe."

"I understand what you're saying, Trudi. But it's also a tradition that goes back at least five generations, as far as Mrs. Nielsen can tell. She said I didn't have to follow along, if I didn't want to. But I kind of do. It makes the ebelskivers a lot more special."

"And it gives you the monopoly," observed Thor, ever on the alert for capitalist transgression.

"I suppose so," Kirsten agreed.

"And you're really going to stonewall us?" asked Sonny with a wry smile.

Kirsten nodded. "Sorry."

Sonny turned to Andy. "You picked up the recipe

from the lady. You must've looked at it."

"Nope, I didn't even glance at the thing," Andy answered. "I was pretty preoccupied with what I'd just heard about Lyle LaPorte."

J. J. kept bringing out trays of ebelskivers until everyone was stuffed. Even Harald gobbled up a few of them, though without maple syrup.

As J. J. took away the last plate, Trudi turned to the proprietor of Ansel's. "Now you're going to have Bev recreate her masterpiece on the outside of the new building, aren't you, Kirsten?"

Andy almost burst out laughing. Aunt Bev was beaming copious thank-yous at Trudi, while Kirsten was forcing a smile.

She looked from Trudi to Aunt Bev, then Andy. He nodded at his sister: *Give Aunt Bev a break, huh?*

"You know, Trudi," Kirsten said, "that might be a good idea. But nothing definite until we know what the building will look like. Okay?"

"That would be just fine," Aunt Bev said. She looked a little giddy. Andy knew she'd never gotten this far with Kirsten before.

"And how are you doing, Trudi?" asked Sonny. "You went through such a horrible experience."

Trudi sipped slowly on her Perrier. It seemed to Andy that she was framing her answer very carefully. Suddenly he had a flashback of Trudi—from that morning at his house—clad in nothing but a smile. He almost hoped that they had indeed done the deed that fuzzy, Biberschwanzbesotted night.

"I'm not sure which was worse, Sonny," Trudi finally answered. "The plan to kill me. Or the betrayal. The way he charmed me, made me believe that I was something special to him. He came up with that whole trip to Wisconsin expressly to…" She trailed off briefly. "It was so cold, so cruel. Just because I admired my uncle and believed what my family had said about him."

"I heard that Carter's trial will begin sometime after Labor Day," noted Thor.

"The guy's going to spend the rest of his life in prison, and that's a fact," Andy said. "Whether you believe that Herb Tremmel did that stuff or not—" Andy had to give Trudi a little something. "—somehow a bunch of bombs got thrown into Carter's family. And now, fifty years later, the last one went off."

Thor, Kirsten, and Carmine jumped in all at once, arguing that Carter was a monster who deserved everything he was going to get.

Trudi put up her hand, and everyone shut up.

"Just like Zeke Haugen and Charlie and Gus and Adonis," she said quietly, "Carter's a victim, too."

"Apart from being a cold-blooded killer," Andy blurted, "he seemed like a pretty nice guy."

Getting up from the table to leave, Trudi leaned over and gave Andy a hug.

"I'll be back to get the house ready to sell," she said. "I'm keeping the farmland as an investment. Then it's good-bye New Bergen. I'm going to move into Carmine's condo down in the Cities and we'll see if we can get along."

"Don't you worry, hon," Carmine said. "It'll be great."

Trudi beamed at him. "Maybe I'll get lucky for once. The Eleanors think I will."

"Both of them?" Andy asked.

Trudi nodded. "Though the First Lady is a little doubtful. FDR made her awfully cynical about relationships."

Andy and Harald accompanied the couple outside. As they were about to walk away, Trudi turned and looked down at Harald.

"You know, Anders, I've been thinking a lot about what happened that night," she said. "How did Harald find us, out in those woods? How could he have known where to go?"

"I don't know, Trud," Andy replied. "I betcha it was just dumb doggie luck."

Trudi shook her head. "No, no. I think that Harald had a spirit guide lead him. Some sort of wraith or fairy. I wish he could tell us."

But Harald, tail wagging, remained inscrutable.

With a final kiss on Andy's cheek and a jaunty, parting wave, Trudi Bock stepped out of his life, on the arm of her six-foot-six Eleanor Roosevelt impersonator—and possibly the man of her dreams.

Chapter Thirty-Seven

Even though it was muggy and hot, Andy and Harald had walked to Ansel's that morning. Now it was time to pay the piper, as they stepped back out into the steam bath.

It had been a fine day, though. The ebelskivers had worked out great—just scrumptious. Kirsten was over the moon. Trudi was happily dispensed with. Aunt Bev would live to rosemal another day. Andy knew that he had a ton of work and responsibility coming his way. His sister would expect 200 percent out of him, as the new gallery and Scandinavian deli took shape—to be called the Nordic. But what a great chance to make an impact on New Bergen and maybe kick-start his own painting career.

Andy had no idea what the place would look like. But Kirsten had an architect in mind—an internationally known guy who lived among the evergreen forests and rocky lakes up by the Canadian border. She had commissioned him to do preliminary drawings. He had won more than a few prizes around the world. His price tag and the construction wouldn't be cheap. But Kirsten wanted the best and could afford it.

Andy didn't get giddy very often. He was too even-tempered, too in tune with the universe's tendency to pop you in the nose when you least expected it. But today, he was walking on cloud nine.

He had come home to New Bergen with his tail between his legs. And sometimes he'd wondered if it had been the right thing to do. But not today. Today it looked brilliant. About all that he lacked was a significant other. And maybe, like Trudi, he'd get lucky.

Out on Skjegstad Street the antiquers were fairly thick, for a weekday during a heat wave.

Across the street a well-dressed older couple emerged from a lighting fixture shop with a handsome Art Moderne table lamp—she bearing the shade, he the lamp itself. They strode along proudly, as if they were carrying pieces of the Crown Jewels.

Up ahead, Andy could see Bob Ludeman, the dealer in Art Nouveau and Art Deco jewelry, crossing Walleye Avenue with a full-figured, very sharply dressed woman. He had one of his mahogany cases under his arm. Doubtlessly full of tempting little treasures to show off while lunching at Ansel's. As he nodded at Andy, in passing, he received a tip.

"Ask if there're any ebelskivers left," Andy said with a wink.

Bob's eyes brightened. "Really? They're ready? They're available?"

By now half of New Bergen knew about Andy's ebelskiver adventure.

"They are indeed, Bob," replied Andy. "As long as the batter lasts. You will be amazed."

He could hear Bob explaining the whole story to his customer, as Andy and King Harald walked in the opposite direction. The woman kept exclaiming, "Oh wow!" and "How cool is that!"

Man and dog hung a right on Muskie Avenue and soon marched past the last few downtown antique shops. The temperature had to be close to ninety, the dew point pushing sixty-five. Very much more of this heat, and everyone would be wishing for autumn to arrive.

For now, New Bergen's shaded streets seemed like a little piece of paradise. Well-maintained bungalows and two-story colonials and Craftsman cottages nestled on their tiny lots. Kids and their dogs were playing up and down the streets, and in their yards. A few of them shouted hellos to King Harald and Andy. This was a scene, Andy thought, that Norman Rockwell might have painted. As wholesome and cozy and all-American as you were likely to get.

About four blocks from home, a sharp, elderly voice broke his reverie.

"Anders Skyberg!"

He halted and looked off to the side.

Coming out of Doc Swanstrom's dental office was an old lady and a younger woman. Mrs. Runestrand and one of her daughters.

Andy suppressed the grimace that wanted to pop onto

his face. He managed a wan smile.

"Hi, Mrs. R," he said, as she hobbled right up to him. "And this is?"

"My oldest daughter, Geraldine Anderson," she said.

Greetings were exchanged, and Andy tried to steer the conversation in the direction of their stinking-hot weather. But the old lady would have none of it. Earthly discomforts held little fascination for Mrs. R.

"I've wanted to talk with you ever since that terrible business at Mud Lake," she said. She gave him her laser stare. "Because of the things you did that night—at the risk of your life—you have done me and my family a great, great service. I just knew that my poor Ezekiel would be vindicated. He was not a murderer, and you proved it. He was not a suicide, and you proved it."

A delinquent, a thug, a stalker, and a blackmailer, Andy thought. But not a murderer. Not a suicide.

"I have always believed there was a reason why the Lord put me there at Gaasedelen Creek thirty-seven years ago. To pluck you out of those waters. Because He knew that one day you would do this great deed for my family."

"But it wasn't just me, Mrs. R. King Harald saved my neck. And so did Cass Conlin. I'm alive to tell Zeke's story because of them."

"Of course, the Lord provided help when you needed it," she said. "But you were the one He chose."

Harald apparently wanted in on the conversation and woofed.

Amazingly, Mrs. R smiled. Andy hadn't realized that

she could.

She bent over and patted the big mutt on the head. "Now you and I have something in common, King Harald," she told him.

Harald attempted to lick her on the face, unsuccessfully.

"We have both saved Anders Skyberg."

Mrs. Runestrand nodded to Andy and the two women walked off down the sidewalk.

"Well, Harald," Andy said, "I guess you can put that on your résumé."

Harald wagged his tail vigorously and looked up at Andy.

"What do you say, big guy? A cold Biberschwanz for me and another Slim Jim for you?"

The dog woofed in the affirmative and started to drag Andy toward home.

Acknowledgments

Every author needs to give his book a reality check. Does it hold together? Does it move well? Is it entertaining? Are there any rough spots? And my various reality checks came from several smart, talented people. I want to thank Marlo Garnsworthy, Kate Collins, Jeri Smith, and Sue Wichmann. Also, I want to thank Kelly Germain for her canine expertise. And a pat on the head for Kelly's best friend, Fiver, who portrays King Harald on the cover of this book.